Brandy,

~~TIM~~ Love your face !

Our Second Chance

Chances Are Series,
Book One

C.D. Taylor

Entice
by booktrope
Seattle WA 2014

Cover Design by Greg Simanson

This is a work of fiction. Names, characters, places, brands, media, and incidents are either the product of the author's imagination or are used fictitiously. Any resemblance to similarly named places or to persons living or deceased is unintentional.

Print ISBN 978-1-62015-502-8

EPUB ISBN 978-1-62015-514-1

DISCOUNTS OR CUSTOMIZED EDITIONS MAY BE AVAILABLE FOR EDUCATIONAL AND OTHER GROUPS BASED ON BULK PURCHASE.

For further information please contact info@booktrope.com

Library of Congress Control Number: 2014913309

To my Mom and Dad: Thank you for taking a chance on adopting a chubby little blonde girl and making me a permanent part of your family. Your love inspires me each and every day.

∞𝑶𝒏𝒆∞

PEERING SADLY OUT THE WINDOW across the skyline of Los Angeles, I couldn't help feeling disconsolate. This was what my life had become; I was nothing more than Emily Mills, the daughter of two powerful movie moguls. I crossed my arms over my chest as I walked to my mostly empty desk.

All that lay there was a stack of scripts and screenplays, staring at me in lifeless black and white. I looked down, wishing that I'd made this office more personal, but there was no point. It was my coffin, and each day I entered I was trapped, knowing the only way out was to run. The only thing that even signified that this hunk of mahogany belonged to me was the nameplate my parents had given me when I started working for them. I picked it up and ran my finger over the grooves of my name, deeply inscribed into the metal. Was that what I'd become? Not a person, but a name? Frustrated, I chucked the worthless thing into the garbage next to my desk. It was just another reminder of how I'd failed; how I wasn't the person I was supposed to be.

I sank down into my plush leather office chair and drummed my fingers on the glimmering wood surface in front of me. Thoughts raced through my mind, bringing a migraine with them. I rubbed my temples, trying to relieve some of the building tension.

Looking in, most people would think I had the perfect life, that I was just another spoiled rich kid who didn't know how good she had it. But I felt smothered. As though someone had shoved a pillow over my face, suffocating me. I'd had it with my life here. I was done with all of it.

I shoved a hand through my long blonde hair, tugging midway down, trying to discharge some of my frustration and alleviate my growing headache. Angry tears pricked at my eyes. I reached forward and shoved the stacks of papers off of my desk, sending them fluttering to the floor. I quickly wiped at my eyes, trying to compose myself, but more tears threatened. It was just another sign of how damn weak I really was.

My mother's signature knock sounded on the outside of my closed door. I took a steadying breath and told her to come in. This was it.

"Emily! What the hell happened in here?!" She looked around at the disarray beneath her Jimmy Choos.

"Uh...they fell." I looked over my desk to the papers scattered everywhere.

"How do piles of paper just *fall* onto the floor like that? I'll have Amanda come in and pick this up immediately."

Ah, yes, my mother's trusty assistant. I felt bad for the poor girl half of the time. If she wasn't answering my mother's phone, I was pretty sure she was wiping my mother's ass with gold plated toilet paper.

"I really don't know." One lie after another — that's what my world had become. "Look, Mom, I need to talk to you about something." The office wasn't the ideal place to have this conversation, but I might not get another chance.

"Okay, I suppose this mess can wait a few minutes." She gracefully took a seat in a chair across from my now uncluttered desk. She observed me with sky blue eyes. They matched mine so closely, as though we shared the same set.

"What is it, Dear?" A wondering smile crossed her Botox-enhanced face.

My nerves ratcheted up about five zillion notches, and I was silently thankful I'd skipped breakfast. "Mom, you know I'm not happy here, right?" The blank look on her face prompted me to go on. "I've been doing a lot of thinking, and I believe it's time for me to find what makes me happy. Don't you agree?"

She looked puzzled. "I'm not sure what to say. I thought your father and I did a good job of making you happy, Emily."

"I'm not talking about material things or money, Mom. None of that matters to me. I want to be able to wake up, look in the mirror and smile for once." I wished I'd just kept my mouth shut. I could've waited until morning and disappeared. It wasn't like they would've noticed anyway.

"I'm not sure I understand then, Emily." She wore a thoroughly confused look on her heavily made-up face.

I crossed the room to look out the window once more, my arms held tightly over my chest. It was a shitty view, nothing but rows upon rows of high-end cars and heat-baked asphalt giving the impression of some sort of mystical hell. But the alternative was looking at my mother. "Mom, I think we both know after the incident with Michael things went downhill with our relationship. I don't know why, and I'm sure you have your reasons for acting the way you did, but it still hurts."

"So you're pegging that on your father and me? That doesn't seem quite fair. In fact, *I'm* a little hurt that you'd say that, Emily. Rehashing old wounds is hardly a way to make yourself happy."

My nerves sizzled into anger. She didn't see my point, as usual. She only saw what she wanted to see. I tried to hold myself together as best as I could, but the hurt and anger piled on top of me like dead weight. "No, I'm not trying to 'peg' anything on you. I just wanted to let you know that I've decided to give my notice." Once the words left my mouth, I couldn't hold the emotions back. Tears began to stream down my still-damp face.

"Giving your notice!" She stood from her chair so abruptly that it fell over. At 5' 5", she stood several inches shorter than I, but when she was pissed, she looked considerably taller. With her shoulders pressed back, augmented breasts thrust forward, she propped her jewelry-clad hands on the slight curves of her hips in exasperation.

"Yes, I am. I have a flight leaving in the morning. Mom, I'm going back to New York. I can't stay in Los Angeles any longer. There's nothing here for me." I couldn't look her in the eye. The fear of what I might see there had me cowering like a bunny hiding from a rainstorm.

"Emily, what's *really* going on? You seem to have gotten a crazy idea and decided on a whim to uproot yourself from your family and move clear across the country. I don't get it."

This was my chance to get everything that frustrated me off my chest. I took a steadying breath and went for it. "First of all, if you'd *acted* like my family, maybe I would want to stay. Second, When Michael decided to take out his drunken frustrations on me, *and* I landed in the hospital, I didn't hear from you except to tell me that Michael wasn't *that* bad of a guy. That *I* needed to be a better fiancé. You left me alone when I needed you the most. You sat to the side like you were a spectator at a game, and I suffered for it. I have done every little thing you've asked of me, including forget who I am. I gave up my dream after failing the bar, just because you and Dad decided it would be best for me to work in the family business. I'm tired of having my decisions made for me. I want to make them for myself. I love you, Mom, but I can't keep putting myself through this." I swiped at my eyes, leaving behind black streaks of mascara that stained my fingers.

"Well, I had no idea you felt that way. I thought your father and I were giving you everything you needed." She removed her hands from her hips, and inspected her nails like she was already bored with our conversation.

"But you forgot the one thing that I needed the most: your support for my dreams and goals. I needed you to push me to try harder and believe that I could become my own person." I hung my head as the tears flooded my cheeks. I was done. I had said all that I needed to, and I really didn't feel any better for it. I felt defeated and vulnerable. Neither of which I wanted to be in front of my mom. "I'm going to take the rest of the day off to get my head together." I grabbed my purse from under my desk and slipped past my mother. The scent of her Chanel No. 5 choked me to the point of gagging.

"That's a great idea, Emily!" She yelled down the hall, causing the other employees in the office to glare at me.

I don't know why I was so hurt by her words. But each time I spoke to her, it was like she was slicing me in half. I couldn't take it anymore. If I didn't get out soon, I was afraid of losing what little bit of myself I had left.

Once I arrived home, I headed straight for the fridge and poured myself a generous glass of wine. Somehow my mother made me hate myself *more* than I already did. I flopped down on my worn sofa, letting the deep flavor of the fermented grape slide down my throat and soothe the migraine that threatened.

I could've used a relaxing soak in my bathtub, but I had so much to do in preparation for the next day. I knew taking even a short amount of time to relax would cut into my timeframe. I gulped down the last drop of wine and set the glass on the coffee table. I refused to let things overwhelm me more than it already had. I knew what had to be done, and I was the only one there to do it. I just wished I were leaving under better circumstances with my parents. I hated having things all knotted up instead of neatly lined out like I'd hoped they would be. But I was only kidding myself if I'd thought things would be easy for me. They never were.

There were moving boxes spread out all over my small bungalow, and just looking at them made me have a sense of freedom that I hadn't felt in ages. I wasn't running away; I was figuring out what made *me* happy. I knew that staying there wasn't going to do that for me. Years of trying had turned me into a shell of who I was supposed to be. I knew somewhere out there had to be happiness, and I was ready and willing to grasp it with arms wide open.

As I started packing up a few odds and ends in a fresh box, I heard that familiar knock on my door once again. There was no use delaying the inevitable. I opened the door, and she strode right in. I watched her scan my living room, and her fuchsia painted lips dropped open.

"What the hell is going on, Emily?"

"I already told you, I'm leaving." I said matter-of-factly.

"I thought you might be bluffing. I didn't really think you were *serious*!" She sauntered around the room, peeking inside the boxes that hadn't yet been sealed. I watched as she brushed the tiny specks of dust off her hands like she might die if it stayed on her skin for very long.

"I wasn't kidding, Mom." I waved my arms around at the boxes littering my small home. "Look around."

"Are you out of your mind? What makes you think that you can survive without the help of me and your father?"

"I will do just fine on my own. Don't concern yourself with my affairs."

"I *will* concern myself. You're my daughter, and I have every right to be concerned."

"Really, Mom? Or are you more worried that I won't be you're little puppet anymore? That you can't parade me around on the red carpet and try to match me up with the next big douche bag out there?"

"You ungrateful little bitch!" Her blue eyes shone with venom.

Inside, I cringed. But I was determined to fight back. "Maybe I am. But like I said before, I'm done with all of this. I can't smile for the stupid cameras anymore and pretend that everything is okay. If you gave even one little damn about me, you would support me no matter what, even if you do think I'm making a mistake."

I watched as my mother paced the room, obviously trying to calm herself down. She looked about ready to snap. "Emily, you know this is a huge mistake. Look at all the things you're giving up. What will everyone say?"

Her concerns had occurred to me, but I was long past the point of giving a damn. "I've made up my mind; I'm leaving for New York tomorrow, Mom. There's nothing you could say or do that would persuade me to stay here. And quite frankly, I could care less what people think about me. I've lived this life long enough to know that most of them are only around for what they can get out of you anyway."

"Why do you insist on being so hard headed? I have worked hard to provide you with a life where you haven't had to want for anything. Now you're planning on boarding a plane and throwing all of that in my face. I never took you to be such an unappreciative girl, Emily."

"Mom, I'm not trying to hurt anyone here. I realize you and Dad have tried to do what's best for me, but it's time I do things on my own. I just want you to support me in my decision."

"I suppose I am having a hard time understanding why you would just up and leave everything you've ever known to start all over again, Emily. It doesn't make sense to me."

"Honestly it doesn't make a ton of sense to me either, Mom." I shrugged my shoulders. "But I *have* to do this. I need this right now. I wish I could tell you why, but I can't."

"I wish you'd think about it a little more. You're making a rash decision, and I know you'll regret it in the end." She faced me.

I turned to her and raised my chin. "I'll regret it *more* if I don't do this."

"Then I'm not sure what you expect from me, Emily. Did you think that by telling me what your plans are that I'd plead with you to stay? I won't sit here and baby you. I think you're making a huge mistake, but obviously you have your reasons. I do, however, think you're wrong about many things. Your father and I did support you when you went to law school. Both times you failed the bar exam, we knew you were disappointed. Neither of us pressed you to keep trying because you didn't seem like you were willing to push yourself. As far as the situation with Michael goes, I stand by my resolve that Michael isn't the monster you've made him out to be. He is a human being that made a mistake. How would you like for someone to constantly hold your faults over your head and judge you for them?"

It was the same old story: I was the wrong one; therefore, I deserved everything I got from him. Furious, I leaned in towards her. "I am leaving.

There isn't a thing you can do about it. I am a grown woman, and it's time to carve my own path. You can either wish me a safe journey or get out. I have things to do." Hearing the same things come out of her mouth cemented my decision to leave.

My mother threw her hands in the air, and I knew what was coming next. "Fine, Emily! But when you get to New York and the grass isn't greener, don't come crawling back to your father and me. We won't be here to help you. The moment you step on that plane, you're on your own."

Her statement hurt, but my mind was set. Even though I was to the point of breaking down again, I wasn't going to let her see me like that. I just wanted her out of my house so I could finish packing. I had a ton of stuff to do and standing there listening to her place blame was wearing me out.

"Goodbye, Mom." I held the front door open for her to make her exit.

"Well, I suppose I will leave you to your devices then. Good Luck." She said on a huff. "Oh, before I forget." She stopped and reached inside of her Prada bag. "I thought you might want this." I recognized the gold glint of the nameplate I'd tossed in the garbage earlier. She dropped it on a stack of boxes by the door. I then watched her swagger out of my home. I was relieved to see her go. The light caught the glittering gold of the nameplate, and tears welled in my eyes, causing my vision to blur. I wasn't doing this. I wasn't letting her little gesture get to me like that. Getting on that plane in the morning was going to be the best decision I'd made in a long time. Over the past few years, I'd saved enough money that I'd be set for a while. It was all coming together. Maybe not exactly as I'd planned, but every plan in life had some sort of flaw.

So many emotions enveloped me after my mom left. I stood there in my living room, waiting for everything to crumble, and it did. I collapsed to the floor. I'd tried for years to have a normal relationship with my parents, but life with them was anything but normal. Weren't a mother and daughter supposed to reveal secrets and cry on each other's shoulders? It wasn't like that with me and my mom. I was lucky if she paid me an ounce of attention, and when she did, nothing I did was ever good enough. My whole life I felt like I was doing everything I could to make her love me more, but it just didn't work. She didn't care about me; I felt like a burden to her. Sometimes I wondered if she thought of me as a huge mistake.

As I sat there letting the cold hardwood of the floor chill my body, I sobbed harder than I had in my entire life. Part of me wanted to run after her and apologize, to tell her I loved her, so we could go back to the way things were. But who would that be benefiting? We would all be pretending and live a constant lie that things were all right. The fact was, nothing was okay.

I wept uncontrollably for several minutes. Severing the entire relationship with my family was brutal, but I told myself that maybe someday we could manage to fix what had been broken. I wanted that more than anything, but for now, I needed to fix myself.

Once I felt like my eyes could spill no more tears, I picked myself up from the floor. I didn't have the time to be weak. I had several small tasks to complete before my departure the next morning.

The last thing left to do was attack the contents of the top of my bedroom closet. Over the years, I had accumulated boxes of junk, and I needed to go through them and make sure there wasn't anything I wanted to take with me on my new journey. At first glance, everything on that shelf seemed so overwhelming. I wasn't an arsonist, but I wanted to strike a match and watch it all burn so I didn't have to mess with it.

I reached up to grab the first box and ended up placing my hand on something else instead. I stood on my toes to see what it was. I spotted an old scrapbook I'd made from my years at NYU. I'd forgotten all about it and must've shoved it in my closet at some point. I pulled it from its cozy resting place. The cover was embroidered with the violet-colored NYU insignia and underneath it was the schools motto in Latin, *perstare et praestare.* I was surprised that I immediately knew what those words meant, even after all the years since college: *To persevere and excel.*

I held the fabric-covered album to my chest and walked to my bed. I sat down lightly on the end and placed the book in my lap. Taking a deep breath, I pulled the front cover open and started flipping through the stiff pages. I glanced at numerous newspaper clippings I'd saved, flyers from student events I'd helped organize, and pages upon pages of photos from my time there. I hadn't looked through this scrapbook in years, but seeing it now transported me right back to some of the happiest days of my life. I'd been able to be myself back then. I'd had a freedom that I didn't have here in L.A. It must have been the fact that I wasn't around my stifling family. I'd had a reason to smile and laugh when I was in college. I was doing something for *myself* when I was there. I was on track to become a successful lawyer, and I was proud of my accomplishments.

My heart nearly stopped when I came upon one certain photograph. I remembered having that picture taken like it was yesterday. It was my last year of law school, and I'd just finished helping a friend move into an apartment. My hair was pulled up on top of my head, with pieces sticking out every direction, and my oversized T-shirt hung loosely off one shoulder. But what caught my attention was the person in the picture with me.

We all have a best friend in life, that one person who lights up our days like they're carrying rays of sunshine in their back pockets, but my best friend just happened to be a guy.

Jake Bradford. We were taking most of the same classes with hopes of becoming successful attorneys when we graduated, and we often found ourselves spending copious amounts of time with each other.

From the first day we met, we hit it off. We just clicked. Were we romantically linked? No. It wasn't as if I didn't want to be; I just always felt like there was some invisible force that wouldn't let us be together. Jake was a good-looking, sweet guy, so there was always a girlfriend around. When there wasn't, I was afraid to make a move on him. I would always be afraid that if something happened between us, our friendship would suffer. I couldn't bring myself to damage that relationship. I told myself that I would rather have him in my life as a friend then nothing at all.

Maybe that made me a coward. Maybe I was just a pansy ass for not standing up and telling him how I felt back then. There were just too many what-ifs. If someone had told me that I wouldn't lose our friendship if we dated, I would have jumped at the chance to be with him. But life offered zero guarantees, so I sat back and watched as he had relationship after relationship. It was a sad reality, but one I'd learned to live with so I didn't lose my friend.

I also couldn't bring myself to believe he had any interest in me besides just being my friend and study partner. Jake had never made any advances toward me or spoke in a way to make me think he found me even the slightest bit attractive. But he was the one person that understood me more than anyone else on the planet.

He could see right through me, and it shook me to the core. I felt like a completely different person when I was with him, more like… myself. Instead of dwelling on something that would never be, I put my energy toward trying to graduate and starting a life that made me happy.

As I sat staring at the photo, I smiled at the two of us looking so carefree and full of life. What I wouldn't have given to take a trip back in time and feel that again. In the photo, I was cuddled into the curve of Jake's arm, his lips pressed against my temple as we both laughed at something someone was saying. All my old feelings of wishing *what if* bubbled to the surface.

I ran my fingers over the smooth surface and couldn't help but wonder what things would have been like if we had actually been more than what we were. I would've never admitted it out loud until now, but I think I'd fallen in love with him back then. Perhaps, I was still in love with him. Was that possible?

After graduating with honors, we said our goodbyes. We resolved to stay in contact via email, snail mail and texts, but our lives became busier than we anticipated. I moved back to California and knew that he'd planned on moving back to his home state of Texas to get started. A small part of me wanted to ask him to stay in New York so he and I could hang out together. I would have stayed in the city for him. But there was also a part of me that needed to run away from my feelings for him, scared that I'd lose him if I acted on them.

Clearly, I just wasn't his type. He would always be my "one that got away." My best friend that helped me through so much that I could never repay him.

When I got home, I lost track of my life in New York. I was expected to date guys that were in my social circle. Once I met my fiancé, Michael, the thoughts of Jake crept in sometimes, but I was always loyal to Michael. I wouldn't betray someone like that. Even having thoughts of someone else was considered wrong to me. Looking Jake up would have made me feel like I was stepping out on my fiancé at the time.

Why was I doing this to myself? It was pure torture wanting something I knew I could never have. I refused to start my new life as a broken and damaged woman; my parents and my past had already inflicted enough trauma to last a lifetime.

I shut the cover of the book quickly and tossed it to the side. But then I reached for scrapbook again, and snagged the picture of us out. I'm not sure why I needed to keep it, but the sentimental side of me wasn't ready to let it go just yet. I was never to live in the past again, but some things I couldn't toss away like garbage. That picture was one of them. When you find something that makes you smile, you want to hold onto it for as long as possible.

∞ *Two* ∞

MY NERVES RATTLED as I boarded the plane that would take me to my new life. My mother didn't try to call and wish me safe travels, and she carried my dad's balls around in her Gucci handbag. I knew I wouldn't be hearing from him either. He never spoke up for himself, much less for me. I loved my dad but his main focus was his business.

I would always carry a certain sadness for the death of my relationship with my family, but maybe I was numb at this point. I wanted to forgive and forget the things that'd happened between all of us, but I couldn't manage to just sweep it all under the rug.

The seats on my flight filled up quickly, and soon we were climbing to an altitude that somehow made me calmer. I packed my iPad for something to do on the flight, and when I pulled it out of my large bag, the photo of Jake and me fell into my lap. I let out a sigh and held it in my hand once more.

"Isn't he a handsome fellow?" The passenger next to me commented.

"Yes, he was, thank you."

"Was? Did something happen to him, Dear?"

I couldn't help but want to talk to my new acquaintance. She was the grandmotherly type, with salt and pepper hair and glasses that sat low on the bridge of her nose. I felt strangely at ease with her.

"Oh, no, nothing like that," I said. "He was my best friend in law school. I haven't seen him since we graduated."

"Is that why you're heading to New York? Will he be there waiting for you?" She looked hopeful.

"No, I'm actually moving there. I have a job and a place waiting for me. I'm excited about it all. A fresh start, if you know what I mean."

I fell silent. I felt a blush crawl up my neck as she waited for me to continue. "He moved back to Texas the last time I'd heard, anyway. He was supposed to set up a law office there." I offered a small smile. I still had a sense of pride for Jake. He'd set out to accomplish his goals and dreams.

"Honey, I know all about starting over. Everyone needs a clean slate at least once in their lives. But can I give you a word of advice?"

I nodded. "Sure."

She grabbed the photo from my hand. "Always tell those who matter how you feel, even if you're afraid to. The one thing I've learned about life is that you can't go through it with regrets. Someday you'll be taking your last breath and wish you'd said or done something, and it will be too late then."

I couldn't argue with her. I'd loved Jake, and I still held a candle for him now. He was such a special man. I had no doubt that some amazing woman had already snagged him up, and he probably had a house full of babies running around climbing curtains and eating crayons. When we graduated, I was fairly certain he was going to ask his girlfriend of two years to marry him. I refused to admit I was jealous: she really was perfect for him. Beautiful, intelligent—hell, I wanted to *be* her just to be even closer to Jake.

"I'm not so sure that's a good idea." I let out a breath I'd been holding while she spoke.

"Well I don't know about now, but if this picture is anything to go by, this man was just as much in love with you as you are him, Sweetie."

What could I say to that? Maybe she was seeing something I wasn't? "Thank you. I'll keep that in mind if I ever run into him." I knew *that* would be about as likely as me sprouting wings and flying south for the winter. Jake was long gone.

The older woman patted my hand with sincerity and returned the picture to me. I tucked it safely into my bag once more and turned on my e-reader. It would be a few hours until we landed in New York and I really wanted to finish the steamy romance novel I'd been engrossed in every night before I went to sleep. The next thing I knew, my eyelids felt like bricks and slowly shut.

The room became brighter. It was like someone was operating a dimmer switch and was setting the mood for what was about to take place. I gently elevated my head from a soft pillow to see the silhouette of a gorgeous male figure standing at the foot of my bed. His considerable frame seemed to dwarf the room, making me feel small and helpless.

A serene heat lit his eyes and made my body melt like an overheated ice cube. He saw right through me and dug deep down into my soul, reading my intense need.

My body and mind were mesmerized by his presence; I was under a hypnotic spell with just one blazing glance. He made no attempt to move. I felt weighed down by an invisible force that I couldn't see or touch. It was as if my body was encased in metal and I was being pulled by the magnet that was this incredible man.

His jaw was strained, as if he were hanging onto his last shred of control with an unraveling thread. Could someone die from just looking at a creature like him? If so, I would have gladly taken my last breath.

I trailed my eyes just a bit lower, and my breath caught in my throat. Apparently, I affected him just as much as he was arousing me. A noticeable bulge strained against the front of his jeans. My visual discovery was cut short by his voice, a soft whisper sending a shock wave of desire radiating through me like an electric charge. "Don't move."

I was still pinned in place by his evocative stare. Slowly, he reached for the zipper of his jeans and tugged it down. The sound of the metal rasping against metal echoed through the room, and my stomach lurched with anticipation. What would he do to me? With me? So many erotic visions orbited around my brain, and my insides were reeling. I wanted this, wanted him. Now.

Once his zipper was down, he removed his pants and let them collapse into a pool of worn denim. He stood gloriously nude. I felt like it was my birthday and this god was my gift, although he was already unwrapped and ready to be played with. His hand wrapped around his hard length and stroked it leisurely from root to tip, the whole time never shifting his eyes from mine. The image was astounding, and my breath hitched in my throat. Just knowing that he was looking at me while pleasuring himself made me feel like I could shatter with pleasure. I felt as though I might combust if he didn't touch me soon.

I could feel the dampness growing between my thighs, and I ached to have him fill the need bubbling inside me like a volcano on the verge of eruption.

A shimmering pearl of moisture seeped from the engorged head of his cock, begging for my tongue to taste the saltiness waiting there. But I obeyed the silent commands in his blazing stare and continued to watch him.

I slowly drew my hand down my sweat-slicked body and positioned my fingers over my sensitive, swollen bud. I could see the corners of his mouth lift in an approving smile; this was what he wanted.

I'd never experienced anything as erotic as what we were doing in that frozen moment. I could feel the tingling sensations of arousal build in my core. The telltale flutters felt as if someone released a thousand butterflies in my stomach. I moved my other hand lower and dipped two fingers into my drenched opening.

I began to pump my fingers in and out, raising my hips, and straining toward completion. The desire was building with incredible force. The urge to close my eyes tightly overtook me, so I wouldn't have to actually see the stars that I knew were going to overtake me.

I couldn't, though; his gaze was locked tight onto mine while he pleasured himself. I kept my eyes wide, locked with his, and watched him fight to keep his self-control. If I was going to lose my mind, then he should go down with me.

I moved my fingers rapidly over my sensitive clit, felt my toes start to go numb, and my breathing turn into furious panting. His groans made every sensation I was experiencing amplified. My insides began to tighten, and the feeling of my release reached higher. The edge was there, and all I needed was to leap over it with abandon.

"Come for me." He whispered.

At his whispered words, I soared. I screamed with intense pleasure as it overtook my entire body. My head thrashed from side to side, as I sought the logic of the sensations that consumed me. Nothing could've been better than this moment. I was riding the high like a surfer taking on the most magnificent of waves.

"Excuse me, Miss." I felt someone gently shaking me. "We're beginning our descent into JFK; I'm going to need your seat in the upright position please." My eyes flew open, and I realized that the passengers in the seats nearby were staring at me, including the kind woman next to me.

Somewhere in between LAX and JFK, I managed to have an extremely vivid dream about *Jake*. Even though I couldn't completely make out his face, I knew who it was. By the current condition of my panties, I daresay it was erotic. What the hell had happened to me that I was having naughty dreams about a guy I hadn't seen in years?

How did I let this happen? Why didn't I ever say anything? I can remember sitting in our favorite coffee shop, half a block from my apartment, and talking about the future with Jake. We'd always assumed we'd be in each other's lives. The idea that his Texas grit didn't meld with my L.A. roots never occurred to us.

He'd listened patiently to me as I'd complained about my nonexistent love life. And I'd listen to his girl problems. And it hadn't seemed like a big deal. We were best friends.

Except that somewhere along the line, I stopped being satisfied with friends. I wanted more. So many times, I looked for an opening, any opportunity to tell him how I felt. But it never came. Or maybe I didn't recognize it. Maybe I'd been too scared of losing him completely, so I'd kept silent. He was my world back then. What if he rejected me? I wasn't sure I could survive it. I would rather have him as a friend than not have him in my life at all.

And now I felt like some sort of failure for not being able to follow through with what I truly wanted in my life. It hit me hard, what that woman on the plane had told me. No regrets. I felt like my life was one big regret. Regrets for not saying or doing the things I wanted most.

∞ *Three* ∞

AS SOON AS I EXITED the aircraft, my phone started ringing to the tone of *"Blow me Away"* by Breaking Benjamin. It was my anthem, and it soothed me in a punk rock sort of way. I loved when it would ring around my mother; she hated my tastes in music. I pulled the device from my bag and didn't recognize the number, but I answered it anyway.

"Hi, Emily, this is Marvin Carlton." It was my new boss. "Listen, I know you probably haven't had a chance to settle in yet, but I have a situation that I need your help with."

My nerves jangled, because not only had I just flown across the country, I was in dire need of a hot shower after my dream on the plane. So much for that idea. "Uh, sure, what can I do to help?" I wasn't going to deny my new boss anything. I didn't want to start things off on the wrong foot.

"I seem to have forgotten some important paperwork at my office for a hearing today. I had hoped you'd be in the city by now. Would you be able to swing by the office and grab them? My secretary's off for the day, and I saved the file on my computer and forgot to print it. Do you think you could do that for me?'"

"That shouldn't be a problem, sir. I'm actually at the airport now. Is there any way you could send me the address, and I'll be there as soon as I can?"

"I'll text it to you. We have until 3:30. The judge has already pushed this back, so your help would sure make my day. I wouldn't have called you, but I'm in a bit of a pickle."

"I completely understand, sir. I'll be there as soon as I can." I hung up from the call and hurried to baggage claim to collect my luggage.

Then I did a wobbly sprint on 5-inch heels through the terminal, hoping a taxi would be waiting outside.

I checked my watch as I loaded myself in an available taxi, noting that I had just enough time to get to the address he'd texted me and then to the courthouse. The entire ride was nerve racking. I'd just gotten off a plane and now I was thrown into the thick of things.

Of course, if I hadn't failed the bar exam twice (twice!), I might have been happily working at a law office instead of taking a job as a paralegal to run errands and file paperwork. Being a lawyer had been my dream. The day that I opened the email telling me I was a complete failure for the second time was the day I turned into something I hated. It shattered my confidence. After that, I had no other option but to work for my parent's production studio in Los Angeles. Technically, I was a production assistant, but that was just a fancy way of saying I was an errand girl. I think that was the moment that I couldn't stand to look at myself in the mirror anymore. I was disgusted at the person staring back at me. I'd thought about taking the exam again, but I could never muster up the confidence to do so. What if I failed again? I didn't think I'd survive it.

As the cab crawled through the over-crowded streets of New York City, I distracted myself with my surroundings. Unlike LA, which was nearly as crowded as it was spread out, you could find nearly everything you needed in a few street blocks in New York City. When I lived here, I didn't need a car – I simply walked everywhere or took the subway.

I should've been trying to organize my thoughts, but the familiarity of the sights of the tight neighborhoods and the smells of the city, both pleasant and unpleasant, made me feel like I was coming home.

I took a few moments to apply a fresh dusting of powder to my oily, travel-worn face, some mascara to highlight my icy blue eyes and a slathering of nude gloss to my lips. I pulled my long golden locks into a ponytail, instead of combatting its extreme frizz. I wasn't a fashion model by any means, but I wasn't a total dog, either. In the past, my mother complained that I needed to lose a few pounds, but in my opinion, I looked healthy. I had an hourglass figure that gave me just the right amount of curves. At least my appearance was one thing I was usually happy with.

The taxi pulled up in front of a high-rise building, and I hopped out. I gave him some extra cash so that he'd stay double-parked until

I retrieved the paperwork from Carlson's office. I didn't want to waste any time.

I entered the office building and headed for the fourth floor. When the elevator reached the lobby of the law office, I walked out and found the reception desk. The office was a ghost town. I peered up and down the halls, looking for someone to help me. I pulled out my phone and called my boss. He answered on the third ring. "Hello?"

"I'm at the office but everyone seems to be gone."

"Shit, it's lunch time. Is there any way you could get into the computer and print the documents? My office is locked and the only other person that has the key is the main receptionist."

"Sure. What's the password?" I walked around the desk and sat down in the rolling office chair behind it.

I typed in the password and luckily it granted me access to the computer system. "Now, find a file marked J984—once you pull that up go ahead and hit the print icon. The printer is in the cabinet below the desk."

I did as he said and within minutes I had the documents printed out. I shut the computer down and headed for the door. I was relieved when my cab was still at the curb. I jumped in and the car sped away from the curb, throwing me back against the cracked vinyl seat.

After thirty minutes of brutal traffic, the cabby pulled up in front of a familiar building with huge pillars holding up its impressive frame. Countless stairs led to its front entrance.

I hopped out of the car, paid the driver who had already set my bags on the curb and took a cleansing breath. As I rolled my cumbersome luggage toward the imposing steps, I could see a short plump man racing down toward me with sweat trickling down his creased brow.

"Miss Mills?" He shouted.

"Hi, Mr. Carlton." I held out my hand to shake his.

"No time for pleasantries—call me Marvin. We need to get back inside; the hearing is set to begin soon. Do you have the papers?" He held out his stubby fingers, into which I deposited the briefs. He snatched them away quickly and then turned to the building. I pulled my bags behind me as I followed him up the concrete steps. I figured I might as well stay since I was there.

Once inside, I trailed Marvin to a small room where another man sat in a leather office chair at the end of a long conference table. There were stacks of file folders and documents piled high at the opposite end of the table. I sat quietly in a chair nearby while the client and Marvin carried on a conversation between themselves. I felt like an outsider sitting in that room. I knew I'd screwed up my chance to be a part of something, and I couldn't help but be angry with myself again.

I scrolled through my phone while I sat there, checking a few emails, text messages and jotting a couple of things in my phone's calendar. I looked up to see my new boss crossing the room toward me. "Since you're here, why don't you come with us and observe? It might come in handy someday."

"Sure." I stood up and followed him and his client out of the room. We walked down a long hallway, my heels clicking on the floor.

As we walked into a massive courtroom, the two men I was with took a seat at a table to the right. I stayed behind and sat down in a row of chairs behind them, settling my purse under my chair. For some reason, nervousness hit me while sitting there. I knew I wasn't part of the case, but being in a courtroom again was intimidating. I hadn't been in one since my internships in law school, and even back then I had anxiety about being close to the scales of justice. I suppose every aspiring lawyer has unsteady nerves at some point or another. The only time I wasn't nervous was when Jake and I were observing together on a case. We would sit back and watch, much like I was today, and he would make me feel at ease by whispering silly jokes or writing goofy little notes and passing them to me. It wasn't very professional, but I think he knew I felt overwhelmed and wanted to calm me down. I wished he were here today; maybe he could tell me that everything in my life would work out and eventually I could be happy.

We waited for the judge to enter, so I glanced around, taking in the ambiance of the room. As imposing as the room was, it was beautiful in its own way. The sleek grain from the wood of the judge's bench gleamed in the soft lighting of the modern fixtures hanging above. I could smell a hint of furniture polish as if someone came in each day to make every item in the large room shine. Each chair in the juror's box was lined up perfectly as if waiting for people to come in and occupy them at any moment. And the unmistakable air of right and wrong hung in the atmosphere almost so palpable you could touch and taste it. It was not only a feast for the eyes; it was one for the senses. It was a room where things happened, where people stood pleading for one reason or another, hoping that justice would be served. Where sometimes even I knew that things weren't always what they seemed. The court reporter sat in her small cubby with her laptop and protected microphone. She looked about as happy to be there as a chicken in a lion enclosure at the zoo. Her small-framed glasses sat low on her wide nose, and she smacked a wad of gum between her teeth sounding like a small child enjoying his lunch way too much. There were a few other people in the room also; I assumed they were waiting for their turn on the docket for the day.

Marvin leaned over the short wooden partition toward me and whispered, "No worries, we'll be out in a flash." He smelled of sweat and breath mints, which wasn't pleasant.

I pasted on a smile and nodded. Across the room, I could see the plaintiff waiting patiently for his attorney to arrive. There were still a few minutes until 3:30.

I heard the double wooden doors of the courtroom open with a resounding creak, and I automatically turned to see a tall, broad man step through. His black suit was tailored perfectly, fitting every inch of him like a glove. His leather briefcase hung from his fingers, and he walked with purpose in his stride. I trailed my gaze toward his face, and as he came closer, I let out a gasp that caused everyone to glance my way.

I would have recognized those blue eyes anywhere. They were the same ones that plagued my dreams and belonged to the man in the photo that was still tucked safely in my bag beside me. *Jake*.

He'd obviously heard me and turned his head, making eye contact with me. His stride stopped abruptly. It was as if his feet were glued to the floor where he stood. One corner of his mouth turned up in a half smile, but not too much that he ruined the bravado he'd come in with.

Our gazes locked for moments. I could feel heat fill my cheeks, my palms became sweaty and my thighs began to squirm. *This* Jake was so much better than the one I'd reminisced about. Sure, he was the same guy, but he'd filled out in so many ways.

Jake was still tall like I'd remembered; his hair was the same sandy brown but was cut in a more professional style. He wasn't the shaggy boy that I'd known all those years ago.

"Are you okay, Miss Mills?" Marvin's voice brought me back to earth.

"Uh yes, I just…I'm fine." I let out a breath I didn't realized I'd been holding from the moment I saw Jake walk in.

Jake dropped his gaze and strode toward his client. He sat down, and then leaned over to his client whispering something in his ear. I couldn't do anything but watch him. How was it that I was just thinking about how I wished he was here, and *poof*, he appeared? Did I have a genie in a magic lamp nearby? Maybe I needed to visit a casino or buy a lottery ticket when I left here. If all I had to do was mentally wish for something, then I needed to make a list of things I wanted.

My brain was *filled* with him now, and my body betrayed me with its sudden reaction. My panties were moist again, and surely everyone around me could see the stiff peaks of my nipples through my blouse. I folded my arms over my chest, just in case. I also crossed my legs tightly, but it did nothing to ease the ache that'd taken up residence in my core. At that point, I hoped this case would be over quickly because what I needed was a stiff drink and a cold shower. I couldn't very well get up and leave, either. Just as the thought crossed my mind, the judge entered the courtroom. *Too late to make my escape.*

∞ *Four* ∞

I SAT SILENTLY while watching the proceedings of the courtroom, but the entire time my eyes were on Jake. As he spoke, he looked so at ease with his surroundings. He had a confidence that screamed "power." His voice was self-assured and every comment he made was calculated and precise. It was like watching a movie being played out in front of me, and Jake was the lead actor. The courtroom belonged to him.

My palms became moist with nervousness as the final words were spoken in the room. Marvin stood up and walked over to shake Jake's hand. The two exchanged some quiet words, and I used that time to make my exit. I felt like I was running as I found the small room where my luggage waited and then made for the exit. I wanted to get out of there before Jake had the chance to find me. I didn't really know what I was running from, but I couldn't be there. I made it outside, and the sunlight nearly blinded me. I got halfway to the curb, and then stopped when I heard my name being called behind me.

"Emily, wait!"

I took in a deep breath and turned around to find Jake. He stood about ten feet away, looking as handsome as he had in the courtroom. "Damn, I didn't realize I was *that* intimidating in there." He laughed as he walked closer to me.

"I'm sorry, I was trying to make sure I got a cab." It sounded lame even to my ears.

"Wow, it's been so long. I didn't realize you were back practicing law in New York. Didn't you move to L.A. with your folks?"

Oh, God, I didn't want to go down this road. It was humiliating enough to have to think about it every single day of my life. But he used to be my best friend. Surely he would understand. "I'm not a lawyer, Jake. I failed the bar. Twice."

"What? You're kidding me right? You had a GPA higher than mine. How the heck did you manage to fail the bar *twice*, Emily?" He laughed.

I was mortified. Of all people, I didn't think Jake would laugh at me for failing. My nervousness quickly turned to anger. "I guess I'm just a fucking idiot," I bit out and turned away from him.

I walked closer to the curb where several taxis were parked, waiting for their next fare. As I reached down to grab one of my bags, I felt a hand on my shoulder. I shot up and turned around, flinching.

Jake must have seen the look of sheer panic on my face because his expression softened. "I'm sorry, I didn't mean to startle you, Emily. Is everything okay?" He looked genuinely concerned.

It was just a gut reaction to shy away and be frightened when anyone put his or her hands on me. I was gun shy after the whole ordeal with Michael. Of course, I didn't think that *every* person I came across would beat the shit out of me like he did, but for some reason I was cautious even so.

"I'm sorry, too, Jake. Sorry that you've turned into an asshole who makes fun of people for their shortcomings. I have to go." I walked away and helped the driver load my bags into the trunk.

"Wait, I didn't mean anything by it. I was surprised. Emily, you can't fault me for trying to make a joke."

"You're right, I don't fault you for making a joke, but I do fault you for not having tact when it comes to talking with someone that *used* to be your best friend. I would've thought you were better than that, Jake."

Jake stood there with a dumbfounded look on his face. Yes, I was being a mega bitch towards him, but didn't I have a right to? It wasn't like he'd come out and said I was an idiot, but it was implied in the way he laughed at my failure. This wasn't the same thoughtful man I'd know in my past; this guy in front of me was a dickhead. His high-powered job had obviously gone straight to his head.

I must have struck a nerve with Jake. He said nothing as I folded myself into the car and closed the door. I looked out the window as it pulled away to see Jake still standing in the sunlight. He was running his hand through his hair while talking to himself.

I faced forward and let out a frustrated breath. What did I expect? I hadn't expected him to waltz into that courtroom and throw my body and mind into a tailspin. This new beginning was meant to cleanse myself of almost everything that reminded me of my past. I knew that the two worlds would collide on some level eventually, but to have Jake be the catalyst of it was throwing me for a loop.

What was he even doing in New York? Back in college, he'd always talked about going home to Texas where he could practice law close to his family. He spoke so highly of his relationship with his parents and brother. Why would he sacrifice what he held so dearly to stay nearly 1,500 miles away? If I had a normal, loving relationship with my parents, I would have stayed without any qualms. But I didn't, and that was the reason I found myself riding in a cab on the way to my new apartment.

∞ *Five* ∞

I FELT A SENSE OF DEFEAT as the cab driver drove me to what was my new home. My entire body was numb. It was as if someone has taken a vacuum cleaner and sucked the life right out of me. The worst of all of it: I never thought Jake would be a prick like he was being. Being laughed at for my failure wasn't the *worst* thing that could've happened to me, but it certainly wasn't the best either. It wasn't like I expected him to throw his arms around me and confess his undying love or anything, but a friendly "how have you been?" or "it's so good to see you" would have been a nice start to things.

Maybe I was being a drama queen about it. I was over sensitive about damn near everything lately. If I wasn't pissed off about something, I was usually crying and feeling sorry for myself. I hated this side of myself. It was like having several different people living in my head, telling me how to feel about every situation I was in. Some days, I wish I could've just found a hole, crawled in it and hid from the world. But this was real life; I needed to start facing problems head on. Running and hiding from them wouldn't do anything but create more problems.

The taxi trudged along the streets of New York, with me trapped in my own head in the back. I replayed everything from the time Jake walked into the courtroom with his self-assured swagger to the moment he put his hand on my shoulder near the sidewalk. Yes, being touched freaked me out, but I couldn't lie to myself and say I didn't feel something when I was. I might have been imagining things, but the spot where he laid his hand still carried heat throughout my body.

Even when Michael and I were together, I'd never felt a sensation like that when his hands were on me during romantic moments. He wasn't my very first relationship; I'd dated guys here and there. But he was the first one who made me feel special. In the beginning he made me feel like I actually mattered to someone. We dated for a year before he asked me to marry him, and when he did I was overjoyed. We seemed to click, but after that things went south. I noticed that I was trying to create a fantasy out of our relationship. I made excuses for his behavior constantly. My friends in L.A. would bring things to my attention about Michael, but I would brush them off and take up for his shortcomings.

Even if I had a rewind button, I don't think I would've been smart enough to change things. I was content being oblivious to his ways, and in the end, I suffered dearly for my choices. It wasn't *all* my fault—I know that now—but had I opened my eyes to what was happening each day, I would have been better prepared for the night he finally snapped.

But I thought things were perfect...well, as perfect as they could be. Michael was honestly the very first man that my parents ever approved of me being with. I think maybe I thought because they were all for the relationship, maybe—just maybe—they would be more supportive of me. But it didn't work out that way.

I had to stop beating myself up over the bad choices I'd made in the past. I would file them away as lessons learned and try to make better ones.

The cab finally reached my destination and pulled up outside of an industrial-looking building in the meatpacking district. I'd looked online for months trying to decide where I wanted to live; the antiquated look and feel of the neighborhood there instantly snagged my attention. I loved that there was an aspect of trendy nightlife, small upscale eateries and shopping boutiques that showcased designs from local designers from around the city. It was a far cry from the mansions and sprawling estates I'd become accustomed to in Los Angeles, but I knew it was perfect, as it would offer a new backdrop for my fresh start.

The façade of the building was a dark grey brick and had a main entrance that could only be accessed with a passcode. There were only three stories, but each one offered floor to ceiling windows. A small local bakery was nestled quaintly on one side and a clothing resale shop on the other. Glancing around the street, I already felt like I'd made the right choice in locations. The sidewalks buzzed with people, some dressed in boho chic, relaxed and carefree and others in business attire. Some walked hurriedly while gabbing away on their phones, and some seemed to stop and take in everything around them like they appreciated the atmosphere. I smiled to myself knowing that soon I'd be one of those people, going to or from work, sipping my morning coffee and tasting the delights that the restaurants nearby had to offer. My troubles seemed to have drifted away for a few moments as I sat in the back of the cab soaking in everything around me.

"Hey, lady, you going to get out? Or you going to sit in my cab and daydream all day?" The driver interrupted my thoughts with his thick Bronx accent.

I pushed the door open and placed a foot on the curb in front of my apartment building. The driver got out and rounded the yellow beast, popping the trunk open to retrieve my luggage. He plopped the bags down and looked to me for his money. I pulled some cash from my wallet and he snatched it up as soon as I held it out.

"Thanks. Lemme give ya a word of advice, Lady: there ain't no time for dreamin' in *this* city. Everything moves fast. If ya don't wanna get ran over, ya better pay attention," he rudely stated and got back into the car. I stood there with my mouth damn near touching the pavement as he peeled away from the curb and merged with honking traffic.

Wow. I hadn't even been there a day, and I had encountered enough impolite people to last me a lifetime. It was shitty that Jake was one of them. I guess if I was going to live here, I'd need to grow a thicker skin or get trampled on.

After I wheeled my suitcases toward the front door of the building I pulled out my phone to find the passcode for entrance into the building. I still had it stored in my phone, in an email from the building owner's assistant.

I'd worked with my realtor mostly online so my mother wouldn't catch wind of what my plans were. Keeping everything a secret was hard; I'd been told that people could read me like an open book. Being dishonest wasn't something I enjoyed doing, but in this case, I felt like I had to. I convinced myself that it was in my best interest to keep things on the down low, and in the end I was glad I chose to do so.

I was told the owner of the property lived on the top floor of the three-story building, and he'd decided to lease the smaller apartments below. Even though they were classified as smaller, the space provided was ample enough for just me. I didn't need something huge, just a place to call home. I did some online research on the seller and found out it was a company called J&B Properties. Given the great reputation of the company, I decided this place would be perfect and signed the papers just a month before revealing my plans to my mother.

I'd been saving for several years while in L.A. At first I didn't really know what I was stashing back money for. I knew that eventually I wanted to strike off on my own, but once I made the decision to go back to New York I was glad I'd kept up with the saving.

I tapped in the passcode for the outer door and pulled my luggage up the stairs to the second floor where my new home awaited. Standing outside my door, I took a deep breath as I slid my key into the lock. When I pushed the door open, I was relieved to see the moving company had already brought most of my belongings in and placed them in various spots around the open floor plan. The sunlight shone through the huge windows, creating a twinkling effect as it landed on the small dust particles flitting through the air. The smell of fresh paint met my nose, along with the scent of the old building. Together they created something that was warm and inviting.

I parked my luggage near the door and walked further into my living space. I spun around like a giddy child celebrating her birthday. Was this what freedom felt like? Was there a point where I would become overwhelmed by all of this? It seemed like I was always waiting for the other shoe to drop. So I mentally calmed my merriment down and tried to act like an adult.

I knew the larger pieces of furniture wouldn't be delivered until the next day, so I had a backup of sleeping on an air mattress for the night.

I took some time getting to know my surroundings and planned in my head where things might go in each room once I unpacked. I managed to hook up the television so I could at least have some background noise while I worked at getting some things put away. Luckily my new place included the use of cable TV. I don't know what I would've done otherwise. Even though I had my nose buried in a book most of the time, I did enjoy my silly reality television. I rifled through a few boxes at first, but between my long flight and the surprise errand for my new boss, I was exhausted.

Tonight I would just relax; I wasn't supposed to start my new job until Monday so I still had Saturday to unpack my belongings and get settled in. I grabbed the TV remote and flipped on the flat screen, browsing through some channels as I went.

I finally settled on a popular celebrity news program. Somehow, watching celebs lives fall apart on national television made me feel better about myself. How sadistic was that? No matter how messed up my life was, shows like that made me feel like I lived a "Leave it to Beaver" lifestyle. Too bad my mother really wasn't June Cleaver.

I wasn't paying much attention while mindlessly unwrapping some knick-knacks when I happened to glance up for a second. On the screen, in my living room, was my ex fiancé, Michael Parker.

"What is that fucker doing on TV?" I said as bile rose in my throat. I turned up the volume so I could hear what he was saying. The churning continued in the pit of my stomach, mixing with a heavy dose of fear that overtook me at the sound of his voice. Every syllable he spoke transported me back to the night when everything changed.

"I just want Emily to know that I love her, and I know in my heart we're meant to be together." The roiling in my gut became worse, so I sprinted to the kitchen to find the garbage can. I emptied the contents of my stomach with several loud heaves and stood up, grasping my aching midsection. Wiping my mouth with the back of my hand, I went back to the television like the glutton for punishment that I was. It was like a train wreck, and I just couldn't take my eyes off of it. This guy *never* quit! Holy shit, I broke it off with him over four years ago, and he was still pining for me like I was his lost puppy. I wouldn't have been surprised to see him holding up printed flyers or a milk carton with my image plastered on them.

His sob story continued for all the world to see. "I'm not sure where she is, but Emily, if you see this, please…I love you, come back home." He pleaded with teary eyes. *What a joke.*

Fury rose in my veins. "Love, huh? Was that what it was called when you beat the shit out of me? Was it love when you cracked my head open on the end table in your apartment and then broke my ribs?" I screamed at the TV as if it were really Michael in the room with me. I grabbed the remote and flung it as hard as I could manage toward the television in my fit of rage. I heard a resounding crack through the hollow room when it smashed into the LCD screen. When I inspected the device, the screen was covered in what looked like a massive spider web. One small circle in the middle where the remote made impact, and smaller lines branching out. *Well damn.*

I was disappointed in myself for acting so childish. I shouldn't have let him get the better of me like that. Even so, I was in disbelief that a celebrity gossip program was rehashing old news. They must have been grasping at straws to find a worthy story to air, but plastering Michael's face all over the screen was hardly worthy. He wasn't even considered a "celebrity" in the circles that counted in Hollywood. Yeah, he'd done a few popular low-budget films, a couple commercials and a week or so stint on General Hospital, but those were hardly roles to write home about. He was a D-list actor who believed he was God's gift to the silver screen.

Our breakup had been the center of media attention for a month or so after it happened, and *not* because of Michael. The stories usually centered on my parents and me since they owned one of the biggest studios in L.A. It was hard to believe they were stuck on a story that'd fizzled out long ago. Either way, seeing it brought back my anger and resentment toward my parents and my ex-fiancé. Watching it being replayed again was like taking a hard jab to my emotional balance.

My parents tried to keep the press out of the situation to help save Michael's budding acting career, but in doing so they pushed me further away. In a way, it was the beginning of the end with my parents. I was their daughter; they were supposed to protect me.

The blame for Michael's drinking problem was placed on me. Each time something would happen, my mom would tell me how I needed to control him. How I should talk to him. I'd tried—I really had. There were several occasions when he and I would sit and discuss what I felt was him tumbling down a slippery slope. For short periods of time he would seem to change his ways. He would either limit his alcohol intake, or not partake at all when we went to an event. My parents gave me a pat on the back when he straightened up his act. My mom would say things like "I see you've managed to rein him in" or "great job on controlling your fiancé." I felt like they thought it was my job to babysit a grown man.

I tried to be the best girlfriend and partner I could, but nothing would've been able to curb his appetite for booze. Not even love. I know I loved him at some point, but eventually I knew it wasn't going to work. I stayed longer than I should because I thought maybe my mom was right, maybe I *was* enough to change him. I forgot that if a person wanted to change, they would make the effort to do it.

For the last several years, every time I closed my eyes, all I could see was him violently kicking me to the floor and smashing my head on the end table on the way down. Even now I could still feel the searing pain as my head made blunt contact with the sharp edge. My image in the mirror horrified me. I didn't recognize the person staring back at me. Two black eyes, a darkly bruised cheek where he'd struck me so viciously, and stitches on the side of my head where my scalp was cracked open like a fresh watermelon. It was like looking at someone else's reflection.

I vowed to myself that I would never let someone lay a hand on me again. I would never let someone else make me feel weak and helpless in my own skin. I deserved better. I even went as far as to take some self-defense classes, and once I completed them I felt stronger. Not just physically, but mentally so. But the one thing that suffered the most was my ability to trust people again. I hadn't had a romantic relationship since then nor did I want one. I guess you could say I was extremely gun shy.

Lately, he'd been trying to get in touch with me. I would get emails from him, saying things like "I'm so sorry, I will go to rehab. I will change for you." And "If I'm going to be a better person, I need you to help me do it." There were times I would get ridiculous amounts of flowers at work with little cards, begging me for another chance. My mother stood by and watched as each bundle would be tossed in the garbage. I wanted no reminders of the horror he put me through.

I had to turn my mind off. It kept replaying the day's events, and Jake always seemed to be at the forefront of everything. I still couldn't believe he would just laugh in my face like that. The man I'd known in my time at NYU and the man I'd faced in front of the courthouse weren't the same. Maybe his time in New York after college made him more brazen than he'd been since the days we quietly studied for our final exams and watched *When Harry Met Sally* a million times together.

Damn, I'd never really realized how closely that movie resembled Jake and me. No matter how many times Jake and I searched for love, we always ended up right back with one another. But I suppose we answered the age-old question of "can a man and woman be friends, without the complication of sex?" back then. Given the chance though, I would've taken that step with him.

As I milled sadly about through my apartment I broke into a smile thinking about the things we'd done back then. Of course I'd been

fortunate enough to visit New York when I was younger with my
parents, and Jake knew that. He also wanted the "Big Apple" experience.
He wanted to visit all the silly tourist spots and eat at the well-known
eateries. Jake thought he would become a *real* New Yorker if he did
those things, and so I acted as his tour guide.

I had a blast taking him to the spots I thought best reflected what the
city was about. Our first stop was Gray's Papaya for a juicy scrumptious
hot dog. Jake nearly flipped out when he saw the almost $2.00 price tag
of the beefy treats, but as soon as he bit into the delight, his eyes rolled
back in his head and a small *not so* manly moan escaped. I think I'd
always taken things like that for granted. I remember standing there
as we devoured our lunch, taking in the classic red uniform shirts of
those who worked there, the smells of the juicy dogs lined up behind
the protective see-through barrier and the funny look of the fries, stuffed
in a Styrofoam cup, slathered in cheese sauce.

After we ate until I felt like I might burst, I talked Jake into visiting
Central Park. It may have been a cliché location to take him, but he
wanted the full experience. When we got there, Jake could hardly believe
that such a place was smack dab in the middle of such a busy city.
Sometimes I had a hard time believing it too. We stopped by the Bethesda
fountain and threw pennies in while making secret wishes. I recall looking
at Jake right before I'd made my wish. His face was so full of concentration
and determination, I was certain he was wishing for something having
to do with his future as a lawyer. Mine on the other hand wasn't. I
plunked my coin into the water with a small splash and made a wish
that Jake would always be happy no matter what. I wanted him to
succeed and see his dreams come true. I watched the copper coin sink
to the bottom of the fountain among the thousands of other hopeful
pieces of money. I wondered what others went there to dream about.
Were they hoping for true love when they tossed their coins below, or
were they just hoping to get through one day at a time?

Afterwards we walked around just admiring the landscape and
soon ended up at a place that had always been my favorite when my
parents took me there as a child. The Alice in Wonderland statue. The
fantasy of seeing the characters from my favorite book come alive in a
sculpture was awe-inspiring. The bronze glow of Alice holding court
with the Mad Hatter and the White rabbit were images I fell back to any
time I'd have a bad day. They always managed to make me smile. The

fact that the artist created the work of art as a tribute to his late wife was such a romantic gesture. To craft something with your own two hands for someone you loved was incredible. I don't think Jake understood the meaning behind it though, and I didn't expect him to either. Men thought differently than women. To us, things held special meanings; to men, they were just another object to take up space. I could still remember the promises he'd made back in our days at college. First of all he made a pact that we would always be friends no matter what. He also told me that one day he would take me through the city and do all the goofy things that tourists do: visit the Statue of Liberty, stand in the middle of Times Square, and even have a hot dog at Gray's Papaya.

Truthfully, though, I celebrated our time at our favorite hangout—the coffee shop—more than anything. One of our fellow students turned us onto *Caffe' Dante* during our second semester of our freshman year, and it was conveniently located near the law school on MacDougal Street. It was just a short walk that Jake and I would use to catch each other up on things we felt like saying. The green awning and the weathered sign were always new and inviting each time we spotted it from the sidewalk. The way the word "espresso" wound around the café name on the deep brown sign always made me giggle. It was placed in a way that made you think someone became lazy or ran out of room while painting the sign. There were a few tables scattered outside that were usually filled with students clicking away on their laptops or small groups of people discussing an assignment that needed attention. Jake and I would always choose a place inside to sit, though. We both loved the smell of freshly brewed espresso overtaking the interior of the longstanding establishment. The fresh pastries and cheeses offered were always a temptation but the one thing I'd always partake of was the cappuccino. The piping hot cup of awesomeness warmed my palms on a blustery winter day and soothed the aches of stress on the days I felt like my brain might explode from studying. I could still remember just sitting there making idle chitchat like it was only him and me in the entire world. The place was normally filled to the brim with the vibe of excited students taking a break from the daily grind of college life. Even though the noise level reached annoying peaks at times there, it didn't really matter. Jake and I transported ourselves to a space where nothing else mattered. The place could have caught fire while we had a conversation, and honestly I don't think we'd notice. The smells of freshly brewed espresso and the scent of fresh baked nutty biscotti drifted through my senses and made me feel at home there with Jake.

I would sit and watch his mouth with so much concentration as he spoke, often wondering what the sensation of his kiss would be like. Would he be an unhurried, slow, passionate kisser? Or would he take charge like a hungry lion pouncing on its prey? My imagination would run rampant with the possibilities when thinking of him and me. But I knew it was just a fantasy. One I'd never *really* take charge of—one of those things that wasn't meant to be.

Even so, Jake was my rock back then; he was always there and never said "no" when I needed something. He would be there to help me lick my wounds after some prick dumped me for someone more apt to be a bikini model. He'd give me proper words of encouragement when an exam didn't go so well and help me to study harder for the next one. I sometimes wondered if Jake knew how much he meant to me and if I meant even a tiny bit more to him than *just* friends...

I once again had to pull my head from the clouds and concentrate on the tasks at hand. I would have loved nothing more than to sit there and daydream about him but that wasn't the reason I came back to New York. I came here to get away from the people who could give a damn less about me in my life. And that was what I was planning on doing.

I worked on unpacking some more of my things, but found myself overly tired after an exhausting day. I wanted nothing more than to take a relaxing shower.

As I unpacked my bathroom essentials from my suitcase, the steam of the shower filled the room and cleared my head just a bit more then I'd expected. I stepped into the inviting spray. My tense muscles relaxed under the pelting water, and I closed my eyes as the warm stream sluiced over my body. The dream from the plane continued to burn my mind.

Jake in the shower with me...washing my body...filling my senses...

Feeling his arms wrap around my stomach from behind me, I sighed as he kissed my neck gently. His rough hands roamed my body like they were mapping out the perfect trail to ecstasy, driving me crazy with desire. He spun me around and lifted me into his muscular arms, pinning my back to the cool tile of the shower wall.

Jake's mouth meandered over every overheated inch of me while he slowly began to push inside my channel, inch by delectable inch. He seared my nipples with his hot tongue while continuing to move in and out of me, achingly slow. I could feel the tension building inside of me like a massive explosion.

My arms twined around his neck for stability, knowing that soon I would fall over the edge, and I needed him to catch me when I did. His hand made its way down between us, where our bodies were so intimately joined, and he began to massage my swollen clit. My head fell back against the wall behind me with a thud, and my entire body began to shudder and convulse around his. Our juices combined as he poured himself inside of me, while my insides pulsed around him so violently that I was gasping for air.

My eyes flew open as the water of the shower began to cool. I looked down and realized that my fingers were buried in my folds, and they were drenched with my slick release. I was still trying to pull precious air into my lungs as I sank to the shower floor and shook with so many emotions. I was stunned and pissed that I would let myself enter into a fantasy about someone who hurt me today. That I would be so ignorant as to let my mind drift to a place it had no business being. I used the side of my hand to punch the wall beside of me, and a sharp pain shot up my arm. Tears seeped from my eyes, not only from the physical pain, but from the emotional turmoil that I had raging within me. The water turned even colder and goose bumps peppered my flesh, making me shiver uncontrollably. I couldn't seem to care. Maybe this is what I deserved.

∞ *Six* ∞

THE NEXT MORNING, I awoke with a renewed sense of self. The whole thing with Jake the day before was still bothering me, but I was determined not to let it ruin my day. I had a lot to do, and keeping busy was the best way to keep my mind off of him and everything else running through my head.

After slurping down several cups of coffee and watching the morning news, I decided it was time to get more organized and start to put things away in my new apartment. The moving company would be there soon to deliver my furniture, so I wanted to make room for everything before they got there.

I heaved boxes into different rooms, starting with the bedroom. One of the cardboard containers was marked "clothing," so that was a good place to start. As I sat on the floor busying myself, placing clothes on hangers, folding sweaters and various shirts the buzzer rang. I pushed the intercom on the wall by the door. "Hello?"

"Yeah, we're here with a furniture delivery for Miss Mills."

I pressed the button to unlock the downstairs door. When they were finished I signed off on the yellow delivery slip and sighed in relief when they were gone. I had a sense of being overwhelmed as I looked around at what could only be described as a "hot mess." I had my work cut out for me but was ready and willing to put in the time to make it all just right.

It took me a few hours of pushing, pulling and lugging things around, but I finally had the big items placed where I wanted them. I was really surprised at how much space there was in my apartment. Even after everything had been delivered, I still had plenty of room. I knew that wasn't typical of a NYC apartment, so I was very grateful for finding this place when I did.

Once the big pieces were where I thought they needed to be, I started unpacking boxes. It was strange, being alone in that apartment just going about my business. For a few moments I sat down and questioned myself, wondering if I had made the right decision to make.

I hated feeling guilty for leaving my parents. A part of me wanted to call my parents and let them know that I was safe in New York, but would they've even cared? Were they sitting by the phone waiting for confirmation that I'd made it okay and was settling in just fine? Or had they forgotten about me the moment I said goodbye.

I did regret not telling my dad goodbye. I wondered if he was hurt by what I'd done. I reminded myself that maybe one day I could salvage the relationship with the both of them. Maybe we could make amends and be a family again. I wanted that so much. But right now I couldn't bring myself to even pick up my phone. My pride refused to let me.

I spent the rest of the day getting things the way I wanted them and put away, along with taking a break to study for the bar. By 6 pm I was exhausted and famished, not to mention my brain was ready for a reprieve. I felt like I could have devoured an entire cow and still had room for dessert with all the energy I'd burned while unpacking.

I didn't cook, so I had to leave to find sustenance. Eventually I'd have to learn the art of the kitchen, but tonight wasn't the night. If I'd tried, the local fire department would have been banging down the door to save me from an epic disaster. I also didn't want to piss off the building owner by burning the place down on my second night. I threw on some clothes that weren't too wrinkled and headed out. As I walked along the streets in my new neighborhood, I passed by a pub where Indie rock music carried through the doors and onto the sidewalk. Spectators packed the small building with their hands in the air, celebrating their love for the songs the band played. I watched as a small boutique owner drug a clothing rack back into her store, closing up shop for the night.

I continued walking and came upon a Thai restaurant where satisfied patrons gathered outside after their meal. I looked up to see the name: "Spice Market." My stomach growled in approval, and I went inside to see if a table was available. The hostess looked to her seating chart and frowned. "I'm sorry, it looks like we're full for the night. But if you don't mind, there is room at the bar."

I took a seat on a tall bar chair and grabbed a menu. Everything looked so appetizing, and by the spicy smells wafting through the place,

I knew I wouldn't make a bad choice no matter what I decided to have. I looked around at the busy eatery and instantly fell in love with the casual, sexy atmosphere. Some customers were dressed up as if they were using the evening there to celebrate something, and others were like me, casually dressed and comfortable. I scanned the menu in my hands one more time before the waitress came over to take my order.

"I think I'll have the butternut squash soup, the spicy Thai slaw and the coconut sticky rice, please." I folded the menu back up and handed it to her. She trotted off to put in my order while I sat sipping on my cool glass of water. I found myself doing a fair amount of "people watching" while I waited for my dinner.

I was in my own little world when I heard someone beside me speak. "Hey there."

I turned. This guy was gorgeous. Tall, with short, dark blond hair and captivating hazel eyes.

"I'm Grant." He offered his hand and a killer smile.

"Emily."

"I'm sorry if this is really forward of me, but can I just say that you're extremely beautiful."

I couldn't help but blush at his compliment. "Thank you. That's a really nice thing to say...especially to a stranger." I laughed.

"I know. I'm sorry if that seemed like a sleaze ball thing to say. I was just sitting over there and you caught my eye. I come here a lot and haven't seen you around."

"I'm kind of new in town. I just moved here yesterday." I had a surge of shyness flushing my cheeks.

"Ah, a newbie. Well, welcome to the City. I hope everything is going good so far?"

"It was a rough start, but I'm sure it'll get better."

"With an attitude like that, I'm sure it will."

The waitress sat my small plates of food in front of me while Grant and I chatted. I pulled the squash soup in front of me first and dipped my spoon in. The perfect blend of spices assaulted my taste buds. A faint moan of delight escaped my throat. I reached over to take a taste of the slaw next, hoping it was as delicious as the soup. I crunched down on the fresh Asian pears littering the slaw while the crispy shallots lent a slight tang to the flavor. The fresh mint twined with the other ingredients making my tongue do a happy dance. I chanced a look at Grant who was engrossed in watching me eat.

"I'm so sorry. I'm being rude." I wiped my mouth with my napkin.

"I'm the one who interrupted your dinner—I should leave you alone." He started to stand from his stool.

I placed my hand on his arm lightly. "Please stay. Honestly, it's kind of nice to have someone to chat with. I've been cooped up in my apartment all day, trying to unpack and move things around. I could use some conversation that doesn't involve me cursing at cardboard." I laughed.

"Only if you're sure. I don't want to be a bother."

"Yes, I want you to stay. Now sit down." I pointed to his vacant chair.

As I worked my way through my meal, Grant and I talked about the neighborhood, some local events coming up, and I told him a little about my job I was starting on Monday. I was surprised at how well we were hitting it off. Chatting with him allowed me to push my worries to the side. I wasn't open enough to share any of my past with him or who my parents were. That's one thing I learned, growing up the way I did. Some people were only out for what they could get from you. I didn't want to think of Grant like that because he genuinely seemed like a nice guy, but I remained cautious.

"So, Emily, I know you're new in town, but I'm going to take a chance here and ask you to dinner."

"I'm already having dinner…"

Grant laughed out loud. "I can see that, you also have some soup…" He reached up and rubbed his thumb across my bottom lip. "Right here."

I flinched, and my eyes widened at his boldness. "Please don't do that." I looked him in the eyes.

"I'm sorry, that was…I don't know what came over me." He looked away as if he were ashamed of his actions.

I felt bad for snapping at him. "Grant, I didn't mean to sound so bitchy. I just have this thing about my personal space." I tried to make up something on the fly. Telling him my entire back story would have made him run like a man on fire.

"I understand, and again, I apologize. So I'm guessing after that, the answer to dinner is a big fat *no*, huh?"

I thought about it. Did I want to give him a second chance? Wasn't that what this whole experience was about for me—about second chances?

"Yeah sure, why not. As long as you aren't on the FBI's most wanted list or anything?"

He held his hands up. "I promise I'm not."

"Okay, then I would love to go on a date."

"Great! I know this amazing French place not far from here called Paradou. That is, assuming you're a fan of French food?"

"It's actually one of my favorites. That sounds great."

"I'll call and make reservations for seven thirty on Sunday then. They aren't as packed then as they would be tomorrow night. Maybe it will be quieter, and we can get to know each other better."

"Perfect." I smiled.

"Emily, it was a pleasure to meet you. I will see you Sunday night." Grant picked up my hand in his and raised the back of my knuckles to his lips. I held my breath. I had to mentally stop myself from having a panic attack. He pressed a light kiss to my hand, and when he was finished, I was proud of myself when I didn't jerk my hand away. I felt slightly triumphant. I was learning to celebrate even the smallest of successes. Eventually the miniscule things would turn into big ones, and I would be on the path to being whole again.

It was going to be weird for me. I hadn't been on a date since I was with Michael. One thing was for sure though, I was fully aware of my trust issues. They were right in front of me like a flashing neon sign, advertising that I was far from ready to completely trust someone. But in a way I was looking forward to it. I needed to get out of my comfort zone and put myself out there. Grant was really sweet, too, and he wasn't a hardship to look at either.

If I was going to start a new life, there was going to be a point I'd have to start letting people in. My walls would eventually need to crumble for me to be happy and feel like I was worth something. Maybe a date with a hot stranger could be the beginning.

∞ *Seven* ∞

SATURDAY MORNING, I spent some time going through important emails and enjoying the sound of traffic buzzing by outside my open windows. The breeze grabbed hold of the sheer curtains hanging above the windows, causing them to flutter and bounce into the living room. Over the sounds of life outside, I could hear pigeons cooing nearby and smell the scents of a bakery, offering its fresh baked treats. Mornings always offered me a time where I could think and plan things. Among other important things in my life, I was the chairperson for a charity I'd started in honor of one of my closest friends, Destiny Schneider. She was the unfortunate victim of domestic violence, and I was devastated when I'd found out what'd happened to her. We'd been close all through high school, and I was the one who'd helped her fill out her college applications, which eventually ended in her being accepted to Dartmouth. She'd dated a guy all through school, but when it was her time to graduate high school and attend college, he refused to let her go. She moved in with him, found out she was pregnant at the age of 19, and was disowned by her parents. When I would come home to visit my family during winter breaks from NYU, I would visit with her and each time I'd feel sad for the situation she was in. I often suggested she leave him, that it wasn't a safe environment for her and the baby, but she claimed that she loved him and things would work out.

The summer of my last year in law school, I watched as her family laid her to rest. One night, her boyfriend came home and shot her point blank in the head while she was sleeping. I stood by watching as her parents cried over her grave, wishing they had never pushed her away.

In honor of her, I formed a charity that would benefit women and children who were the victims of domestic abuse called *The Sweet Destiny Foundation*. I was hosting a fundraiser in a little over a week in New York, and today was a meeting with some of the board members. There were several last minute details to finalize, and after I finished up on my computer I showered and headed out the door.

It didn't take long and I was in a taxi on my way to Le Cirque, our meeting place for the day. When I lived in L.A., we'd always chosen restaurants for our quarterly meetings, and most of the time they were high-end places where the wealthy members could feel comfortable. If I had my way we would have just met at a hotel conference room, but the majority of the board members wouldn't hear of it. It was like they wanted to be seen out and about in the crème de la crème of society. I'd always agreed because those people were the ones who gave the most financial backing to the charity. I learned to pick my battles and starting an argument over a meeting place just wasn't worth my time and energy.

Once I arrived at the restaurant, the hostess led me back to a corner where a table was set for six. I knew there were only five of us attending, but I'd gotten an email from one of the other members saying we had a new donor who wished to be on the board. The more the merrier. I welcomed new members into the fold anytime; the more people that were involved meant there would be more there to lend a hand. Since the fundraiser was so soon, the board members wanted to come in early and enjoy the city for the time leading up to the actual event. We'd always held our fundraiser in Los Angles, and this just gave them all an excuse to board their private jets and scurry across the country for a week. I was sure Fifth Avenue was silently thanking me. No doubt my fellow members would be flocking to the shops there to throw down massive amounts of cash on whatever struck their fancy.

I was the first to arrive, so I ordered water with lemon and sipped it while waiting on everyone else. I nervously glanced at the time every five seconds, but I wasn't sure why I had anxiety over the meeting. It was something I did frequently, and I knew the people who would be there…well, except for the new person. I had my head down, digging in my purse for a mint when I felt someone nearby. I snapped my head up to see who was lurking and when I saw him, my jaw hit the ground.

"Gabe?"

"Hol-ee shit. Emily Mills, how the fuck are you?"

It was Gabe Ellingsworth. Gabe was a good friend in law school. He and Jake were best friends as well. Gabe was a decent guy, and he came from a background a lot like mine: wealth. He also had quite the reputation for being a playboy, and even now you could see him on the pages of gossip magazines and celebrity news programs. Gabe had an I-don't-give-a-shit air about him. He was the spoiled rich boy who partied and fucked his way through life. In a way, I felt sorry for him.

I stood up to greet him. "Wow, it's been so long. How've you been?" I held out my hand; he just glanced at it, and then plunked down in the chair next to mine.

"So, so. Hey, I heard you bombed out on the bar exam. Good goin', put 'er there." He held up his hand trying to get me to high five him.

I slumped into my chair and looked away. "How did you know that?" I whispered. There were few people that actually knew about my failure.

Gabe reached for the breadbasket in the center of the table and rooted around inside, touching ever piece. He pulled out a crusty roll and ripped it in half, like a caveman. Shoving damn near half the roll into his mouth, he leaned his chair back on two legs. "Jake told me." He smiled, showing hunks of bread lodged in his front teeth. I cringed.

Why did my past follow me around like a lost puppy? I hadn't even been here a week, and it seemed that everyone knew about me botching my exams. I knew Gabe was a bit of an asshole in college, but he was even more so now.

He sat chomping away on the bread and finally spoke again. "Hey, don't feel bad. I graduated and didn't even take the damn thing. Fuck a bunch of law school shit. I only went to get my parents off my ass."

"Gabe, what are you even doing here? I have a meeting in a few minutes, and you're in the way." He needed to leave before he embarrassed me in front of my donors.

"I have a meeting, too; some charity bullshit my mom said I should be involved in. She said it would polish my image if I did something good once and a while." He grabbed the silverware and started to use them as drumsticks on the table.

My stomach twisted in knots as I realized Gabe was the new person on the board. *Well, fuck me.* I wasn't going to sit there and take shit from Gabe, especially since he referred to the charity as "bullshit."

I reached over and snatched the cutlery from his fingers and grabbed the back of his chair, pushing him forward until all four legs were on the floor. "First of all, this charity is not bullshit, Gabe. You need to grow up and stop acting like a brat. Second, if you don't want to be a part of it, the door is right over there. Feel free to walk your annoying ass right out of it."

He looked at me wide eyed. "Shit, Emily, I'm sorry. I didn't know it was your gig."

"This fundraiser is something I've planned and designed with my team for a year. I'm not going to sit by and let you trash-talk it."

He put his hands up in defense. "Okay, okay. Jeez, what's with you? You used to be so passive; now, you're like a damn pit bull."

"Things change; people change, Gabe," I said quietly.

"Look, if you don't want me here, I'll leave."

"Gabe, I can use all the help I can get, but I need you to take things seriously if you stay. I can't babysit you."

"Then I'll stay and behave. I'd rather keep my mom off my back for a while longer anyway."

"Fine. Now, please do me a favor and not say anything about the bar exam when the other board members arrive. I would rather avoid the humiliation."

"My lips are sealed," Gabe promised.

The others in our party arrived and for two exhausting hours, we went over the details of the fundraiser. Gabe managed not to make an ass out of himself, and everything seemed to be ironed out. Once the others left, it was just Gabe and me again.

"So what's the deal with you and Jake?"

"We don't have a deal."

"He does. We met for beers the other night, and the guy was acting weird. He said something about seeing you at the courthouse."

"I don't think this is any of your business." I rolled my eyes.

Gabe got up from his chair and looked down at me. "Suit yourself. But that fucker has been hung up on you since college. I think it's only fair that you put him out of his misery." He strode off toward the front door.

I sat there in shock. What the hell was Gabe talking about? Surely he was drunk or high and just spouting things he had no clue about.

∞ *Eight* ∞

ON SUNDAY MORNING, I woke up wanting to get out and about before my date with Grant. I needed to find a dress for my charity function the following weekend, and I knew I'd be too busy at my new job to do it during the week. I filled a travel mug with coffee, threw on some clothes and put my hair up in a loose ponytail.

My mother was always bitching at me for the way I dressed and my "lack of sophistication," as she liked to call it. Personally, I didn't care what the labels inside my clothing said. As long as they fit and were comfortable, I was fine with whatever brand. She saw things differently, though. Everything in her closet was custom made by famous designers, and her jewelry was the biggest collection of gems and diamonds I'd ever seen.

I could afford to pay the high prices for fashion, and at times, I did. But I would've rather used my money to help my charity, rather than fill my closet with clothing and shoes I really didn't need. I shopped mostly at vintage and resale shops in L.A. I could own upscale designer clothing for a fraction of the cost, and no one knew. But sometimes I shopped at regular discount stores, too. My mom probably would have fainted if she knew I basically wore someone else's clothing. It was a secret I kept from her. Not making waves in the parent pool was a task I worked on daily.

My newfound freedom made me feel slightly better about myself already. The fact that I was having dinner with a smoking hot guy that evening was just a cherry on my sprinkle-covered sundae. I was more excited about dating than I'd been in months. The thought even crossed my mind to find something fun to wear for my dinner with Grant.

I headed out for the day and walked a few blocks before hopping the subway to Fashion Avenue. Once above ground, I pulled out my phone and hit the app to find a fun place to shop. Since I was in love with vintage fashion, I became giddy when a store called "Resurrection" popped up. The website boasted famous designer fashions from Versace, Dolce & Gabbana and Chanel. *The perfect place.* I smiled to myself.

I navigated the street and weekend pedestrians, the traffic more relaxed than the typical weekday flow. The entire storefront of Resurrection was made up of glass, showcasing beautiful vintage clothing on sturdy mannequins. When I entered, I noticed a framed picture of two celebrities on the counter. They were both wearing dresses that had been found here. Jessica Simpson donned a short pink vintage Herve Leger cocktail dress, and Nicki Minaj stood next to her in a colorful Jean Paul Gaultier number.

I browsed through the racks of stunning gowns set against a backdrop of bright crimson walls and black carpet. Pushing hangers back and forth, I tried to find something that piqued my interest, but nothing screamed, *wear me, Emily!*

"Is there something I can help you find?" I turned to see the sales girl with a bright smile on her face.

"Well, I have an event coming up, and I need something formal, and beautiful, of course."

She scanned me from head to toe. "Size 6, right?"

"Yes, how did you...?"

"I've been in retail since I was 17; I have an eye for things like that." She laughed. "I have a couple of gowns in the back that you might want to take a peek at."

I followed her through the store until we came to a small rack with eight dresses hanging from it.

"Personally I love this one; it's vintage Chanel." She pulled a stunning red gown from its hanging place and held it up.

"It's beautiful, but I'm not sure I'm bold enough to wear that color. Maybe something in black?"

She hung the gown back up and flipped through the rack again. Her face brightened when she landed on another garment. "What about this one?"

I couldn't see the shape of it clearly while it was on the hanger, but what I could see was amazing. "I can put this in a fitting room if you'd like." She must have seen the look in my eyes.

"That would be great." I agreed.

She placed the gown in a dressing room. "I'll be back to check on you in a few minutes."

"Thank you," I said and stepped into the room where the dress waited. I quickly shrugged off my clothing and pulled the black fabric from its hanger. As I stepped into the gown, it felt like it was made just for me. I pulled it all the way up and reached around to slide the zipper up my back. I opened the door to walk outside and heard a gasp.

"Oh. My. God. That looks sublime on you!" The sales girl admired.

"Here, take a look." She motioned to a floor length mirror to the side.

It was nothing shy of incredible. The mermaid cut of the dress hugged every curve like it was crafted solely for my body, the three quarter length lace sleeves made my arms look like a dream, and the way the neckline hung just off the shoulders added the right amount of sexiness.

"We literally just got that in this morning. I knew it wouldn't be here long. Vintage *Givenchy* doesn't last long around here. A lot of times we have things shipped to our store in Los Angeles, and they end up being worn on the red carpet."

"How exciting." I congratulated.

I toyed with the sleeves of the dress and ran my hands down my sides, feeling every curve of my body underneath the gown. It really reminded me something the beautiful Grace Kelly might have worn. I felt like a Hollywood screen angel.

"I'll take it."

I went back into the fitting room and changed into my own clothing. I was excited that I'd found something so gorgeous to wear to the fundraiser. After I paid for the dress, I decided to grab some lunch and find something to wear for my date with Grant that evening.

It didn't take me long to find a boutique tucked between arts stores and cafes. After searching for only ten minutes, I came out with the perfect outfit for the evening.

∞   ∞   ∞

I made it back home with just enough time to shower, shave and make myself presentable for my date with Grant. I was giddy with excitement while putting my makeup on and couldn't stop smiling into the mirror. It was a look that was starting to grow on me. Is this what it was like to be happy? If so, I liked the change so far. Once I approved of my finished product, I slipped into my date dress, threw on some heels and grabbed my purse, glancing at my phone as I walked out of the building. Grant had sent me a text that made me smile: **Is it weird that I feel like an excited school boy about tonight?**

I quickly typed a message back: **If it is, then I'm weird for feeling like a schoolgirl. ;-)**

I felt a little silly for smiling so much, but then again, it was refreshing. I'd been a depressed lump of human being for the past few months; it was high time I was able to feel great about *something*.

I took off down the sidewalk as the evening air wisped across the exposed skin of my shoulders, causing me to shiver. I wasn't really cold; it was more of a nervous tremble. Yes, I was eager about my date; but inside, I had a level of anxiety that made me feel like I might throw up. The night I'd met Grant couldn't really be classified as a "date" but this was no doubt one. The last date I'd been on was with Michael, and that was the night everything went to hell in a hand basket. I didn't need to think about that though. *Only positive thoughts tonight.* As I strolled through the streets, I soaked up the atmosphere around me. Even for a Sunday night everything was busy and booming with excitement. Several couples held hands as they strode to their destinations, chatting and appearing to be enamored with each other. You could feel the romance in the air as some stopped on a corner to steal a kiss and look into each other's eyes with love and passion. I wanted that someday. I wanted to find a special someone to share a romantic evening with, just walking along and conversing about really nothing at all. It would be great to be so comfortable, even to be able to not talk at all. To find a person that could almost read your thoughts and feel the emotions radiating off of you. I had no idea if Grant was even that person. I wasn't willing to think that far ahead; that would've been ignorant on my part. I was just planning on sharing a meal, and getting to know him. It wasn't like I was planning my wedding or anything.

My heels clicked on the concrete as I continued toward my destination. As I neared the restaurant, I spotted Grant waiting for me outside. He hadn't noticed me yet, but I stopped for a moment to take in his handsomeness. He was dressed in a pair of crisp black pants that hugged every leg muscle, his white buttoned-up dress shirt clung to his chest and arms, and a slight shadow of hair darkened his jawline. He really was a piece of hotness.

When I finished enjoying the view, I continued toward him. He spotted me, and his entire face lit up. In that moment, I felt beautiful. There were plenty of stunning women in the same vicinity as the two of us, but the way he looked at me made me feel like I was the only woman in the world. It felt good to be wanted. It was something I could get comfortable with real quick.

"Wow, you look incredible, Emily." He eyed me up and down.

"So do you. You clean up nicely," I teased.

"Shall we get this date started?" Grant turned and opened the door to the restaurant. We reached the hostess podium and waited for the couple in front of us to be seated. The hostess quickly came back to check us in, and soon we were seated in the garden.

It was an enclosed space, made to look like a botanical garden that had been brought indoors. Tables lined the sides of the tent-looking enclosure and clear, twinkling lights provided enough lighting to give the space a romantic appeal. Our table for the evening sat near a tree that happened to be growing right up through the retractable roof of the space. I chose the seat closest to the large tree, and Grant came around and pulled out my chair while the waiter held a menu in front of me.

After we ordered drinks, I looked over my menu. My stomach grumbled loudly as I scanned the choices.

"Sounds like someone is hungry. I should've made our reservations earlier."

"Oh, no, this is perfect. I did a lot of walking today, so I'm sure I burned off everything I had for lunch."

"So you were able to get out and about today?" He asked.

"I was. I have an event to attend next Saturday, and I had waited until the last minute to find a gown. I tend to procrastinate quite a bit."

"You and about every other human being on the planet." He chuckled.

"I'm trying to change my ways."

"I wish you the best of luck with that." He joked.

I finally decided on my order as the waiter made his appearance once more. He jotted down our selections and hurried away.

"So Emily, tell me about yourself." Grant prompted.

"Well, I'm 29, I moved here from Los Angeles, and I start a new job tomorrow."

"Oh really, where?"

"Carlton & Brewster; it's a law firm in Chelsea. I have an assistant position until I take the bar exam; after that I'll be hired as an attorney."

"Wow, a lawyer. Impressive."

"Not quite a lawyer, but I'll get there." I shrugged. I wasn't going to tell him that I blew my shot at becoming a lawyer several years back. I really didn't think it was any of his business. "So, what do you do?"

"I'm a day trader for TD Ameritrade. It's been rough the past few years, but things are starting to look up. The economic meltdown in 2008 almost killed us, but everyone goes through rough patches once in a while." He smiled confidently.

"Don't I know it," I said, almost under my breath.

We talked a little more, and soon our entrees arrived. My stomach rejoiced when the steam of my chicken paillard reached my nose.

"This looks delicious," I commented as I reached for my utensils. I looked up at Grant, but my gaze went beyond him. I squinted my eyes, thinking I must have been seeing things. I dropped my fork and it hit the plate with a loud clatter. None other than Jake strolled into the restaurant with a leggy brunette on his arm. My jaw must have been lying on the floor.

"Is everything okay?"

No, everything was *not* okay. I'd just managed to put Jake out of my head, and he shows up and screws with me even more. Not to mention the skank hanging all over him. She looked like he'd just plucked her off the street corner and offered her a hot meal in return for services rendered. Her skirt was bordering on indecent. Her tank top barely contained her breasts, and her shoes resembled those of a cheap stripper in Vegas.

"I think I'm going to find the ladies room." I stood and hurried away from the table so I didn't have a full-blown panic attack. When I found the bathroom I hunched over the vanity and stared at my flushing reflection.

What if Jake decided to ridicule me in front of my date? He had no qualms with doing it in front of the courthouse the other day. Oh god, this was a disaster. I took a few deep breaths and calmed myself down. This wasn't fair to Grant. I shouldn't be acting like a teenager. I got myself together and went back out to our table. When I got there

I was shocked to see that Jake and his prostitute of a date were seated at the table right next to Grant's and mine. *Well, fuck.*

Maybe he wouldn't notice me. Maybe I was just being paranoid. With those hopeful thoughts in mind I sat back down. Grant raised an eyebrow in curiosity.

"Want to talk about it?" He took a swig of his beer.

"Not really." I did the same with my wine.

"Emily, if you want to leave, it's fine."

My face flamed as he said my name, and Jake turned around in his chair. I closed my eyes and tried to mentally transport myself anywhere but where I was sitting.

"Small world." Jake smiled.

Grant turned around to face Jake, and I saw something on Jake's face that looked like aggravation.

"Excuse me, do we know you?" Grant asked.

"You don't, but Emily does." Jake bit out.

Grant turned to me with a questioning look on his face. "Yes, I know him. We went to college together." I tried to keep the answer simple.

"Well, if you haven't noticed we're on a date here, so why don't you turn back around and mind your own business." Grant told Jake.

"Listen buddy, Emily and I have been friends far longer then you've been around, so I suggest you shut the fuck up." Jake bit back.

The scene in front of me was unfolding like a take from a bad soap opera. I wanted to crawl under the table and hide until it was over. The patrons around us were staring, and Jake's floozy date was just sitting across from him smacking her gum between her loud pink lips. Grant abruptly stood from his chair and faced Jake with anger in his eyes. I didn't know what to do. I knew if I didn't say something, the situation would escalate, and one or both of them would end up in jail. Jake didn't need that. He could ruin his reputation and ultimately his career; I couldn't let that happen.

"Grant, please, let's just go," I pleaded.

"No. This bastard wants to start shit, then he can finish it, too." Grant began to roll up his sleeves.

Jake stood from his seat at the invitation. "Emily, you sure have found a winner here. Pretty boy likes to solve things with fighting."

Now, I was pissed. First, Jake makes fun of me failing the bar, and now he has the balls to make fun of my choice in dates. *Fuck that.*

"What is your problem, Jake? Have you just turned into the world's biggest asshole or what?" I pushed my chair back and stood. "Excuse me, but I'm leaving." I grabbed my purse and started to walk out. I could hear the two of them still verbally abusing each other.

"So what's it going to be, Man, you want to take this outside and finish things? Or are you going to stand there and be a pussy?" I heard Grant provoke Jake.

The next thing I could hear was the sounds of a fist hitting something. I twisted back around to see Jake holding his jaw, and when he pulled his hand away, blood trickled from the side of his mouth.

"Oh my god!" I screamed. At that point, I didn't care if I was making a scene or not. I ran back over and pushed Grant out of the way. "What's wrong with you?" I poked Grant in the chest with my finger and yelled.

"What's wrong with *me*? This douche interrupted our dinner by being an asshole."

"Have you ever heard of being the bigger person? The two of you are acting like adolescent boys, not grown men." I scolded.

As Jake stood there bleeding, Grant stood there about to breathe fire, and Jake's date collected her purse and walked out. The manager of the restaurant showed up. "Excuse me, I'm going to have to ask you all to leave. You're causing a scene in front of the other customers, and we can't have that."

Grant grabbed my arm. "Come on, Emily, let's go."

I wrenched my arm away. "No, I'm not going anywhere with you." I stormed out and stood on the sidewalk. My heart rate was through the roof, and my breathing hiccupped and labored.

Grant exited the front doors, walked right past me and down the street. He didn't even bother to say good-bye, but then again, why would he have?

"Damn, what a night." I heard Jake say behind me.

I spun around and gave him my best "eat shit" look. "*Really?*"

"I'm sorry, but that guy was an asshole, Emily. Any man who won't let you *even* talk to an old friend is a dick."

"You had no right to treat him like that, Jake." I felt tears begin to prick my eyes.

"And he had the right to be all possessive over you?"

"How would you have felt if some strange guy started talking to your date? I highly doubt you'd be okay with it." I pointed out.

Jake reached up and wiped a streak of blood from his busted lip. "Damn, that's going to hurt in the morning." He chuckled.

I dug through my purse and found a travel pack of tissues. I pulled one out and dabbed at his lip. "Serves you right."

Jake became silent while I tended to his injury, and I could feel his warm breath on my hand. His chest moved up and down rapidly, and as I looked up into his blue eyes, I saw a fire that I'd never seen before. My breasts felt heavy, and the all-too-familiar wetness increased between my legs.

"I'm sorry, Emily. I should have left you alone."

I pulled my hand back and stuffed the bloody tissue back in my purse. "I need to go."

I had to get out of there. Jake once again had my body tied up in knots, and I didn't need to be there. Maybe he was right: maybe Grant was an asshole for being possessive with me. But didn't he have the right to be? After all, we were on a date. I could see why he might feel like I was his for the evening. But why would Jake even care? It wasn't like I'd ever been *his*.

But standing there looking into his eyes made me want to be.

∞ *Nine* ∞

MONDAY MORNING WAS the big day. My first full day at my new job. Excitement and fear coursed through me as I went about my early morning routine. Coffee was the number one priority. I set the pot brewing and opened the door to grab the newspaper on my doorstep. I cozied up to the bar in my kitchen and flipped open the inked pages to see what kind of news New York had in store on a Monday morning. The most interesting news I could find was the start of baseball season. I guess it was that time of year; it was already May after all. My coffee machine gurgled, telling me that my caffeinated angel was done and ready for consumption.

Sunday night was nothing shy of a disaster. When I got home from the failed date with Grant, I sat on my sofa and cried until I was out of breath. It was stupid for me to act like a baby about the whole deal, but I couldn't believe that yet again Jake wasn't the person I thought I knew. Sure, Grant acted a little weird, but Jake didn't have to go all caveman asshole on him. The entire time I wiped tears from my face, I couldn't help but wonder why Jake acted the way he did. He was obviously on a date, too, so why did he focus his attention on my date and not his? I also recalled my juvenile reaction to Jake's date. What did it matter that he had a two-dollar hooker hanging on his arm? It wasn't any of my business who he chose to associate himself with. I honestly thought Jake would've had higher standards than that. Apparently, I was dead wrong. Maybe he'd turned out like Gabe, fucking anything with two legs, a nice rack and a willing vagina. But either way, it wasn't my concern. What *was* my concern was that I was scheduled to start work the next day. I needed to clear my mind of everything that went down the night before and do the job I was hired to do.

∞   ∞   ∞

While going about my morning rituals Monday morning, I reached up and opened the cabinet where my coffee mugs were housed and nearly screamed when the door flew off the hinges, landing on the floor at my feet. *Well, damn.* I'd been there only a few days, and I'd managed to damage something already. It looked like the hinges had completely come out of the wood in which they were planted. I picked up my phone and called the rental company.

I left a message. "Hi my name is Emily and I live in apartment B at 1231 West 13th Street. I've seemed to have had a mishap with a cabinet door in the kitchen. If there is anyway someone could come and fix it that would be great."

I hoped someone would be there while I was at work to take care of the problem. I mentally hoped I didn't destroy anything else. The maintenance man would report me to the landlord for destruction of property. That would just add to the pile of bad juju I'd had since I moved to New York. I was contemplating finding a shop that sold rabbits' feet or bringing in a priest to bless everything. With the way things were going, the broken cabinet, running into Jake the asshole *twice* and the incident at Paradou the night before, I needed something to keep luck on my side.

When I felt like my body was filled with enough caffeine to successfully begin my day, I hopped in the shower. As I was drying off with my favorite fluffy towel, my phone started ringing in the other room. The ringing stopped before I could grab it, so I dialed my voicemail. It was the rental company, letting me know someone would stop by today to fix the cabinet.

Well, that was fast. I called for a cab to take me to the office, and while I waited I popped into a small bakery next door to my building. Everything in the pastry case looked inviting, but knowing I still had to fit into my amazing gown at the end of the week, I chose a small oatmeal raisin muffin and a medium green tea with lemon and honey. The warmth of the paper cup filtered through my palms, calming my rising anxiety over the prospect of my first day of work. Of course I was ready but the thoughts of something new still scared me. I knew I could do the job and was grateful that I would have the chance to work toward finally becoming a lawyer, but the chance that I might fail again worried me. I supposed that only made me human though.

My ride pulled up a few minutes after I'd gotten my breakfast and I climbed in. I had the option of taking the subway, and maybe I was a little spoiled because I'd rather use my money for a cab, but I just preferred the car instead of riding on a train with a ton of strangers.

We pulled up to the same building I'd come to when Marvin needed his paperwork; I paid the driver and got out. I smoothed the front of my black pencil skirt and made sure my cropped jacket was in place and walked through the doors of the lobby. "Here goes nothing...or *everything*." I said under my breath. Crossing the lobby, I could see the hustle and bustle of others just like me, making their way to work for the day. Briefcases hung from the hands of men and women and people talked loudly on their phones, causing the large area to be filled with sounds of tension and business. Some had their hands full of their morning cups of coffee or tea just like I did, and a few were munching on wrapped baked goods. It was all a bit overwhelming. I'd experienced all of this when I did my internship in college, but somehow it had seemed less overpowering. I did intern with Jake right by my side back then though; maybe it was the fact that Jake calmed me down and made me feel at ease with things like this. I wish he had been that soothing the night before instead of causing a massive scene and getting all of us kicked out of a restaurant. I took a deep breath and cleansed my thoughts.

I packed myself into the elevator with about fifteen other people and the machine began its ascent to my floor. Nervousness slid over me when the doors opened. Here I was, someone who previously had hob-knobbed with celebrities getting ready to enter the world of the working class citizen. It was nerve racking and exhilarating all at once. I put one foot in front of the other and walked through the pristine set of glass doors. Once inside I found myself in front of the same reception desk as a few days before, and behind it sat a girl that looked no more than twenty-one.

She looked up for a moment to eye me up and down. "Um, can I help you?"

"Yes, I'm Emily Mills, here to see Marvin. I'm his new paralegal."

"Have a seat over there." she pointed to a row of chairs, "I'll let him know you're here."

It wasn't long before Marvin came through another set of doors and greeted me. He looked less stressed out then he did Friday, but I knew in this business that could change in a heartbeat.

"I trust you had a good weekend?" He greeted.

"Yes I did. I spent most of my time unpacking and getting things organized but all in all it was good." I smiled.

"That's good to hear. I can't thank you enough for bringing that paperwork on Friday. Sometimes things like that slip my mind. I've been in this business forever, maybe it's time to retire." He laughed.

"I'm sure it was just a fluke." I reassured him.

I followed him down the hall until we came to a large door with a placard stating Marvin's name. He led me inside and motioned to a chair in front of his cluttered desk. Stacks of files stood catty corner to each other, used paper coffee cups sat in small piles and wrappers from fast food joints were wadded up and tossed on the top of the wood surface. I cringed at his lack of organizational skills. I wasn't the best at keeping clutter at bay, but Marvin's desk looked like the beginning stages of an episode of *Hoarders*. He began to push things around and then picked up one of the cups and took a swig. The disgusted look on his face told me he'd grabbed the wrong one by mistake, but to my surprise he swallowed the mouthful anyway. My stomach roiled as I considered how old the contents might have been.

"Sorry for the mess, things have been insane around here lately." He apologized. "I'll get you settled into your office in a bit, but first I wanted to go over a few things."

"Okay, not a problem." I assured him.

"When were you planning on retaking the Bar?"

"Well, the next one is in a few months and I've already signed up. I've been doing some studying, but since the move I've slacked off a bit."

"No big deal, we actually have a couple of other paralegals who have an education like you do. They're already scheduled to take it; you're more than welcome to study with them during business hours. We like to hire them with an education, some have it and some don't but the ultimate goal for those that do, is to pass and have a job here, so we make sure and give some time to that."

"That would be great, thank you." I was grateful for the offer. I needed all the time I could find to study. I was determined to pass.

"Don't feel bad for failing the first time either, trust me, it's not unheard of. In fact I can give you several examples of well-known people who failed the bar at least once. John F. Kennedy Jr., Hillary Clinton, and even our current First Lady. But as you see, they all have or had great careers in the end."

Marvin's kind words really touched me. I'd never thought of it that way. I was being hard on myself for failing something so important, and I gave up. I wasn't going to let anything stop me this time. I was determined to keep taking it until I passed. "Thank you, sir." I smiled.

"I would normally put you downstairs with the other paralegals, but I'd like to keep you on this floor and have you work directly with me. The others float around between me and my partner, but I think you're more suited to my style. I hope that's okay with you?"

"That's no problem at all." I assured him.

He lightly banged his hands on his desk and stood. "Okay, since we have that squared away, let's get you settled into your office."

We walked down the hallway until we came to a door just four down from his own. He pushed it open and revealed a small office that contained a desk, chair and a small sofa to the side. On the desk sat a MacBook laptop, which looked brand new.

"You're more than welcome to bring photos or personal belongings in to spruce up the place; just try and not overwhelm it." He went around the back of the desk and pulled open a drawer. "Here's the password for the computer." He jotted something down on a sticky note. "And I'll have my secretary get you a key card. The legal library is upstairs on the sixth floor so you'll need the card to gain access. If you need to stay after hours to study or do any sort of research, you're more than welcome to, just let my secretary know in advance. I'd hate to lock you up in this place for the night." He chuckled. "We have an employee lounge on the second floor for lunches and break times, but you're also allowed to take lunch in your office if you see fit. Do you have any questions so far?"

"Um, not yet. But I may later."

"You know where to find me if you do. My secretary Molly will be more than willing to help with anything you need, too. Now if you'll excuse me I'll leave you to get settled in. I'll send Molly in with your key card in a bit." Marvin came back around the desk and left my office.

I went to the window and looked out at the blooming city below. We were only three floors up but I could still see the people below me going about their Monday morning business. I felt strange. Yes, I'd worked in L.A., but this was different. I wasn't working for my parents, nor was I under their rule. I smiled to myself knowing that I was doing this on my own. And soon I'd retake my exam and with any luck, I'd pass and become an actual attorney. Sure I was upset when I'd failed, but I managed to pick myself up enough to get my paralegal certificate. That was something else my parents never knew about. I knew I'd need some sort of job when I decided to make my big move, and working in a law office was something I knew how to do. It was the best option to get my foot in the door and eventually retake my test. I had the money to sit at home and do nothing, but I wasn't built like that. I was happy that Marvin was so understanding and willing to help out in any way he could. Knowing that made me feel more at ease with my decisions. I considered myself lucky that he was willing to hire me. Being from the same alma mater helped, but I think he saw something in me that sometimes I didn't really see myself. It was the first time I'd applied for a job online. And the fact that he hired me on just my education, resume and a phone interview said a lot I suppose.

I spent the first hour getting to know the computer system and organizing the things in my desk to my liking. I didn't have much in the way of family photos or trinkets so decorating my office space might have been pushing it. I laughed when I thought about buying picture frames that had images of happy families already in them. Would anyone notice?

Eleven-thirty rolled around and a light knock sounded at my office door. "Come in." I said.

The door swung open and a woman in her early forties came through. "Hi, I'm Molly, Marvin's secretary." She greeted.

I stood from my chair and extended my hand. "I'm Emily Mills, it's nice to meet you."

"I have your key card for the legal library, if you have time I can take you there and show you around. Marvin is still in his meeting, so I can give you a quick lay of the land." She offered.

"Sure, that would be great. I need to get away from the computer anyway." I joked.

We traveled down the hall and Molly explained a bit about everything. "Most of these offices are empty right now. We just moved to this location about nine months ago. The plan is to hire more attorneys eventually and fill them up. We have a few law graduates like you who are hoping to get hired on after they pass the Bar."

We stepped inside the elevator and went to the sixth floor where the library was located. "Any time you need access here, just swipe your card and the door will click." She demonstrated the action and sure enough the door clicked, and she pushed it open. The smell of books immediately caught my nose.

The walls were lined with shelves housing rows and rows of legal books, journals and files. In the center of the large room were tables with state-of-the-art desktop computers all hooked to individual printers. In one corner of the space was an area with a Keurig coffee maker complete with a K-cup tree and disposable cups. We were alone in the library, but I knew from my days at college that wouldn't last long. Legal libraries were the hub for research for any law student. They spent most of their time huddled over a computer or with their nose buried inside of some legal book. No doubt I would soon be in that position right there in that room.

"You're more than welcome to use the coffee maker. And I'm sure you'll be trapped in here most days so you'll need the jolt of caffeine." She laughed. "If you need to take something out of here, be sure and check it out in the computer system. The bosses are sticklers about keeping track of everything."

We left the library and hit the elevator once more. Molly pushed the button for the floor we needed and the doors closed. "There are also stairs you can use in the building, but I prefer the elevator. I wouldn't want this baby coming out before it's fully cooked." She patted her stomach, which showed a slight noticeable pooch.

"Oh, congratulations! When are you due?" I asked with excitement.

"I still have another few months, but my others were early so I'm nervous this one will be too. Do you have any kids?"

"No, it's just me." I smiled.

"Not even a boyfriend?"

"Nope, I'm as single as they come." I laughed.

"Well, if a beautiful woman like you can't find a man, then I don't think there's hope for the rest of the world."

I blushed at her compliment. She was really sweet and I knew we would get along great.

When we came to the second floor we exited the elevator and rounded the corner. An open room sat empty with several tables and chairs dotting the space. A full-size refrigerator sat on a wall with a countertop filled with a microwave, toaster, coffee pot and a small sink.

"Not too much to see in here, but at least you know where everything is now."

"I really appreciate you showing me around." I thanked her.

"It was my pleasure. Oh, but one word of advice...if you bring something for lunch and use the fridge, be sure and write your name in big letters on it. God love Marvin, but that man would eat a damn cat if it wasn't labeled." She rolled her eyes.

"I will keep that in mind." I chuckled.

"Well, let's get back upstairs, the boss man should be out of his meeting and I'm sure he has plenty of work waiting for us."

When we got back to our floor Molly went to her desk and I to my office. I felt more at ease with everything after my tour and couldn't wait to do some actual work. Just as I logged back into my computer I heard another knock on my door, followed by Marvin coming right in.

"Emily I need another favor. Jeez, I feel like I'm underutilizing your skills lately." He tried to laugh it off. "I need these documents taken to an office in Midtown. I called the messenger service we normally use but they can't get someone here until later this afternoon. Would you be able to take them for me, I'll give you the cash for a cab."

"Yeah, I can do it." I didn't really want to do it, he was right, he *was* underutilizing my skills. I wasn't an errand girl, I was a paralegal. But telling him no wouldn't have looked good on my part, so I agreed.

He placed a manila envelope on my desk, with an address written on a sticky note on top. "There's a confirmation letter in there, just have the secretary sign it. And the address is on top."

He left my office and I grabbed my purse to head out. Once outside I hailed another cab and one rapidly pulled up to get me.

"Where to?" The driver grumbled out.

"Midtown, East 55th Street, please." I read off the address from the yellow note on the envelope.

We sped away, and I held the documents on my lap. I didn't really know where I was going, but hopefully the driver did and I would get there safely.

When we pulled up to the address I'd given him, I paid him with the cash Marvin had given me and walked toward a high-rise building. When I entered the lobby through the huge glass double doors, I stopped dead in my tracks.

Right in front of me in huge gold lettering was the name: Bradford Law Office LLC.

Shit.

Unless there were several lawyers with the last name Bradford in the city, I knew I was standing in Jakes office. Why did we keep crossing paths? Was I being punished for uprooting my life in L.A. by having to deal with my former best friend? It sure felt like it. I wasn't sure how long I stood there with the envelope pressed to my chest and a dumbfounded look plastered all over my face. I started when a female voice spoke.

"Can I help you?" She asked.

I turned to face her where she sat behind a U-shaped desk with a beautiful smile on her face. Her teeth were all straight and white and her hair was the most amazing shade of auburn I'd ever seen. I could see a smattering of freckles on her porcelain cheeks, peeking out from under her light makeup.

"Uh yes. I need to drop these off. I'm with Carlton and Brewster." I held out the papers.

"Oh, okay." She took them from me and slid the top open. She then pulled the papers out and started to read the confirmation.

"I just need you to sign that copy saying you received those." I spoke quickly because I wanted to get the hell out of there.

It seemed like it was taking her forever and a day to read the letter and I impatiently tapped the toe of my shoe on the marble floor. There was an eerie silence as she continued to scan the document and suddenly it was interrupted by the one person I really didn't want to see.

"Hey Eliza, I'm headed out to grab lunch, do you want...Emily?" Jake looked shocked to see me standing there in the lobby of his office. I couldn't say I blamed him. I was floored that fate seemed to hate me as much as it did.

"Uh, I don't want *Emily* for lunch," Jake's secretary broke the silence in the space.

Jake laughed at her and then looked back at me. "What are you doing here?" He questioned.

"She is dropping off some paperwork from Mr. Carlton." The woman named Eliza butted in.

"Is that where you're working?" Jake's face softened.

"Yes, I started today."

"He's a good man, I've known him ever since I opened my firm." Jake complimented.

"I just need the confirmation signed and I'll be out of your way." Jake pulled the paper from Eliza's hand and signed his name to it. He handed it back to me. "You're never in my way, Emily."

"Thanks." I snatched the paper up, turned and started to walk away.

"Have lunch with me." Jake spoke and stopped me dead in my tracks.

"I can't, I have to get back to work."

Jake pulled out his cell phone and dialed a number. "Hey Carlton, it's Bradford here, thanks for getting that paperwork to me. Listen, I actually know Emily Mills—yeah, the woman you sent over…would you mind if she stayed and had lunch with me? You wouldn't? Okay great, I owe ya' one." He hit the red button on his phone and shoved it back into his pocket. "Looks like you don't have to get back right away now."

"Jake I don't think this is a good idea. We work for competing law firms. Isn't there a rule against fraternization?"

"Your boss said it was fine, now come on, I know this little bistro a few blocks from here." He started walking toward the door and it was like my body was overriding my brain and I followed him. "Eliza, I'll be back in a couple hours."

"A couple of hours? It doesn't take that long to eat lunch, Jake." I scolded.

"I know, but we need to talk."

Why did I have to walk into Jake Bradford's office? Why didn't the ground just open up and swallow me whole right then? After everything I'd already been through, now I had to sit through lunch with Jake and probably watch him be a complete douche bag in some way or another again. This was not the day I'd planned when I rolled out of bed this morning. All I wanted was to have a nice calm day at work, get my feet on the ground and go home to a glass of wine and a relaxing soak in my bathtub. I was learning very quickly that nothing went according to plan. Life had a way of reaching up and biting me on the ass when I least expected it.

Jake and I left the building and I walked beside him down the sidewalk. It seemed so natural to be with him. Just like watching those couples the other night. I briefly wondered if anyone thought we were like those romantic couples. Probably not judging by the scowl on my face.

He didn't say anything as we made our way to his lunch place of choice. But when we got there he opened the door for me and I slid by him to get through. The scent of his cologne hit me in the face and caused a shudder to rack my body. Damn he smelled yummy.

The sign at the door said, "Please seat yourself," and Jake took the lead to a table near the back. He pulled out a chair for me so I skated in. I hung my purse on the back of my seat and crossed my legs under the table. When Jake sat across from me, I clenched my thighs tighter, my body betraying me with its interest.

Jake had always been a good-looking guy but now...he was sublimely handsome. It almost hurt to look at him he was so damn sexy. His grey suit snugged against his muscled form, the sunlight from the bistro windows shone on his hair making it look glossy and thick. The slight stubble on his jawline made me want to reach across the table and run my fingers over it, just to hear the sounds that might come from his throat. But it was his eyes that had me engrossed the most. They always had. It was like looking into a crystal ball and seeing myself staring back at me. I had to look away. If I didn't, I would spend the entire time looking at him. I distracted myself with the menu instead.

"I always get the turkey club; they have the best in the city in my opinion." Jake pulled the paper menu away from my face. "Unless you just feel like rubbing the menu on your nose." He smiled, and I couldn't help but return it.

The waiter came to take our order, and of course I went with Jake's suggestion.

"So, what did you want to talk about?"

He blew out a breath. "I wanted to apologize for the way I acted Sunday night. I let myself get out of control."

"Apology accepted. You could've just told me that back at your office instead of dragging me to lunch."

"Is it that big of a hardship to have a meal with me, Emily? We used to do everything together...*including* lunch." He sipped his water.

"No, I guess not."

"Then why don't you relax and stop acting like you've got a giant stick up your ass."

"Why don't you stop being an asshole every time you see me?"

"I'm sorry. I really don't know why I've acted like that. I have been an asshole. But I'd like to change that, if you'll let me?"

"It's really hard for me to trust people now."

"It wasn't difficult to trust some guy you just met and go on a date with him."

"Why is it a problem for you that I went on a date? You never had a problem with it before. Now you go all caveman and have a freak-out session when you see me out. I don't get it."

"I can't explain it. That guy just rubbed me the wrong way. I don't think he's any good for you."

"Maybe he's not, but that's *my* mistake to make, Jake, not yours. I didn't say shit about your date, even if she *did* look like you plucked her off a street corner."

Jake laughed. "Do I detect a hint of jealousy in your voice, Miss Mills?"

"Trust me, Jake, I would never be jealous of someone like that woman," I said in a snarky tone.

"Okay, I won't talk about your dating life and you won't talk about mine. Is that a fair trade?"

"Sounds fair to me," I agreed.

"But I do want to talk about you and the bar exam. What happened?"

"I failed." I said flatly.

"I know that already, Emily. I just don't get it though. You had one of the highest GPA's in our class; you were pegged to become one of the best damn lawyers out there."

"I guess we all fall from grace at some point in our lives. That was my tumble. But I'm picking myself back up, and I will try again. And if I fail *again*, I will continue to try until I pass it."

"I'm glad to hear that."

"What about you? I thought you had big plans of moving back to Texas and starting a firm there?"

"After graduation I got a job offer from a firm here in the city, I worked for them for a year and a half and then decided to strike out on my own. My mom tried to talk me out of it, but I knew I could do more here in New York. Don't get me wrong, I'm going to go back to Texas eventually."

"I'm glad. You'd always talked about your home and how much you loved it there. I'd hate for you to be trapped here for the rest of your life. Especially with your family being so far away." I felt sad when I talked about family. Jake had the opportunity to be with his. If I had that chance, I would've taken it in a heartbeat.

"My parents understand and support my decision. Besides, I talk to them about once a week. They know I want to go back home. And I will."

Our sandwiches arrived, and we were both silent as we devoured the food. I hadn't realized how famished I really was until that first bite hit my tongue.

"I told you this was the best club in the city." Jake wiped his mouth with a paper napkin and smiled.

"It's really good."

"So, I heard you were engaged," Jake said as I took a bite of my food.

The bite of bread became lodged in my throat and I started coughing. Jake stood up and began to pat me on the back. I managed to take a swig of water to wash it down, and Jake once again sat across from me.

"Judging by that reaction, I'm guessing it didn't end well." Jake laughed.

I didn't want to talk about my time with Michael. I didn't even want to *think* about it. My pulse started to rise, and my vision became blurry.

"Emily, are you okay?"

I abruptly stood from my chair and snatched my pursed from the back of it. "I need to go." I bolted for the door like my shoes were on fire and the only relief was the outside air. I gulped in oxygen when I found the outside and tears sprang to my eyes. I furiously wiped them away knowing my makeup was now a mess. Jake caught up with me and turned me to face him.

"Fuck. What is going on with you, Emily? Every time I see you, you're either crying or pissed off. This isn't you. This isn't the woman I fe…that I was friends with."

"I don't know, Jake. I don't know why I'm a disaster or why my life is fucked up like it is." I continued to sob in front of Jake and every other person walking by.

"Let me help you. What can I do? I'll do anything, just name it."

"The best thing is for you to walk away, Jake. Don't get involved with my screwed up life. It isn't fair to you."

"Let me be the judge of what's fair and what isn't." Before I knew what was happening, Jake's hands were on the sides of my face and his lips were on mine. My eyes closed and dizziness took over my brain. I didn't even know if it was truly happening or if I was dreaming again. What I did know was that where his lips connected with mine felt like embers of a fire had touched me and were searing every inch of my body. My mouth opened to him as if I'd kissed him so many times before. His moist tongue swept past my lips and twined with mine making the dizzying effect magnified. I couldn't move my body. I was trapped in a place where I'd always wanted to be, and it was a place that scared the life out of me.

Rational thought seeped back in and I suddenly pulled away. I touched my now swollen lips and looked at Jake. His eyes were glazed over, his lips were also puffy, and his breathing seemed just as labored as mine.

My flight instinct chose that moment to kick in and I bolted. I didn't walk or jog, I took off running through the throngs of people on their lunch breaks milling from one destination to another. I didn't look back.

∞ *Ten* ∞

AFTER I FELT LIKE I was far enough from Jake I flagged down a cab, and it sped away with me inside. I pulled a tissue from my purse and wiped my tear-streaked face. I then worked on putting my makeup back where it should be so I didn't raise questions when I made it back to the office. What happened? Why did Jake kiss me? It wasn't as if I didn't enjoy it, quite the opposite actually. It was the most phenomenal kiss I'd ever experienced but I freaked. I freaked and I ran. Wasn't that what I wanted: to be with Jake? Now I had a taste of him, literally, and I wasn't sure what I wanted. Confusion swept through me as I replayed the entire episode. The sensations of him touching me, the feel of his breath mingling with mine...it was all too much.

At first, I couldn't figure out why it scared me so badly, but as I thought about it more and more, I realized why it did. Jake never forced himself on me, but he took control, and that's what frightened me. I tried to shy away from situations where I didn't have control, but I hadn't seen the kiss coming. I didn't have the chance to react.

When would I stop running scared? I surely wouldn't be like this for the rest of my life, would I? If so, I would never be happy; things would always make me run and I would die alone with 50 cats to keep me company. I needed to do something about my fears. Before, they weren't a big deal. I kept to myself, didn't interact intimately with anyone really, but now they were converging in a perfect storm and blocking my chance with someone I'd fantasized about forever. This *had* to stop.

Luckily I'd cleaned myself up just as we pulled to the corner outside of my office building. When I got inside I took the elevator to my floor and practically sprinted to my office. I flung the door open, threw my purse in a desk drawer and plopped down in my leather chair with a sigh.

"Ah, you're back." Marvin popped his head in the door. "I have a deposition in thirty minutes and I thought you might like to sit in?"

"Absolutely." I pasted on a smile. Sitting in with him was the last thing I wanted to do, but I needed the experience, so I agreed.

"Good. Meet me in Conference Room C in thirty."

I took a few minutes and went to the ladies room to freshen up before the deposition. I ran my fingers through my hair, put on a thin coat of clear gloss and used the facilities. When I pulled my skirt up and my panties down, I was shocked to see how Jake's kiss really affected me. My pink satin panties were soaked with moisture from my arousal. My body heated with the thoughts of how he did that to me. No one had ever worked me up enough to do that. Even during sex, I'd never become *that* wet, let alone with just a kiss. I couldn't wear them now. I didn't need the reminder while I sat in with my boss and his clients.

I shimmied them down my legs and over my heels. I wadded them up and concealed them in my fist long enough to make it back to my office. When I got there, I shoved them into the side pocket of my purse and closed it. It felt strange standing at work with no underwear on, but luckily I'd just gotten a fresh wax, and my pussy was smooth as glass. Thank god for small miracles.

It was just a few minutes until the deposition, so I went down the hall to find the conference room. I passed in front of Molly's desk where she sat pecking away on her computer.

"How was lunch with Mr. Bradford?" She looked up as I passed by. I stopped and turned toward her with a questioning look. "Oh, Hon, everybody knows *everything* around here." She giggled.

"Apparently. It was fine." I replied dryly.

"Just *fine*? Honey, I've seen Jake Bradford, and anytime spent with him would be more than fine." She got all starry eyed.

"Aren't you married?" I looked at her wedding ring on her finger.

"I'm married, but I'm not dead. Jake Bradford is one of those fantasy men. I know I'll never have someone like him so I like to live vicariously through others."

"I hope you don't tell your husband about men like him."

"Nah, but I'm sure Carl has his own stash of mental fuck buddies. He wouldn't be a man if he didn't."

I couldn't help but laugh at Molly. But I wasn't going to tell her I'd run from Jake like a bat out of hell after he kissed me. I wouldn't have put it past her to reach up and bitch-slap me.

"I'd better get in there." I pointed to the door down the hall.

"Okay, have fun. I'll see you tomorrow. I have to leave early for a doctor's appointment. I'm hoping this little one is turned just right so we can start planning the nursery." She beamed with pride as she spoke of her pregnancy.

"Good luck." I said as I walked to the end of the hallway.

I got to the door of the meeting room, pulled it open and stepped inside. I looked around the room seeing Marvin and a couple of other people I didn't know. As I looked further down the long wooden table, my eyes felt like they popped out of my head.

Grant was sitting at one end of the large oval table. The same *Grant* I'd been on a disastrous date with the night before. He caught my eyes, and the edges of his mouth turned up into a mischievous grin. My face flamed, and Marvin glared at me. I broke the eye contact with my disastrous-yet-still-sexy date and found a seat near the door. I crossed my legs and felt an ache forming between my thighs. *What is with you today, Emily?*

I managed to take notes and listen while Marvin deposed Grant. To my surprise, someone was suing his firm for millions of dollars that they'd allegedly swindled. I really couldn't concentrate on the details for the fact that I was practically drooling over him. Molly talked about a mental fuck buddy—well, Grant was that and then some. I knew Jake had felt Grant was no good, and maybe he was right. But besides giving Jake a busted lip, he hadn't really done anything to me personally. I really did want to give him a second chance, but now he was tied up in a lawsuit with the firm I worked for. I knew beyond a shadow of a doubt that Marvin would not look favorably on that. Not to mention that I shouldn't have been thinking about Grant anyway. I'd just been kissed silly by my dream guy not even two hours earlier. What type of person did that make me?

When the end of the deposition came around, I stood with Marvin and shook everyone's hand. I quickly left the room. I was stopped part way down the hall by a hand at the small of my back. *Grant.*

"Hey babe, sorry I didn't tell you I'd be here today. After you told me you were working here, I knew you'd put an end to our date."

"You were right on that assumption." I continued walking.

"So how about a drink after work to apologize, my treat?"

"Thanks for the offer but that's not a good idea."

"And why not?" he ran his hand over my backside causing a flutter of excitement and apprehension to run through me.

"Well for starters, you're a client. That's a huge conflict of interest, Grant. I really wish you would've told me last night."

"I said I was sorry, Emily." He gave me a sad face.

"Well like I said, this isn't a good idea. We can't continue to see each other. I know it was only one date but if you could please not say anything I'd appreciate it. I could lose my job over this," I pleaded with him.

"I understand you're point, but I still see the way you look at me. And the way you were squirming in your seat in there. Tell me you don't want me. Tell me that you wouldn't like to have my hands all over you right now."

Oh my god. He was turning me on even more with his low seductive voice. I shouldn't have been aroused by his forwardness. I should have been appalled and run away. Why wasn't I running away from him? I sped away from Jake and Jake didn't even talk like Grant did. He was slow and sensual, not crude and crass.

"Grant it's just not the best idea…"

He suddenly grabbed my arm and yanked me into a vacant office, then shut and locked the door.

"What are you doing…?"

I felt his lips crash onto mine in a bone-melting kiss. The tango of our tongues felt so wrong but also so damn right. I mentally compared the kiss to Jakes. It wasn't the same at all; no, Grant took what he wanted and didn't apologize for it. He reached around me and grabbed my ass with his large hands, and squeezed hard. He pulled me into his front and I could feel the hard press of his cock against me. I closed my eyes and let the sensations overwhelm me. I shouldn't have been there, doing that. I knew better. But for some ignorant reason, I didn't care. I wanted to get lost in the arms of *someone*. I didn't want to be the good girl right then; I wanted to do something reckless and irresponsible and not give a flying fuck about the consequences. I had to prove to myself that I wasn't that scared little canary in a cage anymore; no, I was a bird of prey, going after what I wanted. And dammit, I would have it.

I felt Grant snake his hand down the front of my skirt and lift the hem slightly. I found myself closing my eyes and fantasizing again about Jake.

The cool air in the room brushed my bare skin as Grant pulled my skirt up high enough to expose everything to his gaze.

"Damn, now that's hot."

I gave him a lazy smile.

His fingers ran over the silken finish of my intimate skin and I let out a shuddering breath. Grant tapped my inner thigh and I automatically spread my legs further at his silent command. He petted me gently and then ran a finger through my drenched lips. "Holy fuck, you're wet." He continued to make languid strokes with his fingers.

He pressed his fingers along the outer rim of my sex, and teased my swollen clit with his thumb. I arched my back to get closer, I needed more. He dipped one, then two fingers into my moist opening and pressed his concealed cock against the side of my bare thigh. I gasped at the feeling of the pressure building inside me so quickly. His thick digits filled me up and gave me a delicious pleasure bordering on pain. I knew I was tight; I hadn't been with anyone in over four years. Grant didn't seem to care though, he plunged his fingers inside of me deeply, causing me to whimper.

It had been so long since I had actual contact with a man, I knew I wouldn't last long. I was just embarrassed that I was so wanton, but I needed an orgasm like I needed oxygen.

Finding that all too sweet spot just inside, he began to rock his fingers. I began to tingle and ache; his hands were taking me where I wanted to go. I hadn't realized that I'd needed this so damn bad. I began to ride his hand like my life depended on it.

He continued the delicious torture, kissed my neck ever so lightly, and I felt myself shudder. My release was getting ready to sweep over me like a hurricane over the ocean. He thrust his fingers into me harder, and pressed the pad of his thumb roughly over my clit. My orgasm flooded over me and I was at its mercy. As the first waves of my release crashed into me, I cried out. "Ahhh, Jake!"

I knew as soon as that name flew out of my mouth, I was screwed. Grant didn't even bother bringing me down from my orgasm, he quickly pulled his fingers out of me and stepped back. I stood there breathing heavily, trying to focus my vision again. I grabbed the hem of my skirt and yanked it over my exposed flesh. "Grant, I'm so sorry."

"I'd have to say that's never happened." A storm brewed behind his eyes.

"Please Grant, I don't know what happened. Just…"

I didn't have a chance to even make up an excuse. Grant flung open the door of the office and stormed out. I was left wondering what the hell had happened. One minute I was experiencing an erotic moment and trying to be a bad girl; the next I was shouting out Jake's name. I should have chased him down and apologized, but I couldn't risk Marvin asking me questions I didn't want to answer. If he found out about Grant and me, my employment would be terminated and I would be left trying to figure out a way to dig myself out of yet another hole. So I just stood there like the coward I was.

∞ *Eleven* ∞

THAT EVENING, I went home to lick my wounds and try to forget about the fact that I was a first-class dumbass. That was the only explanation I could come up with for acting the way I had that day. It seemed like every decision I was making was the wrong damn one. I was beginning to think I was destined to fail at everything and inevitably end up moving back to L.A. and begging my parents for forgiveness. I had a lot of things to deal with and work on, and it might have taken me a while to iron things out. But calling it quits wasn't an option.

I walked up the steps to my apartment feeling like the weight of the world was on my shoulders. I only had myself to blame though. My heart started pounding in my chest when I found my door ajar, and I could hear sounds of someone inside. Panic rose inside me, and I wasn't sure what to do. Was I being robbed? Should I call the cops, or should I go in?

I chose the latter and pushed the cracked door open enough to peek through. I couldn't see anyone, so I thought maybe I was hearing things. I thought back to that morning and wondered if I'd accidentally left the door open by mistake. No one would've been able to enter the building without the passcode, so that only left my downstairs neighbor and the person who lived upstairs to have access to my apartment. I hadn't met either of those tenants. I thought back to my self-defense courses and tried to put myself in the "brave zone," like I'd been taught. I steadied my breathing, put my shoulders back in a confident stance, and looked around for something to defend myself with.

The only thing remotely capable of being used as a weapon was an umbrella propped against the wall by the door. It would have to work in the pinch I was in. Picking it up, I moved slowly toward the kitchen area. I crept around the island and could hear someone whistling. Okay so I *wasn't* crazy, I did hear someone in here. I slipped off my heels so I could be stealthier; tip toed closer to the sound and put my back against the wall, just around the corner. I could hear the roar of my pulse in my ears, and as I stood there I tried to calm myself. It wasn't working. Before I could even react, the perpetrator moved around the corner. Then he was within reach. I sprung forward, swinging the umbrella into his torso. It bounced off his arm.

He barely flinched and then turned around to face me. "You might want to find a better home security system, Emily. An umbrella is hardly intimidating."

It was Jake…in my apartment. What the hell was he doing there? How did he get in? Then all of a sudden my brain put two and two together. The name Eliza rang a bell, which was the name of the woman who left the voicemail about my apartment that morning *and* the name of Jake's secretary. That couldn't have been a coincidence. The initials J&B, as in J&B Properties came to mind—Jake Bradford…*Jake* was my landlord. *Well, holy hell.*

"You're cabinet door is all fixed up." He smiled and walked back around me to the kitchen again. "Try not to be so rough on the place. I would hate to have to come down here every time you decide to tear something up. But at least I'm just right upstairs." He winked.

I still stood there with my jaw on the floor, holding onto the umbrella for dear life. I couldn't fathom the fact that I'd come all the way to New York, found a place to live, a job…and everything I did led me back to Jake.

"I didn't know it was you who lived here until this afternoon. My secretary Eliza takes care of the paperwork with my apartments. She told me you had a mishap in the kitchen and needed a repair." He leaned down and placed some tools into a small red toolbox. "When she told me it was you who lived here, I damn near shit myself." I could hear Jake's Texas accent and it made me smile.

"Thank you," was the only thing I could manage to say. I was still flabbergasted that I was living just below Jake, he was my landlord, and he was standing in my apartment. The sleeves of his white dress shirt were rolled halfway up his arms, there was a slight sheen of sweat dotting his forehead, and the toolbox in his hand screamed sexy cowboy.

"I'll get out of your hair." Jake started walking toward the door.

"Wait." I called.

He turned around and looked to me with imploring eyes. "Can I maybe order you dinner since you fixed my cabinet?" I felt like I needed to make amends after running at a full sprint away from him earlier that day.

"Fixing things is part of my job; no need to repay me." He reached for the doorknob.

"But I want to. Please?" I felt like I was begging. "I have some things to explain, and if you're willing to listen, I think I'd like to tell you." Something in me felt like I could trust Jake. He'd apologized for his previous behavior. At least I hoped he could.

"Yeah, okay." He agreed. "But I'm buying," he insisted. He pulled out his phone and hit a number on his speed dial. I smiled as he placed a delivery order for pizza and then hung up. "Hope that was fine with you. I remember how you liked your pie when we were at NYU."

It touched me that he'd carried that knowledge with him all those years. He knew my favorite toppings were bacon, black olives, fresh basil and extra cheese.

"Thank you, Jake. You didn't have to do that; you could've ordered what you liked. I would've eaten it."

"Those toppings have grown on me since college. I've found myself ordering them more often than not."

That thought made me do an internal happy dance. Jake actually ate his pizza with *my* preferred toppings—how incredibly sweet.

Jake brushed past me and went to the fridge; he opened it up and scanned the contents like he lived there. "At least you have *something* to drink in here." He held up my bottle of wine.

"I would have stocked it full of *Shiner Bock* if I'd known you were right upstairs, Jake."

He looked at me and raised an eyebrow. "You remembered my favorite beer?"

"Of course. Some things are hard to forget, Jake." I moved to his side and pulled a couple of stemmed glasses from the cabinet.

"Then why did you forget *me*?"

He asked the one question I'd been asking myself since college. "I never forgot you, life just…happened."

"That's a bullshit excuse if I've ever heard one," he bit out.

"What do you want me to say? I moved back to L.A. after I failed the bar, and as you know, I was engaged. I couldn't very well try to look you up when I was with someone else."

"We were friends, Emily. I thought you would've at least kept in contact for that reason."

"Things just became complicated, Jake." I turned my back toward him and started to pour us each a glass of the dark purple liquid.

"Then enlighten me. I'm pretty good at understanding complicated. You said you had things to explain. Well, I'm here. Time to start explaining."

He was right; I did need to clear things up. Jake deserved to know why I wasn't the same person I'd been all those years ago. Was I afraid he wouldn't accept me after I told him? No, I was terrified. But if I didn't take that leap and put trust in the one person who'd always been there for me, I was doomed to fail again. I didn't want or need that.

"Maybe we should have a seat in the living room first." I motioned him that way and watched as he plunked his frame into a chair across from my sofa. I took a seat on the couch and placed my glass of wine on a coaster in front of me on the coffee table. Jake pulled a coaster free of its holder also and put his on a table near him that held a lamp.

"I just want to start by saying what happened earlier today when you kissed me wasn't because of you. I don't want you to think I ran because it was dreadful or anything like that."

"That's good to know. I thought maybe I was in dire need of a Tic Tac." He laughed, making me feel more at ease. Jake always managed to do that for me. He was my warm fuzzy blanket on a frigid winter's day, my huge plate of comfort food after a shitty week at my job or my big bowl of Ben & Jerry's after a tragic breakup. Jake was everything all rolled into a gorgeous man. Which was, of course, part of the problem.

"So, why did your fiancé break off your engagement?" Jake prompted.

"He didn't; I did. Some things happened, and I couldn't stay in the relationship." I picked up my glass of wine and took a small sip to postpone a few moments while I collected myself. Jake sat across from me waiting patiently for me to continue. I hated talking about that part of my life and to reveal it to Jake was, in a way, embarrassing. I felt tears begin to well up in my eyes as I began to speak again. "At first Michael was great—we got along and had what I thought was a loving relationship. It wasn't long though until I saw the true side of him."

Jake stopped me. "Emily, you don't have to tell me if you don't want to. I can tell it upsets you."

"No, I need to. You need to know why I ran, and why the things you've said have hurt me so much."

"Then I'll listen." He sat further back in his chair, and his expression softened.

"Michael liked to drink, a lot. He would get out of control when he drank and at first I just brushed it off. His words would become belligerent and hateful, but being the doting fiancé, I stood by him. It wasn't until a couple of years into the relationship things got out of hand. We went out one night, had a nice dinner with drinks, of course. Michael wouldn't stop drinking, and so I urged him to let me take him home to sleep it off. He finally agreed.

"When we got back to his place he got mouthy, and I took it. I shouldn't have. I should've just left. But I didn't. He grabbed me and started to force himself on me. It all started with a kiss, and I pushed him away. The next thing I knew, he was hitting me. He shoved me to the floor, and on the way down, I hit my head on an end table. But that wasn't enough for him. He continued to kick me in the ribs while I lay on the floor bleeding." I took a deep breath and wiped the tears from my cheeks that'd started pouring the moment I began talking. "He did have the decency to call an ambulance after he'd hurt me, though. But I'll always have this…" I pulled my hair away from the place where a nasty scar lay, right behind my left ear. "As a reminder of that night."

I could see the fury on Jake's face as I showed him the evidence of my misfortune. He soon got up slowly from his chair and knelt next to me. He brushed the hair away from my face and ran his fingertips across the angry red mark. "I'm so sorry, Emily."

"I've spent the past few years telling myself that I could've fixed him...that I could've been better somehow, so he wouldn't have wanted to treat me like he did."

"That's bullshit. No one deserves to be hurt like that. There's no excuse for it. And for you to try and make an excuse is unfair to you."

"I know that now. But I've been trying to put my life back together since then. It's been hard to wake up every morning and look at this scar. I hate it. I hate what he made me become."

"Where is he now? Please tell me he's in jail for what he did to you."

Jake waited for my answer. I knew he wouldn't like what I was going to tell him, either.

"No. He's not in jail."

"And why the fuck not?" Jake raised his voice, causing me to flinch.

God, I didn't feel like getting into the whole deal about my parents and Michael. I was emotionally wrung out already and didn't know if I could compose myself long enough to tell *that* side of the story. "Jake, can we just drop this for tonight?" I felt like I was begging.

He stood back up and looked down at me. "Yeah. But I want you to know something. Not all men are like Michael. Not everyone wants to hurt you, Emily. I don't want to hurt you, and I never would."

"I know that Jake, but hopefully you can understand why I ran from you."

"I do. But you need to know that just because you experienced that doesn't mean you need to construct a wall so that no one else can be with you. That's not fair to anyone."

He was right. But it wasn't like I could just decide to break my walls down right away. I'd built them quite sturdy and wasn't ready to just huff and puff and blow them down. Jake understood that, hopefully.

A silence fell over the room for a few minutes but was luckily broken by the downstairs buzzer.

"Pizza's here. I'll run down and get it." Jake headed for the door.

I sat there, wondering how I ended up there. How was it that I pined for Jake all those years, and there I was sharing the deepest, darkest time in my life like we'd never been apart? It was as if those eight years hadn't even passed by. I was glad that he was there. I forgave him for being an asshole; so I felt immensely better about that. But the one thing I wasn't willing to do was open myself up completely to Jake.

∞ *Twelve* ∞

AFTER JAKE LEFT MY APARTMENT the night before, I felt so much better. It was good to get things off my chest and explain almost everything to him. Sure, I wasn't ready to delve into the complete saga of my screwed up life just yet, but I'd told myself that eventually maybe I could trust Jake enough with everything. We talked until around two in the morning and to be honest, I was sad to see him go even though I knew he'd only be upstairs. It was a comforting thought to know that only my ceiling and his floor separated us. Jake had always been so good to me, and that hadn't changed. He apologized again for the things he did and said a few days before, and I knew he was sincere.

He'd talked about his life on the ranch in Texas and how growing up he'd helped his parents. There was such pride in his voice when he'd talk about his home life. I'd always envied him for having a good family life and parents who seemed to love him and his brother with every fiber of their being. Sure, they didn't have much growing up, but they had the one thing that I'd wanted more than anything: love.

Who wouldn't be envious of something like that? When you came from a past like mine, the grass always looked greener on the other side. The biggest lesson I'd learned, though, was that money didn't buy happiness. I tried for years to get my mind set the way my mother thought. I tried to squeeze into the mold my family was cast from, but I never could quite fit.

When I was a teenager I liked the fact that my friends were jealous of the things I had and where we lived. I went to private schools all of my life. My parents made sure that I had the best education possible, and I was always grateful for that.

When it came time to fill out college applications, they'd pushed for me to stay in California, but I'd wanted the chance to spread my wings and fly. It was intentional when I applied to NYU. I wanted to move across the country and have a life away from the shadow of my family for a while. Those college years were the best years of my life. Not to mention I met Jake. I wouldn't have traded my experience there for anything in the world.

When I went to bed after Jake left, I lay there thinking about him. It was so natural, having him in my space like he belonged there with me. I drifted off and began to dream once again.

I sensed his presence yet again. He was close, his eyes piercing holes through my soul, even in the dark of night. His manly smell filled the room, making my attraction to him heighten. My breathing became labored as the anticipation mounted. Erotic thoughts raced through my mind and turned my body into an inferno of lust-filled need.

I could see only his silhouette, but I knew who he was. He stood there, taking in the sight of my naked body on display just for him, all laid out on the sheets, ready and willing. I felt a brush of air, and then the bed dipped with the weight of his glorious masculine body.

I was more nervous than I had ever been, even though he'd visited me before. His body loomed over mine and before I could protest, he took my mouth in a burning kiss. I was so damp that my own moisture seeped onto the sheets where I lay.

Reaching down he trailed his tender lips to my strained and puckered nipple. The sensations of his teeth tugging on my distended areola had my heart ready to pound through my chest, and he kept up his relentless torture until I was moaning and pleading for release. He moved his hands leisurely down my torso, and I felt a tingle everywhere he caressed me.

He was branding me with his own personal form of an ecstasy-laced drug. It felt as if I had hot wax drizzled all over my already heated body, and it burned and singed me to the core. Pleasure and pain were both overtaking my senses like a mad storm of unrelenting need. I let him work his sexual magic on my over-sensitive skin.

Each one of my nerve endings were about to incinerate when he gently dipped his fingers into my soaking sex, swirling my own juices across my clit in a languid motion. He then entered me with two fingers and pumped his digits in and out.

"Ready for me?" he sensually whispered into my ear.

I was so ready; I wanted him beyond anything I ever had before. He encouraged my thighs to part, making way for his delicious body. My heart beat a symphony against my rib cage. Then he leaned down, and slowly pushed his fully engorged cock inside of me. His warmth radiated through my entire body, and I was on the verge of exploding around him.

Even when I thought he was fully seated inside of me, I felt his cock glide deeper into my passage. He was submerged to the hilt. I felt every sultry throbbing inch fill me up, making me feel irrevocably complete. My body began to clamp down around him, and he let out a strained groan of pleasure that had my senses on elevated alert. I couldn't believe I could affect him as much as he did me.

He began to thrust in and out of me, scraping my already sensitive flesh. I lifted my hips, meeting him stroke for stroke, trying to get him even deeper inside of me. We were fusing our bodies together in a dance of supreme ecstasy. It wasn't about a hasty fuck for him; he wanted possession of my body and soul.

My climax built, and it wouldn't be long until I shattered around him.

"Come with me." He moaned. His voice hurled me over the edge of blinding pleasure. I lost feeling in my extremities as I let out a keening cry of release and felt him harden even more inside of me. He spilled himself within my pulsing depths, coating me with each thrust while working me down from my high.

Even in the dark, I could tell he felt something for me...Lust? Love? I didn't know. What I did know was that I never wanted him to leave.

I was jolted awake by the incessant buzzing of the front door. *What the hell?* I threw my feet over the side of my bed and shrugged into my pink fluffy robe. I padded to the front door, not quite awake yet, and pushed the intercom button.

"Hello?"

"Hi, I have a delivery for Emily Mills." The man said.

I pushed the button to let him up. Moments later, he was knocking at my door. I cracked it open to be cautious, and he stood there with a vase filled with what had to be three dozen crimson roses.

"Are you Emily?" He looked at his clipboard and back at me.

"Yes." I reached out and took the flowers from him and he pushed the clipboard in my free hand.

"Sign here please."

I did as he asked and handed it right back to him. He hurried away and I shut the door and clicked the deadbolt. I carried the vase to the kitchen, curious to see who would be sending me roses on a Tuesday morning.

I placed the flowers on my kitchen island and plucked the small card from its plastic holder. The plain white envelope had my first name printed on the outside. I lifted the small flap and slid out the card, turning it over to read the note handwritten on it:

I know we've had a rocky start, but I'd like to try again. Grant.

Images of what transpired between Grant and me wafted over my brain, making me flush with arousal. I knew it was a terrible idea to see him again, but I really did need to apologize for blurting out Jake's name as I came around Grant's fingers. Apparently, he wasn't as upset with me as I'd originally thought. But I couldn't leave it the way it was, not in good conscience anyway.

I would see him one more time, and hopefully, he would forgive me. Then I would break things off. He had to understand that it was a conflict of interest for the two of us to continue to see each other. He seemed like he had a good level head on his shoulders. My only fear was for myself. Would I be able to resist him? I hadn't done a good job of it in the office the day before. It was hard to say no to someone as sexy as him when I'd been going through the longest dry spell I'd ever experienced.

I made up my mind that I would send him a text when I got to work. Maybe sometime during the week we could meet for dinner and I could feel better about calling out another man's name in the heat of the moment.

∞ *Thirteen* ∞

ON WEDNESDAY I'D GOTTEN to the office early. I knew that Marvin probably had a ton of things for me to do, and I wanted to get started early so I didn't have to stay too late. I was hoping that I could leave on time at 5 because I needed to get some things squared away for the fundraiser on Saturday. I had to touch base with the caterer and band and make sure the wait staff was in the loop of what their role was. I needed for this event to go off without a hitch. It was the biggest event of the year for the charity, so success was imperative.

I'd been so busy the day before that I'd completely forgotten to text Grant to thank him for the roses and see if we could meet up one night during that week. I stayed after work for two hours and was able to grab some study time in the library. The time spent with my nose in books and online made me feel like I was right back in my days at NYU. This time though, I felt more confident.

That morning, I settled in at my desk and before I could even get my computer booted up, my desk phone rang. I picked up the receiver. "Emily Mills," I answered.

"Hi Emily, it's Grant."

"Grant, I'm so sorry I haven't called or texted you to thank you for the flowers. They were beautiful."

"You're welcome. I felt bad for storming off the other day, and I needed to make it up to you."

"You had nothing to make up for; it was my fault that things went south. I'm really sorry, Grant."

"It was an honest mistake. I thought about it, and I'm not mad. It could happen to anyone."

It made me feel good that Grant was being so accommodating. He didn't have to accept what I'd done. He had every right to never speak to me again.

"Well thank you for understanding. Listen, I was wondering if you might want to have dinner maybe tomorrow night? I think there're some things we need to discuss." I tried to sound positive even though my plans were to break things off with him.

"Yeah, sure, I'm free after seven." I could hear the click of computer keys in the background, telling me he was at work.

"Okay great. I work in Chelsea, so how about we meet outside Chelsea Market around 7:30?"

"Sounds good, I'll see you there." He hung up.

I felt a little better knowing I could make nice with Grant soon. Of course I still had to keep it a secret. No one at my office could know I was meeting him or that I'd been on a date before. And I for sure didn't need it getting out what'd happened in that vacant office down the hall. I'd lose my job and all credibility. I needed to work on damage control. I hoped that Grant would just walk away, and we could be civil.

When I left work that evening I stopped by a Chinese takeout place and grabbed some cashew chicken and fried rice to take home for my dinner. I needed to get home quickly to get work done for the fundraiser on that following Saturday.

As I kicked off my heels in my apartment, a loud knock sounded at my door. I knew again it must have been someone in the building because otherwise they would've buzzed downstairs. My pulse kicked up at the prospect of it being Jake on the other side of the door. I flung it open with enthusiasm and my facial expression dropped when I saw it wasn't Jake. It was *Gabe*. I looked past him to see if he was alone.

"Hi Gabe, how did you get past the door downstairs?"

"I know the code." He pushed past me and into my apartment.

"Come on in." I said sarcastically.

I watched as he surveyed my place and headed for the kitchen. I followed him in and found him pulling my takeout containers from the plastic bag they were in. "Why are you here...smelling my food?" Gabe had one of the white cartons open and was sticking his nose in, taking a whiff.

"Mind if I eat this? I'm starving." He asked.

I walked over and pulled a fork from the silverware drawer and I shoved it at him. "Be my guest."

Gabe snatched the utensil from my hand and went to the living room where he plunked down on the sofa like he owned the place. I watched as he dug into *my* dinner like he'd never had a warm meal before.

"Is there something I can help you with, Gabe? Or do you normally show up at people's homes and devour their food?"

"I was in the neighborhood and thought I'd stop by. Jake told me you lived here, and he wasn't home yet."

"So I was the next victim on your list?"

"Yeah, pretty much. But I also have a surprise for you."

"I'm not sure I want your surprises, Gabe." I rolled my eyes.

"Oh, I think you'll want this one." He teased.

"Well then, spit it out." I crossed my arms over my chest in annoyance.

"I got rid of your shitty jazz band you booked for Saturday night."

"You what!" I yelled.

"Seriously Emily, that crap was bores-ville. No one wants to donate money or sit around in a room for a few hours listening to elevator music. They had to go."

"Gabe, that band was the best in the city. What the hell am I supposed to do now?" I felt my blood pressure rising as I spoke to this lunatic in my living room.

"Jeez, take a chillaxative, Emily, I've got it covered."

"Then enlighten me, Gabe. How the fuck do you have it covered!" I couldn't keep my voice at a calm level anymore.

"I made some calls and now you have the one and only Michael Bublé performing Saturday night...you're welcome, by the way."

My anger was quickly replaced by excitement. "Wait, how did you get him to do this? It's really last minute."

"He's friends with a cousin of mine, I made a call and he's on a break from his latest tour. He also offered to do it gratis; that way all the money you raise won't have to be spent on entertainment."

I fell into a chair. "Wow, thank you, Gabe, this is amazing."

"You're welcome. Now if you'll excuse me, I'm going to go break into Jake's place and fuck around on his Xbox until he gets home. I'm sure there're some hookers on Grand Theft Auto that need to be run the fuck over." He jumped up from the sofa and went to the door. "See ya' 'round."

I couldn't help but chuckle. Even though Gabe had done something so nice for me, he was still the same juvenile idiot he'd always been. You could put lipstick on a pig, but underneath, it would always be a smelly, curly-tailed creature.

After he left I cleaned up his food mess on the coffee table and grabbed my laptop. I still needed to email the caterer a head count for the fundraiser and send out a letter letting the other board members know about the change in entertainment. I logged into my account to check my mail first. I scrolled through some spam and stopped when I found an email that made me slump back on the couch. It was from my dad. I leaned forward and clicked it open and started reading:

Dearest Emily,

"I know it's only been a matter of days since you've struck out on your own, but a lot has happened here. I've realized that I've been naïve to so many things around me and now I hold regret for many of them. I was never the perfect father to you and I know now that you've suffered greatly for my lack of concern. I let your mother dictate my actions and reactions to many situations, which have put you in a position of pain and suffering. If I was any sort of man I would've stood up for you and been there when you needed me the most. For that I'm sorry. I know that forgiving me isn't something you can do right away, but I do hope in the future we can mend the relationship that has been broken. I take the responsibility for my actions. Please know I would do anything to make sure you are happy.

Your mother and I have not seen eye to eye on many things over the years, as you know. But I've sat by and let things go, when I should've been standing up for what was right. Most of all, I should've been standing up for my own daughter.

After you left I decided that I'd had enough of sitting idly by and letting your mother dictate my actions. I know this probably doesn't come as much of a shock to you but your mother and I have filed for separation. I don't know if things will ever be repaired in our lives, but I do know that I was given the choice to stay with her or have a relationship with my daughter. I chose you.

Life has taken us down this path for a reason, and I truly hope you can find it in your heart to forgive my transgressions. I am proud of the woman you've become, Emily. You have an inner strength that I someday hope to possess myself. Just know that I am here if you need me, and I will hop on a plane anytime, day or night, to see you."

With much love,
Dad

I hadn't even made it halfway through the letter and tears poured from my eyes. I couldn't believe that my dad was finally standing up for what he wanted. Like me, he'd had enough and was claiming his independence. I sat there with the computer open and sobbed. It was a mixture of happiness and sadness all rolled into one big cry fest. I'd always wished my dad would stand up for himself and now my wish had come true. I actually had an opportunity to have a relationship with my father. It was like I had been given a gift, and I wanted to act on it right away. I reached forward and allowed my finger to hover over the reply button on his email.

I thought for a minute and then pulled my hand back. Everything was too fresh. I needed time to process this. I didn't want to send an emotionally charged letter back to him. And truthfully, I didn't want to email him at all. I wanted to hear his voice. I sat back once more and made the decision to wait. I would find time to call him one day and be able to hear if he was truly sincere. It wasn't as if I doubted him, but my trust issues gave me pause like they always did.

∞ *Fourteen* ∞

THE NEXT DAY I ARRIVED at work a few minutes late and went right to my office. Molly came in shortly after and placed a doughnut wrapped in a napkin in front of me.

"I figured you needed sustenance." She joked.

"Thank you. How was your evening?"

"Oh, same old, same old. Wrangling kids, cooking dinner. Just another day in paradise. How was yours?"

I didn't want to get into to the whole deal about my dad. I felt comfortable with Molly, but not *that* comfortable. "Uneventful," I lied.

Molly plopped down in one of my chairs and crossed her arms over her slightly protruding tummy. "Well, this kid is apparently going to be a soccer player. It keeps rolling around in there like crazy."

I laughed. "Were they able to see what you're having?"

"Heck no. This little one had its tush pointed directly at us. No biggie, though; I go back in a few weeks to try again. Hopefully things will be different."

"There's always the color yellow." I suggested.

"Very true." She smiled. "So, have you talked to Mr. Hot and Handsome anymore?" She waggled her eyebrows.

"Actually, yes. It just so happens that he owns the building I live in, and he lives in the apartment above me."

"You don't say! How convenient."

My cheeks heated at the direction of the conversation. "Yeah, it's nice to have someone I know living so close."

"Sure it is; you can just knock on each other's door and have a booty call."

"It's not like that with Jake and me. We're just friends." I fibbed.

"I didn't say you had to marry the guy, but a *friends with benefits* deal would be fun."

"I'll think about it." I really wanted to end this conversation.

"Well, keep me updated. How's the studying going? I saw you stayed the other day."

"It seems to be going fine. I'm pretty much just refreshing myself on everything. I'll be glad when I get to take the test again."

"I'm sure you'll do fine. You have more guts than I do. If I'd failed it once, I would've given up, much less twice!"

"I did give up, but realized that I really wanted to be a lawyer so I finally decided to take it again. I just hope it turns out differently this time."

Molly was super easy to talk to. It was like I'd known her my whole life and we were best girlfriends. In a way I envied her—she had her life in order complete with a husband and children. I wanted that someday. I wanted to be able to get off work and go home to someone who really cared about me.

"Well, I have a feeling about you, and I think you will pass the exam and become very successful."

"Thank you for your confidence in me, Molly, that means a lot."

"Well, I'd better get back to my desk before Marvin starts screaming and gives himself a stroke. If you need anything just call, or scream down the hall." Molly got up and walked out.

During the day I worked on some documents that were sent my way by Marvin, then I went to the legal library and did a couple hours' worth of research on a case I was helping out with and made a few phone calls to gather information for Marvin. Five o'clock came around and I went back to the library.

"So, Emily, are you more nervous over the essay questions or the multiple choice section?" One of the other paralegals asked.

"Both, I think. If you blow one section, it doesn't matter about the other, you're pretty much done."

He nodded and then returned to his work.

By the end of the study session, I felt a little more comfortable with everything. I knew I had plenty of time to study before my actual test so I felt okay with things for now.

I looked at the time on the computer I was using and saw that it was 6:45. I was meeting Grant later and wanted to get to Chelsea Market in plenty of time. I got up from the table and headed for the door.

"Emily, can I talk to you for a minute?" One of the paralegals stopped me.

"Uh yeah, sure." We exited the library doors and stood in the hallway. "What's up?"

"I know this is none of my business, but I don't want you to get in trouble..."

I had no idea what she was talking about.

"I saw you the other day. With that client."

Oh god. Bile rose in my throat and I became dizzy.

"Listen, I won't say anything, I just thought you should be careful. I know we aren't supposed to be dating active clients, and I don't want you to get fired."

"Thank you, it was a mistake. I'm actually meeting him tonight to break things off. We'd only been on one date, and he failed to tell me he was a client."

"Okay, like I said, my lips are sealed. I like you and think you have a good head on your shoulders."

I nodded and thanked her again. I was thoroughly embarrassed. I'd been caught. I really hoped she wouldn't say anything; I was going to take care of the issue soon and just needed time to fix everything.

I left work feeling uneasy; it wasn't the best idea to meet Grant again, but I now knew that breaking it off with him was for the best. I couldn't afford to get caught again.

Grant was waiting just outside Chelsea Market when I arrived. I couldn't help but appreciate the way he looked so delicious in his black tailored suit and grey striped dress shirt. He wore no tie and had the top two buttons of his shirt open, showing just the slightest amount of tan skin. He was leaned against the brick front of the building checking his watch for the time.

"Hi, I'm not late, am I?" I knew I wasn't.

He pushed himself off the wall and walked a few feet toward me. "Nope, right on time." He smiled. "Hope you're hungry. I read about this place inside called Green Table and they are supposed to have a veggie pot pie to die for."

"Sounds great." I walked ahead of him and he put his hand to the small of my back.

We strolled through the market watching the groups of people gathered at the various eateries, carrying armloads of fresh produce, baked goods and take out containers. I even saw the Food Network star Bobby Flay walking by with what looked like part of a filming crew.

"Hey was that...?" Grant looked over his shoulder.

"Yeah it was." I laughed at the star struck look on his face. "They film a ton of the food shows here."

"Very cool. I've never actually been here before—guess I need to get out more." He joked.

I soon found the restaurant we were looking for and the smells that filtered out were divine. My stomach grumbled at the thoughts of digging into the local offerings. Grant opened the glass door and ushered me inside. The reddish orange of the walls were bright and inviting, welcoming us in for what I hoped would be a great meal. I'd only managed to eat the doughnut Molly had laid on my desk so my hunger was about to drive me insane.

We took a seat at one of the small tables and began to scan the menu. My mouth watered at the selections printed in front of me. Everything was made from organic and local ingredients grown right here in the city.

"I think the grilled cheese sounds pretty good," Grant placed his menu back on the table.

I went with my original choice of the potpie and after we put in our orders we sat in awkward silence for a few moments.

"I guess I need to apologize again for the other day. I'm really sorry." I ducked my head in shame.

"Like I said before, it's water under the bridge. It could've happened to anyone." Grant assured me.

"Well I appreciate you being so understanding, most people would've told me to fuck off."

"I'm not most people, Emily; besides, I really like you."

"And that's what we need to talk about, Grant. This thing between you and me just won't work. You're a client of Marvin's and I can't afford to break the rules and get fired."

"You broke the rules the other day when you were moaning in my arms in that office."

His words flamed my skin. "It was a mistake; I was caught up in the moment. I can't let it happen again."

Grant was silent as our food was delivered to our table and we dug in. I was still nervous with the conversation. He obviously wasn't willing to take no for an answer just yet.

I took a few bites of my food and pushed it away. "Do you want me to get fired over this? I could lose my job and be out on my ass. Is that what you want?"

"I think you could manage just fine if you didn't have a job, Emily."

"What's that supposed to mean?" My head shot up.

Grant leaned over the table, his face mere inches from mine. "Do you really think I didn't look into you? The daughter of movie moguls in L.A. The heiress to a shit ton of money when your old man croaks."

The color drained from my face. It wasn't like I was trying to hide out in New York; anyone who knew my name could plug it into a search engine and find out who I was. What alarmed me was that Grant had a tone about him that told me he was now looking for something other than just a few dates.

"What do you want?" It was the same story with anyone who knew I came from money. They wanted something, whether it was cash, or their 15 minutes of fame.

"I don't want anything besides you."

"What does that even mean, Grant?"

"Like I said before, I really like you. I think you and I click. It would be a shame to break this off and not see where things could lead."

"So basically what you're saying is that if I break things off with you, you'll rat me out to my boss and get me fired?"

"I'm not saying that at all, Emily." He took another bite of his sandwich and smiled.

My creep-o-meter was off the charts now, Grant looked like the villain in a comic book, and I felt uneasiness wash over me. What was I to do though? I needed my job in order to take my exam and build my reputation. If I was fired, the reason would be publically known and I wouldn't be able to find a job in the law field. My name would be ruined. I thought about it and knew I only had once choice in the matter. I would date Grant and hope that he would keep it a secret.

"Fine, but this has to be low key, Grant. If my boss finds out, I'm screwed anyway."

"Deal." He gave me a satisfied smile and threw back the rest of his drink.

Yet again I found myself in another fucked up situation. Grant may have been sexy as hell, but he was turning out to be a class-A dick head.

∞ *Fifteen* ∞

SATURDAY MORNING I WOKE UP still exhausted with my mind filled with anxiety over everything that'd happened the past week. It was all converging on me like a cloud getting ready to spill rain. I wasn't sure how to make sense of it all. But I didn't have time to dwell on all of it that day. I had my fundraiser that evening and I needed to pull myself together and put on the best damn event I possibly could. I'd put my heart and soul into making my charity a success; this event was just the culmination of everything. It would determine the amount of funding the charity would receive for the year to help women in need. I had so many people counting on me to make sure it went off perfectly.

I spent the morning trying to relax and put my mind where it needed to be. I made a few calls to confirm last minute details and sent a few emails to make sure the silent auction items would be there in plenty of time, and after I got my tasks done I headed to the salon for my few hours of pampering.

When I walked out of the salon I felt like a million bucks. I was getting glances from passersby as I stood on the sidewalk flagging down a taxi. Men were taking a second glance, which made me feel desirable and sexy, something I hadn't felt in quite a while.

When the cab dropped me off back at my apartment building I immediately went upstairs and pulled my dress from the vinyl bag it had been in since I'd purchased it. I was ready to slip into it and feel beautiful.

I milled around my place for a few hours until it was time to get dressed.

I slipped on my dress with ease, put on my jewelry and shoes; then stepped in front of the mirror. I had dressed up so many times before, but *this* time was distinctive. I actually *felt* beautiful. Almost like a fairy tale princess. My golden hair was swept up into a smooth bun resembling a style that Jennifer Lopez might wear on the red carpet. My face was airbrushed to perfection, eyes lightly smoky with long dark eyelashes and a hint of pink dusted on the apples of my cheeks. But the *wow* factor was the lipstick I was at first hesitant to choose. I wasn't normally daring per se, but I wanted to make a bold statement and I was elated with my final decision. The crimson shade highlighted the bow of my lips, showing their lushness and bringing everything together perfectly. I smiled at myself in the mirror, knowing that I'd managed to step out of my box for at least one night.

"It's a shame that all the princes are actually frogs." I laughed to myself in the mirror.

Around six, I went downstairs to meet the limo that was picking me up.

Arriving at the Plaza Hotel was sort of surreal. Of all the elegant places I had ever visited, I never had one take my breath away like this. I could just imagine the people who had stayed there, or even the happy couples who decided on this place for their day of wedded bliss. It made my heart pound, just thinking about all the emotion that the walls had seen over the many years they'd been standing.

I was sure there was a fair share of love and tears that were embedded within the architecture of the building. It made its charm that much more inviting and magnificent.

The grand feel of the flags outside waving in the evening breeze and the red carpeted steps leading to the landing that would take me into the lobby was all like a dream I'd been privileged to have. Even when my parents and I had visited the city, we'd never stayed here. They'd rented a penthouse apartment on Fifth Avenue, and now I wished they would've at least brought me here once. Sure, I'd seen plenty of photos when I was looking for a place to hold this event, but they didn't give it justice. It was truly like something constructed for a movie set.

I picked up the hem of my dress and went through the doors of the hotel. The lobby was breathtaking, but I walked straight through to my ultimate destination, The Grand Ballroom. When I reached the doors I was taken aback by just how grand it really was. Ornate crystal chandeliers hung opulently from the high ceiling. The massive pillars on each side of the room held up gorgeously intricate archways all trimmed in cream and gold adding to the richness of the colossal room. Expensive tapestries framed the archways showcasing damask patterns done in a golden spun fabric while smaller light fixtures hung on the pillars, adding just enough lighting to the space. A stage sat at one end of the room with a huge set of curtains matching the others in the room, pulled back. That would be the place where I'd have to speak later. The thought made me nervous. I pushed my anxiety aside and scanned the room again, this time taking in the amazing décor that my team had created.

Each round table was covered in white linens that were floor length, along with a gold cloth topper draped over them. In the center of each table were tall clear glass vases containing dozens of long stemmed red roses. Each bouquet held wires from which hung small sparkling crystals that caught the light, creating a twinkling effect throughout the room. Each place setting was set perfectly with fine china that reflected the gold and cream pattern of the entire place. Name cards were placed near the plates, along with a stemmed champagne glass for the toast later on.

I walked over to the wall where long covered tables held the items for the silent auction. Numerous high end products and services had been donated but some of them I hadn't known about. I checked out each one as I strolled along the edge of the tables. There were so many things that I knew would fetch decent dollar amounts to support the charity. A gorgeous diamond ring from Tiffany's, signed sports memorabilia from the Yankees, an all-expense trip to Paris and dinner with several well-known celebrities were just some of the offerings for the evening. I quickly wrote my name and bid on a couple of the items before most of the guests arrived. One in particular that I hoped I won was tickets to a Yankees game in a Luxury Suite. I'd always wanted to go to a major league ballgame, but my mother said it was something that "common" people did. I didn't care how common it was, I thought it would be fun to cheer on a team and hear the roar of the crowd during a homerun. I mentally crossed my fingers that I'd win.

People started filtering in the room, some alone, and some couples. Most made their way to the open bar, grabbing a cocktail before the night's festivities began. If I knew one thing, it was that buzzed rich people gave more freely of their money than sober ones did. I hoped that would be even truer during the event. We needed the money. It would help so many people who really needed it.

I scanned the room for someone that I knew personally, and couldn't spot anyone just yet. It was common knowledge that the cream of the crop of society normally showed up late because they wanted to make an entrance and draw attention to themselves. I decided to visit the bar for something to calm my nerves before the throngs of people overtook me.

I stood at the bar and ordered a cranberry/vodka. After gulping down my first and *only* drink of the night I decided on perusing the room a bit.

"Oh, Emily! You look absolutely divine tonight!" I heard from a few feet away.

As I scanned around for the face to match the voice, I found Mrs. Waverly. She'd always been a generous contributor to the cause and had friends in high places that would donate as well. I always made sure to send her an invite every year. I made my way over to her. "Mrs. Waverly, thank you so much for coming, it's great to see you again," I politely answered.

Waving around the room she said. "This is absolutely amazing. You should be very proud of yourself, Emily."

"Yes, incredibly proud indeed. Although I can't take full credit, everyone had a hand in helping out. I'm thankful I have such an amazing team to pitch in."

"How is everything going? I heard that you moved to New York." Great. She wanted to be nosy. I knew the news of me moving would be spread around like peanut butter on toast. I just hoped it wouldn't take away from the real reason we were there. "Everything is going great. I'm all settled in and happy." I smiled.

"Well that's just great. Look Dear, I'm sure you have a ton of people to talk to so I won't keep you. It was so nice to see you again."

"Thank you again for coming Mrs. Waverly. I hope you enjoy yourself tonight." And with that she was off, probably to the bar. That would've been my guess. From the things I'd heard she kept herself buried in the bottom of the bottle so she didn't have to deal with her marriage that was in shambles. I wanted to head that way too, but made myself a promise that one drink was plenty.

I moved around the room a bit more as guests arrived. I said some hellos and pointed people to the silent auction tables, which were packed with guests placing bids. I looked around and happened to see a guest that I was glad could make it. I moved through the crowd to get to her.

"Amy, I'm so glad you made it." I placed my hand on her shoulder.

"Emily, everything is so pretty, thank you for inviting me." She sent me a shy smile.

Amy was a prime example of the amazing work the charity did. She was living proof of the positive results we'd had in the past and hoped to have in the future. The first time I'd met Amy was in L.A. at one of our many women's shelters, she had come in with her 6-month-old daughter. I'll never forget the look on her face when she asked for help from us. Her terrified bruised face spoke volumes about what she'd been through and in that moment I wanted to kill the person who had done that to her. I can remember taking her daughter and holding her close to me while Amy cried and relived her story to me and one of the volunteers there. Her husband of three years had taken out his aggression on her and the time she sought help from us had been the worst. The only thing Amy had done was refused to have sex with him. He'd come home from a late shift at a factory and Amy was asleep. Her baby was in her crib beside the bed. Amy worked long hours as a waitress and when she told him she was too tired, he started beating her. After he decided he'd inflicted enough violence on Amy, he went after the baby. Amy was able to get up from the bed and push him away, he was down long enough so she could grab the child and run. She did what she had to do to protect her baby. I admired her for that. She left everything she'd ever known to make sure her child was safe.

When she came into the shelter she literally had only the clothing on her back. We helped her contact the police, and her abusive husband was arrested and was then serving eight years in prison. She was so scared though, and she had nothing. She refused to even go back home for fear he might find a way to retaliate.

I personally helped Amy move to a different part of the city, find a great job and childcare and sat with her in court when she filed for divorce. That was four years ago. It was so great to see her be a part of a night where our work helped people like her.

"How have you been?" I asked Amy.

"I'm wonderful, Emily, and I have you to thank for that. If it wasn't for all of this, I don't know that I would've even been alive tonight."

"It wasn't just me, Amy, but thank you. How's your daughter?"

"Sara is growing *so* fast it's hard to keep up with her some days." She laughed.

As we stood there talking a man came up behind Amy and put his arm around her waist. "There you are, I thought I'd lost you in this crowd of people." He leaned down and kissed her temple.

"Emily, I'd like you to meet Eric, my husband." Amy beamed as she looked at Eric. I could tell she'd found happiness and I was elated for her.

"Oh my god!" I practically shrieked and threw my arms around her. "I'm so happy for you." I held out my hand to shake Eric's.

"It's a pleasure to meet you, Eric." I smiled.

"Emily was the one who helped me. She was my guardian angel.," Amy explained.

Eric pulled me in for an unexpected hug. "I don't know how to thank you enough for what you've done for Amy. She and Sara have been the light of my life. I don't know what I would do without either of them." He looked down lovingly at Amy.

"I'm so happy things worked out and that you two found each other. That's amazing." I felt tears well up in my eyes.

"We also just found out a week ago that our family is expanding too." Amy and Eric beamed.

"Oh, congratulations!"

"Thank you." They both said in unison.

"Well I hope the both of you enjoy the rest of your night, I think I'd better start making my rounds before everyone thinks I went off to hide." I gave the happy couple another congratulatory hug and said my goodbyes.

Seeing such a success story in front of me was a perfect beginning to the night. I didn't always get to hear about the wonderful things the charity was doing, but knowing that Amy had found happiness made me feel like a proud parent watching her child succeed in the world.

∞ *Sixteen* ∞

ONCE I'D MADE SOME ROUNDS and talked to a few other people in the ballroom, I settled at the edge of the dance floor, watching the throngs of people milling around and seeming to have a great time so far. I was thrilled at the turnout and at the amount of guests placing bids on the numerous auction items. I was curious to see how much the baseball package was up to but I refrained from being nosy just yet. I told myself that I'd look just before the bidding ended at 9 pm.

I had a smile on my face as I turned toward the entrance of the ballroom and my body froze its stance. My heart began to flutter out of control at who was standing there. My palms turned sweaty, my knees knocked together like two wooden sticks and my chest became tight with anticipation. All I could do was gawk at the person who just entered the room. Jake was, for some reason, at my event and he looked divine in his perfectly tailored tux.

I couldn't believe that Jake was there. He was the last person I expected to see when I turned around, but I really wasn't surprised at my body's reaction to him. In fact every time I'd seen him since I'd move to New York I'd felt like a kid in a candy store. He elicited so much arousal from my body that I was beginning to wonder if I was crazy. I wished I could've just gone up and told him how I felt about him, but after revealing the things that happened with Michael the other night, I wasn't so sure Jake even held any kind of want for me. He'd left my apartment that night and didn't give me so much as a hug. But maybe that was my fault. After all, I kept pushing people away with my trust issues including him. He had every right to walk away; I carried enough baggage to fill the cargo hold of a Boeing 747.

I don't really know why, but seeing him there made me want him even more. By the looks on some of the female guests' faces, I could tell they thought the same thing. Behind Jake, bringing up the rear, was Gabe. He was already doing his usual scan of the room looking for probably the newest notch on his bedpost. I mentally prayed that he would keep his juvenile ways under control for at least *one* evening. I didn't need the embarrassment of Gabe getting caught in the coat check with some willing piece of ass.

Jake smiled and confidently sauntered towards me. Each step he took ratcheted my pulse up to just this side of heart failure, and I tried to slow my breathing so as not to look like I was hyperventilating. When he finally stood in front of me, I let out a puff of air and smiled.

"Hey there." He said.

"Hey yourself. What are you doing here?"

"Gabe invited me, I guess he needed a wingman for the night, you know him."

I looked behind Jake and Gabe was already going in for the kill on some young blonde. "Yes I do." I chuckled.

"I keep telling him that someday a woman is going to grab him by the balls and never let go. He doesn't seem to believe me though."

"Most people won't until it actually happens."

"Very true statement, Miss Mills."

"You should visit the auction table, there are a lot of great items over there. I'm sure there is something you'd like."

"I think I've found something I like already." His voice dipped lower and my cheeks flamed.

"And what's that?" I had to ask.

Jake leaned forward and whispered in my ear. "You."

"I'm not up for auction, Jake." I whispered back.

"Then I guess I'll have to find some other way of getting you to dance with me." He looked disenchanted.

"I think I can manage a dance, Jake."

"Well then we shall start with a dance and see where the evening takes us." It was an unspoken promise that I wasn't sure I could commit to.

Jake grabbed my hand and swept me onto the nearby dance floor. We ended up close to the middle when he pulled me around, pressing my chest to his. One hand held me even closer to the hard muscles of his chest. The other hand twined with mine as we swayed to the sounds of Michael Bublé crooning *"I just haven't met you."* I found myself trying to get even closer to him if that was even possible. It was like I was made to fit him the way we danced together in unison. The entire world melted away as if we were out there gliding on our very own cloud.

"If you get any closer, we might have a problem." Jake chuckled in my ear.

It took me a few seconds to figure out what he was talking about, but when I did I tried to pull away. "Oh, I'm sorry." I was embarrassed.

Jake drew me back to him. "And if you leave now, I'm going to be standing here looking like a pervert in the middle of a dance floor." I could feel his hardness pressing into my thigh through the fabric of my dress.

We continued to dance as the song played on. It was so right being in Jake's arms. Even though we'd had some differences during the past week, I knew without a doubt Jake was there for me. And feeling the way I affected him had me achy and on edge.

There was no doubt about it, I wanted Jake. I wanted him to have me in any way he would take me. I just wasn't sure about crossing the boundary of friendship into something more. If things didn't work out, what would we be then? Would we both just walk away and never speak to each other again? I'd gone all those years missing my best friend; I didn't know if I could handle going through that again.

I had to take a breather and think for at least a few minutes. The song ended and I backed away. "I need to use the ladies room."

Jakes eyes were full of desire and want. I was certain mine were too because I felt that way from the top of my hair to the tips of my toes. He nodded, and I walked away on now shaky legs.

In the bathroom, I closed myself in a stall and stood there, pressing my forehead against the cool metal of the stall door. It didn't help much; my body was like an inferno, my skin ready to disintegrate in flames with another brush of Jake's hand. I went to the vanity area after I used the toilet and washed my hands. Glancing into the mirror I saw a woman staring back at me who was unrecognizable. She was sexy and striking, her lips were extremely kissable, her body looked amazing in her remarkable gown and her eyes held emotion that I hadn't recognized in quite some time. She was *me*. I stared at myself knowing that I loved what I saw. I felt like I had finally found a small part of myself. Did I attribute that completely to Jake...no. But I did know he had a little something to do with it. He made me happy, and that was something I hadn't been in such a long time.

After I finally felt like I had regained some measure of self-control, I headed back toward the ballroom.

"Hey, Babe, fancy meeting you here."

Grant. I swung my head around and there he was, standing with an evil grin and looking like the Grinch who stole Christmas.

"What are *you* doing here?"

"Not much, was just on my way to your event." He winked.

"I'm sorry but you have to be on the guest list, and as I recall you're *not.*"

"Well that's the thing, I know a lot of people in this town and therefore was able to snag an invite. How lucky of me," he replied smugly.

My stomach was in knots, I wanted him to leave, but also knew he would cause some sort of scene if I insisted too hard. What the hell was I going to do?

"Fine. Just leave me alone." I snapped.

"Well, since we're dating and all, I thought you might like to have me here as your plus one for the evening."

"You promised you'd keep things low key if I didn't break things off with you, Grant."

"Damn, I suppose I did. Well, in that case, I'll just pretend I don't know you, how's that?"

"That's fine." I was relieved.

"But don't make plans for afterwards, I haven't seen you since Wednesday, I'd like some quality time with you." He said while walking by me.

I felt like the floor was jerked out from underneath me. I wanted to be anywhere but there at that moment. I knew Grant was blackmailing me and I also knew it was illegal, but I was caught between a rock and a hard place. Pretend to be with him and keep my job and dreams of becoming a lawyer, or tell him to take a hike and risk losing it all. I'd already lost everything once; I wasn't willing to take that chance again. Somehow I'd figure a way out of the mess I'd found myself in, I just wasn't sure what that *way* was yet.

I went back inside the ballroom after my run in with Grant. Everyone seemed to be having a good time; they were dancing, drinking and socializing. But that did little to calm my nerves. I wished I could just escape from it all and crawl inside myself. But I had a job to do. I wasn't going to run scared anymore, it was time to face things head on and hope for a positive outcome.

"How about another dance?" I turned to see Jake once again, and suddenly I felt safe from all of my woes.

"I would be delighted." I giggled.

He swept me toward the dance floor, took my hand in his and wrapped his other arm around my waist pulling me close to his chest. I could smell him, and God, he smelled wonderful. It was a mixture of pine and the smell of something very clean and masculine. It was a scent so individual to Jake. If I could've bottled up his fragrance, I would've doused myself in it anytime I needed comfort. It was *that* intoxicating.

Feeling his body heat in such close proximity to mine was heaven *and* hell. It felt only natural that I should lay my head on his shoulder while we were dancing, so I did just that. I was almost afraid of what his reaction would be until I heard him breathe a welcoming sigh. He was fine with it. And so was I.

"Do you ever wonder why we never became an item in college?" he asked.

"I know why we weren't. You were always with someone. I could've sworn you were going to marry the girl you dated our final year."

"I thought about it, but I wasn't ready to settle down. I wanted to get my career off the ground and make sure I was stable before making a life changing decision like that. It wouldn't have been fair to her otherwise."

"So in other words, you were trying to be selfless?"

"Not selfless, just smart." He smiled.

"Did you love her?" I had to ask.

"I think in a way I did. We clicked, and things were really good. But I never took her home to meet my family."

"I'm guessing that's the telltale sign that things are *really* serious?" I joked, but Jake had a staid expression on his face.

"I'm protective of my family; I refuse to let them get close to someone who won't be around in the long run. My mom gets attached to people rather quickly and had I taken anyone home, she would've been picking out china patterns and names for grandkids."

"Then it's probably a good thing you never took anyone home."

"A good thing indeed." Jake playfully spun me away from him and brought me back. "I don't think I've told you how gorgeous you look tonight."

"Well thank you, Jake, you don't look so bad yourself."

"Hey, I had to go out and buy this monkey suit just for this occasion. I think I deserve a little more credit," he chuckled.

"If I'm being completely honest, I'd say you're the best looking guy here. You look hot."

Jake looked around the room. "That's really saying something since most of the men here have their AARP card already."

"I'm sure when you apply for yours, you'll look just as amazing."

"Highly doubt it." He spun me around again.

As we talked and teased, the song ended and I knew it was almost time to give my speech for the evening. "Thanks for the dance, Jake. Now it's time to make a speech and haggle these nice people out of some money." I winked.

"Good luck, knock 'em dead. Oh wait, here..." He reached inside his jacket pocket and pulled out a plain white envelope. Jake handed it to me as I began to walk away. "I thought this might help out."

I was curious as to what was in the envelope. I figured it was a monetary donation for the foundation, and every little bit would help.

Curiosity got the best of me and while I was being introduced, I lifted the flap of the plain white envelope and slid a check out. My mouth dropped open when I saw the amount of money Jake had just donated. *$500,000.*

I'd never expected Jake to donate so much money to the charity. I felt guilty that he'd just given away his hard earned money, and I didn't know what to say. I stood there with a dumbfounded look on my face as the master of ceremonies introduced me.

"And to start the evening off, I would like to introduce the chairwoman for this amazing charity. Please welcome Miss Emily Mills." The room erupted in clapping and cheering while I took my place behind the microphone.

I cleared my throat and began to speak from the only place I knew, the heart. "I'd like to thank each and every one of you for taking a few hours out of your day to come here and support what's not only had an impact on so many women's lives, but mine as well. During the past few years I've been taught what it's like to have nowhere to turn when you are at your lowest point. I've watched women and children walk through the doors of our shelters and seen the faces of those affected most by domestic abuse. We strive to help every single person who needs it." I took a deep breath before I said the next part. This would probably be the hardest thing I'd ever done, but in order for me to heal I knew it was necessary. "It was only eight months ago that I myself was in a situation much like the women who walk through our doors." A hush fell over the entire room and I know I could've heard a pin drop. "I found myself beaten and bruised, wondering what I'd done to deserve such a treatment. I couldn't look myself in the mirror because I knew somehow I'd let it happen to me. So many women aren't as lucky as I was."

"I was able to heal on the outside but still have so many scars on the inside. I personally don't know if I'll ever be whole again, but in helping others who have experienced the same ill fate as I, I know my efforts are not in vain. I look around the room and see faces of so many who have come out on the other side of their situations with hope and a renewed sense of self. I wish that someday I too can wear a smile and be as happy as they are."

"So tonight, I don't want you to think of this as just another time you're asked to open your checkbooks. I want you to look around and see those faces that are being helped by your contributions. If you choose to give, please know that every single dime is going to a cause that *does* reach out and protect those who need it. Think to yourself, what if this was *your* daughter? Your granddaughter, or niece? Wouldn't they deserve a chance to make their life whole again with the help of an amazing organization like this?

"Again, I would like to give you my deepest heartfelt thanks for being here." I stepped away from the podium and let out a breath. The room was still silent and all eyes were trained on me. I smiled even though inside I was dying a slow agonizing death. I didn't know how many minutes ticked by until finally I heard one solitary clap at the back of the room. I squinted my eyes to see who it was and when I saw the man standing there, I started sobbing.

My father was there. Supporting me, cheering me on. The entire room then broke out into a standing ovation and loud claps. I wiped the tears from my face and walked down the stairs, exiting the stage. I wove through tables, bumping into guests as I went but I didn't care. My dad was waiting for me and when I finally got to him after what seemed like the longest walk in my life, I threw my arms around him and sobbed into his suit jacket. I could hear clapping still around me, but all that mattered was that my dad was there…for *me*.

∞ *Seventeen* ∞

"EMILY I'M SO PROUD OF YOU, what you did up there was so brave." My dad hugged me tightly.

"Dad, I had no idea you'd be here, but I'm so happy to see you." I cried even more.

Knowing that my dad stood there and listened to my speech made me feel prouder than I'd been in so long. He traveled across the country to support me. The emotions overwhelmed me like a flood. I pulled away and looked into his eyes. What I saw there was the truest form of love.

"I know my showing up here won't repair everything, but I'm hoping it's a start." He reached up and wiped the tears forming under my eyes.

I said the only thing that came to mind. "I love you, Dad."

His face softened, showing me a different side of my dad than I'd seen before. He'd always had a stoic expression that didn't portray much emotion at all. At times it was frightening. But what I saw in front of me made me believe he wasn't the man he'd been while with my mother.

"I think I'm hogging all of your time." He pulled away and looked over my shoulder.

I turned my head to see Jake standing there with a somber look on his face. I knew I must've looked like a mess, but it wouldn't have mattered to Jake. He walked up to us and put his hand on my arm.

"Emily, are you okay?" Jake asked.

I wiped away more tears. "Yes, I'm perfect actually." I smiled. "Jake, I want you to meet my dad, Richard Mills." I introduced the two.

"It's nice to meet you sir." They shook hands.

"If you two don't mind, I think I need to go clean myself up a bit."

"Take your time." My dad said.

I left them together in the ballroom talking about who knows what while I visited the ladies room again. I took a few minutes to make my face presentable and apply a fresh coat of crimson lipstick. I pushed back a few loose hairs that had worked their way down from my bun and opened the door to leave. I walked a little way down the hallway and lost my breath when someone grabbed my arm and pulled me into an empty corridor. My back forcibly hit the wall, knocking the rest of my breath clean out of me. When I managed to get my wits about me I looked up to see Grant staring down at me with fury written all over his face.

"What the hell are you doing, Grant?" I bit out.

"I told you I wanted some quality time with you. I think now is as good a time as any."

"You need to let me go. Now." I was beyond pissed. I could feel the anger rise in my veins causing me to breathe harder. I'd been here before...one night not long ago, with Michael. Fear caused my blood to run cold and my body start to tremble.

"What the fuck is your problem? I can't leave you alone for five seconds without you rubbing all over some other guy like a cat in heat. I guess you're just a little slut, aren't you?"

I'd had enough. I pushed as hard as I could against Grant's chest, causing him to stumble backwards a bit. I raised my voice, not giving a damn who heard me.

"You do *not* get to speak to me like that!"

"We had a deal, you do what I say, or you can kiss your job goodbye." He stood there glaring holes in me.

"Fuck you! The only person who tells me what to do is me." I stepped forward and dug deep for the courage I needed. "And by the way, the *deal* is off, Asshole." I twisted my body around and started to walk away.

Grant just couldn't let things go He grabbed me again by the arm and tried to pull me back. I wrenched my arm out of his punishing grasp, reared my fist back and let it go. I heard a resounding crack as my knuckles broke through the cartilage in his nose and blood poured out of both nostrils like a faucet. Grant was beyond furious.

"You broke my goddamn nose, you bitch!" He yelled.

"You're damn right I did. You're lucky that's all I did." I shook my hand as it began to swell. It wasn't sore yet, but once my adrenaline level returned to normal, I would be in some serious pain.

Grant held his gushing nose and spoke in a muffled voice through his hand. "You'll pay for this, you stupid cunt."

He stomped off with a blood soaked shirt, leaving me standing there with a swollen hand and a rapidly beating heart. My chest heaved up and down while I tried to calm myself, and suddenly tears sprang to my eyes.

"Emily, what happened?" Jake found me bawling in the small space. "I just saw that guy you were with the other night; he was bleeding, and it looked like someone broke his damn nose."

I held up my injured hand. "I-I hit him." I managed to say around my sobs.

Jake grabbed my hand lightly and inspected it while my dad came up behind him. "Emily, you need to get this looked at. Come on, I'm taking you to the hospital." Jake was overly concerned.

"No, I have to stay until the event is over, I can't just leave."

"The hell you *can't*. Dammit, Woman, you're hurt and you need to be checked out." Jake insisted.

My dad stepped around Jake and took my hand in his. "Listen to what he's saying. Go get this checked out, Emily." He lightly dropped my hand and rubbed a falling tear from my cheek. I nodded slightly.

Jake pulled out his phone and dialed a number. "Hey, Man, Emily got hurt and I need to take her to the ER, can you handle things while they wrap up here? Okay, thanks Man—I owe ya' one." He placed the phone back in his pocket.

"Who was that?" I was curious to see who he spoke to that would take over.

"Gabe."

"Oh no! I'm not leaving everything in his hands, Jake. He'll have this place turned into a frat party with naked women dancing on the tables." I tried to slip past him.

Jake put his hands on my shoulders and looked me in the eyes. "Stop it. Gabe will be fine. You need to trust people, Emily, I think you'd be surprised with what they can do."

He was right; I did need to start trusting people in my life, but Gabe? The thought of leaving him in charge sent a sickness through my body.

"Emily, this is not up for negotiation. I'm taking you to the hospital and that's final. Now come on."

Before I knew what was happening, Jake lifted me into his arms and was carrying me toward the lobby. Several bystanders gawked our way as we headed for the door and then outside. The valet recognized me and quickly motioned my limo over, opening the door so Jake could place me inside. I sunk into the leather seat, exhaustion hitting me all of a sudden, making me feel like I could fall into a deep sleep right there in the car. Jake slid in next to me and pulled me onto his lap. He placed his hand on the side of my head and lightly pushed it onto his broad shoulder.

"That was a beautiful speech you made back there." Jake pierced the silence in the car. "I don't know that I could've ever revealed a story so personal in public like that."

"I had to. It was time to tell it, Jake. I needed to show people that I'm not the perfect person they all think I am. I have issues and scars just like everyone else."

"You're such an amazing person, I'm lucky that I was able to connect with you again, Emily. I missed so many things about you. Your giving nature, your smile…I missed it all." He stroked a finger down my cheek.

"I missed you too." I looked up at his face in the dim light of the car. "Can I ask you something?"

"You know you can ask me anything, Emily." He smiled.

I wasn't sure how to get out what I wanted to know. I was in pain, but something was plaguing my mind. I knew Jake was attracted to me, he made that fact abundantly clear, but what I didn't know was where we went from there. What would happen between us? I'd lived my life by a certain plan, and I suppose I needed some security of sorts. I did know that I wasn't ready for any sort of long-term relationship. I was still healing from everything in my life and to drag someone else into that wasn't fair to them. I'd told myself from the beginning that I would hold off on any sort of commitment until I knew beyond a shadow of a doubt I could emotionally handle it. Now wasn't the time. Molly's words of "friends with benefits" came to mind. Would it be selfish to ask Jake for something like that? I didn't want him to feel like he was wasting his time. He deserved to be happy above all else.

I decided that the best thing I could do was just lay my cards on the table and hope he didn't push me off his lap and jump from the moving vehicle.

"I guess I don't know how to ask..."

"Emily, if you don't ask me for what you want, I won't know if I'm willing it give it or not."

I took a deep breath and let it roll off my tongue. "I want to just be friends with you but I want...benefits, for now." I closed my eyes and waited.

Jake was silent for a few moments and I knew it was probably not a good sign. He let out a deep sigh. "Friends with benefits? Damn." He didn't sound happy.

"I'm sorry, I know that was a stupid thing to ask for. I just thought we were both aware of our attraction to each other and, well, I don't know what I was thinking. Please forget I said anything, Jake." I rested my head against his shoulder once more and shut my eyes.

"Okay. If that's the only way I can be with you for now, then I'll do it."

"What? You would do that for me?" I was shocked.

"I don't think you realize the things I would do for you, Emily." He still didn't sound thrilled, but I was. I was excited, aroused and nervous all balled into one. I'd forgotten about my hand too, until I reached up to caress his stubble-laden cheek.

"Ouch." I pulled my hand back and rested it on my stomach."

"Take it easy there, Rocky." Some of the humor came back in his voice and it made me smile.

∞ *Eighteen* ∞

"I'M GLAD IT WASN'T anything serious." Jake commented after he took me back to his apartment. He'd been so attentive and caring at the hospital, sitting with me in the waiting room, helping me onto the gurney in the exam area and holding my non-bruised hand while I had X-rays taken. It was a relief that there was nothing majorly wrong after giving Grant my best right hook to the nose. The doctor went over the X-ray results with me, and it was just some bruising and swelling from the blow. He recommended I keep some ice on it and take over the counter pain relievers to help the swelling subside. He expected that the majority of the puffiness would be down by morning, which was a relief.

Jake insisted I stay with him for the night, he said he'd feel more comfortable if I was in his apartment, even though mine was just downstairs. I was so drained that I didn't bother to argue. Truthfully I wanted to be near him after our talk in the limo. I knew nothing would happen between us that night due to my injury but it didn't matter. Just being around him made me feel safe and secure.

I sat on Jake's couch as he busied himself with something in one of the other rooms. I looked around and took in the atmosphere of his place. It made me smile to see things that represented his home in Texas, from the weathered barn wood of his coffee and end tables to the pictures of his family placed on nearly every flat surface. He was proud of his roots and I was glad he'd had an amazing upbringing. Even though I didn't feel like mine was the best, I hoped that eventually my dad and I would be able to have a relationship of a normal father and daughter. Maybe someday my mom would come to her senses, but I couldn't make her change.

"I put clean sheets on my bed, you can take it and I'll crash on the couch." Jake came out of a room with a pillow and brown blanket.

I was disappointed that he wanted to sleep separate from me. "Okay." I agreed even though my tone was laced with discontent. I lifted my fatigued body from the sofa and walked down the hallway toward the room he'd come from. I turned back around and looked at Jake who was still standing there watching me. "Goodnight, Jake."

"Night, Emily." He looked away and started to throw his blanket and pillow on the couch.

I found his bedroom and walked over to the bed. The burnt orange comforter was thick and inviting, begging me to crawl underneath and sleep for days. His bedroom furniture was finished in a deep oak and it too had photos sitting around, reminding him of his childhood and adolescence. I went to the dresser and picked up a photo of what I knew was Jake and another man who looked similar to him, dressed in military fatigues.

"That's Tyler." Jake came to stand beside of me and we both stood there gazing at the picture.

"You miss him." It wasn't a question; I could plainly see the sorrow in his eyes for his brother.

"Yeah, but he'll get to come home soon and all will be well in the Bradford house again."

"I always wondered what it was like to have a sibling. My mom didn't want any more children after me, she said it was bad enough that I'd ruined her figure."

Jake screwed up his nose. "That's a horrible thing to say to a person." He took the frame from my hands and placed it in the same spot it'd come from.

I shrugged my shoulders and walked back to the bed, pulling the plush comforter down. I sat on the edge watching Jake.

"I just need some sleep pants." He pulled open a drawer and grabbed some plaid print pants, then went to the door. "Well, goodnight." He left the room and more disappointment came over me.

Should I ask him to stay? Damn, I'd never been in a situation like that before, I wasn't sure of the "friends with benefits" protocol. I mulled it over in my head for a few minutes and decided that I would do what Jake had said, *"ask if I wanted something."* I hopped up and went to find him. He sat on the edge of the sofa with his elbows planted on his knees and his head hung.

"Are you okay, Jake?" I said softly. I was worried that I'd done something to upset him.

His head snapped up and he then turned to look at me. "I'm fine, did you need something?"

Boy, did I ever. But I knew he wouldn't give me what I *really* needed. I moved my feet on the floor with nervousness before spitting out my request. "I want you to sleep with me."

"Emily, you're still hurt, remember? I don't think that's a good idea."

"I'm not talking about sex Jake, I just want you next to me, please?" I felt silly for asking but I needed him.

"Okay." He stood from his spot and grabbed his pillow. I felt him close behind me as I went back to his bedroom.

"Oh, I need to go downstairs to grab something to sleep in." I couldn't believe I'd totally forgot to mention pajamas.

Jake went back to his dresser and dug out more clothing, when he found what he was looking for, he threw them across the room to me. "Here, just wear mine for the night."

The thought of wearing something that belonged to Jake was making certain parts of my body heat up like slowly simmering water on a stove. I would be sleeping in his bed, wrapped in something he wore, with him right next to me. It was my biggest fantasy come true...*almost.* I sat the clothing on the bed and tried to reach around my back to pull the zipper of my dress down. I grunted and groaned as the tiny piece of metal proved to be more of a challenge then I'd anticipated.

"Here, let me get that." Jake stood behind me and reached for the hidden zipper. His fingers worked it down until I could feel the cool air of the room chill my overheated flesh. Once it was fully open, Jake didn't move. He stood behind me letting me hear the deep rumble of his rapid breathing. I started to imagine so many ways that this scenario could play out. Each one caused moisture to pool inside my panties, and I began to squirm. Jake's hand touched the exposed skin of my back gently and goose bumps raised over my entire body as he trailed just one finger down the length of my spine. Damn he'd barely touched me and I was primed to go off like a rocket to the moon. He continued the simple torture and I couldn't take much more. I shivered and then turned my body to face his. My dress had slipped lower causing the tops of the cups of my black lace bra to be visible. I pushed my breasts out more trying to get some sort of contact with my front to his. He was so close I wanted to reach out and touch him but he'd already warned me that he had no intention of going down that road with me that night.

Our eyes connected, and I silently implored him to touch me. He obliged by pulling the top of my dress down further, making it catch on the slight curve of my waist. Jake stepped forward and ran a fingertip across the creamy swell of my breasts. I sucked in a breath. Each stroke left a burning path that shot straight to my groin.

I let him explore as much as he wanted even though it was killing me to not have control. It was like I'd been bewitched and put under his spell of seduction, and it was the most intense sensation I'd ever felt.

"Can I kiss you?" He breathed.

I nodded, unable to form words at that moment. I held my breath as Jake leaned his head down and placed his moist, warm lips on mine. The fusion started out slow and soft, but soon turned into something hungry and desperate. His hands began to run all over the bare skin of my body, and I dipped my fingers through the silky strands of his hair. Wetness began to soak the fabric between my legs and I pressed them together to help alleviate the ache. He began to glide his palms over my bare back and then I felt the familiar snap that released my bra. I became nervous. Jake, my best friend, was going to see me naked. What if he didn't like what he saw? What if he compared me to every other woman he'd been with in the past? I didn't have a perfect body, I was soft and curvy, so what if he wasn't used to something like that. What if he expected me to be thinner? More angled? My anxiety climbed higher and to shield myself from disappointing him, I quickly grabbed the cups of my bra and held them firmly over my breasts.

"What are you doing?" Jake looked confused.

"I don't want to disappoint you, Jake." I looked toward the floor.

Jake put his fingers under my chin and made eye contact with me. "How could you ever think I'd be disappointed in you? God, Emily, you're gorgeous. Sometimes it hurts to look at you, you're so damn beautiful."

"Really?" His compliments gave me confidence and made me strengthen my resolve to go through with whatever we were doing.

"Yes really. But I won't push you. If you don't feel comfortable, we can stop."

"I don't want to stop, I ache." My response came out automatically. And *damn,* I ached. I needed an orgasm like I'd never needed it before. I dropped my hands from my breasts and let the garment slide down my arms, landing between us at our feet.

I watched as Jake's eyes dipped toward my uncovered skin and he smiled with appreciation.

"Like I said, *beautiful.*" He kissed me again but this time he tested the weight of each breast in his hands as he fused his lips to mine. I mewled in satisfaction and pushed them further into his working hands.

It felt like we were floating as our bodies moved toward the bed. He pressed me into it, and then reached for the rest of my dress to finish removing it. When he was done, I lay there on his bed in nothing but my satin thong. He leaned over and kissed the delicate skin behind my ear as his hand slid down my stomach and landed on the satin covered flesh between my legs. I arched up to meet his light petting.

Jake sucked in a breath as he grazed his fingers over the soaked material, the sound causing my nipples to pucker. He rewarded them with the moist dart of his tongue, swiping and laving at the pink buds. I closed my eyes just as his hand dipped underneath the cloth covering my intimate area, caressing my smooth skin. He worked his fingers over my swollen clit, making me moan and writhe. Just when I thought it couldn't get any better, Jake sealed his lips over mine and entered me with two fingers. I gasped at the mixture of pleasure and pain as he drove them in and out of me, coating his hand with my dampness. I cringed slightly as he pushed deeper inside, searching for the spot that would cause me to cry out.

"Am I hurting you?" He broke the kiss and asked close to my ear.

I rolled my head to the side to look at him. His eyes were glazed over and they held a bit of worry behind their striking blue color. "A little, but its fine. It's just been a while." I was embarrassed to admit.

"Tell me to stop and I will, Emily." He warned.

"No, don't." I begged.

Jake didn't need any more words after that. He began his sensuous torture to my body again, and I was soon on the cusp of a blinding release. My body tightened around his soaked fingers and he struggled to keep the pace he'd set. My toes started to go numb, signaling that I was so close to orgasm. This is what I had waited for, a moment like this with Jake. Me in his arms, him inflicting erotic pleasure upon my body. It was all so surreal.

My breathing soon became labored, my pulse shot through the roof and I knew that soon I'd been coming for Jake for the first time ever.

"You have no idea how sexy you look right now." He growled.

His words pressed me over the edge into the best kind of oblivion. I balled my fists up in the rumpled sheets below us and arched my back as I felt myself begin to see stars behind my eyelids.

"Oh God, I'm going to come!" I yelled as the first pulses washed over me. A keening cry released from my lips. He leaned his blazing forehead on my shoulder and suddenly he let out a shout of his own, followed by a sexy twitch of his entire body. When he pulled his fingers from my opening, he kissed me once more and rolled to his back. Our chests were moving up and down rapidly as we worked to bring our breathing back to a normal range. I lulled my head to the side to see him.

Jakes face had a look of supreme satisfaction written all over it. I was excited to see that pleasuring me made him happy. But I also felt bad. He'd gotten nothing out of the whole thing. He'd focused his attention on me, which wasn't fair to him. He had to have been hurting.

"Jake I feel so selfish." I pointed out.

"Why?" He rolled his head to the side to face me.

"That was all about me, you got nothing out of that." I made a sad face.

Jake lifted his head and looked down toward his legs. "I wouldn't say I got nothing."

I followed his line of sight and was shocked to see a moist spot on the front of the black tuxedo pants he still wore. My mouth hung open in surprise. I had no words to describe my satisfaction in seeing that I made him come without even touching him.

"I'm floored, *too*. That's never happened." He broke the silence.

"Never?"

"Nope, never. I guess you just do things to me, Emily."

His words made me feel a certain pride. I didn't consider myself a sexy person by any means, but judging by the reaction Jake's body had, I must've had some level of sex appeal.

"I think I'm going to hop in the shower and clean myself up." He raised himself from the bed and went to the bathroom attached to his bedroom. He shut the door and soon after, I got up from the bed and removed my completely soaked panties. I threw on the boxer shorts and T-shirt he'd given me to sleep in and crawled underneath the covers. It wasn't long and I felt my worries of the day slip away and my eyes start to close. As I drifted off I took comfort in the fact that when Jake finished with his shower, I'd be snuggled up to him in his bed for the rest of the night. The feeling was one of extreme contentment.

∞ *Nineteen* ∞

THE NEXT MORNING I awoke warm and happy. Jake was wrapped around my body, his arm thrown across my stomach and his leg over mine. I lay on my back looking up at the ceiling, wondering how I'd become so lucky as to have someone like Jake in my life. It was an odd situation to be in, the whole "friends with benefits" thing, but it's what I needed and could handle for the time being. I really wasn't sure if I could emotionally handle something more. I knew the feelings I'd had for him, and knew they would never change, but I couldn't bring myself to give him anymore of myself besides friendship and sex.

"What are you thinking so hard about this early in the morning?" Jake spoke in a raspy, sleep-laden voice.

I rolled my head to see him in all his sleep-mussed glory. His jaw was covered in stubble, his captivating eyes were rimmed with a shadow of sleepiness and his hair was rumpled up, sticking out from every direction possible.

"Nothing, just trying to wake up." I fibbed.

"How's your hand feel today—let me see." He reached over and picked up my injured hand. "Looks better than it did last night."

I held it up for my own inspection. "It doesn't hurt too bad." I turned it over and took a good look. The bruising wasn't as terrible as I'd thought it would be, and I honestly wasn't in much pain at all. I was happy that the swelling had subsided and it looked like a normal-sized hand again.

"Are you sure you don't need a Tylenol or something? I have some in the medicine cabinet." Jake offered.

"It's fine, really. I could use a shower though."

"Yeah sure, there're towels in the linen closet in the bathroom, and I'll lay out some sweat pants and another shirt for you to put on. While you're showering I'll go make some breakfast. Anything you don't like?"

"I'm sure whatever you fix will be fine. I do like meat, though." My cheeks flamed as soon as the comment left my mouth.

"Good to know." he smirked.

I got up from the bed and padded to the bathroom. I turned on the shower water and pulled my clothing off, placing them on the counter by the sink.

The spray of the shower felt heavenly on my aching muscles as it rained down on me while I stood there still not believing that I was actually with Jake again. Jake's body wash and shampoo were sitting on the ledge of the shower stall and I lifted one to my nose, taking in a huge whiff of his scent. Something about using his stuff and being in *his* shower was so arousing. The intimacy of being in his personal space made me feel honored and cared for. I knew it wasn't anything serious between us but either way, I told myself to be grateful for the time that I *did* have with him.

Once I felt clean enough I dried off, finger combed my hair and stepped back into Jake's bedroom. On the bed lay some heather grey sweat pants, and an NYU tee shirt. I smiled at the gesture and quickly dressed feeling the softness of the clothing against my shower damp skin. I found my way to the kitchen where the smell of cooking food filled the space. My stomach grumbled in satisfaction reminding me that I'd not eaten anything since breakfast the day before. I was too busy trying to prepare for the fundraiser, forgetting that I needed to eat.

Jake was leaning against the counter, flipping pancakes on a griddle. I stood there for a second taking in his obvious domestic ability. He looked divine, and I really wouldn't have minded having *him* for breakfast instead of what he was cooking. His pajama pants hung deliciously low on his hips, the firm muscles of his back moved seamlessly while his arms worked the utensil in his hand. I happened to notice a small tattoo just below his shoulder blade. As I moved closer, I could tell what the ink actually was. It was the word "family" inscribed in a scroll font.

"Hey, hope you like pancakes—it's my specialty. I also fried up some bacon…since you like meat." He interrupted my visual inspection.

"Sounds good. Is there anything I can help with?" I offered.

"There's some juice in the fridge, could you grab it?"

"Sure thing."

I opened the fridge and was surprised at the abundance of food in it. I guess I expected to find some old Chinese takeout boxes and cans of beer, but it was stocked full of *actual* groceries.

"Anything else?" I asked.

"Nah, these are about done so have a seat."

"Where did you learn to cook?" I inquired.

He let out a laugh. "My mom. She always said that we Bradford boys needed to know how, just in case we met a girl that was crap in the kitchen."

Jake pretty much described me to a "T." I was a horrible cook. Sure, I knew how to boil water, but that was about the extent of my abilities. Turning on the coffee pot in the morning was like climbing Everest in my book.

"You're lucky, the only things my Mom taught me were how to determine if a Coach bag was legit and how to walk in heels."

"Some would say those are valid talents." He winked.

"Yeah, well, cooking skills might have come in handy at some point, you know."

"Well maybe sometime I could show you a thing or two. I'm no gourmet chef, but I could help if you want. It might actually be fun."

Oh God. Spending time with Jake in the kitchen might not be the best idea. If it involved chocolate sauce, or whipped cream...I licked my lips at the thought.

"Sure, that sounds like fun."

He moved the food to the table and my stomach growled at the sight and smell of it all. Pancakes, bacon and fresh sliced melon. I had died and gone to heaven.

Jake filled his plate and looked at me. "Eat up. I can't put all this away by myself Trust me, I've tried."

I was starved, but was also extremely nervous around him for some reason that morning. His face was so kind when he looked at me, it was like there was something beyond friendship there. I *had* to be imagining things. We'd made an agreement—friendship and sex—that was it. Most men would've celebrated the fact that a woman didn't want a messy commitment. There were no chances of things getting complicated. We could date, be friends and have hot sex...I hoped.

I dug into the buffet of savory delights he'd prepared and sighed when the morsels hit my taste buds. "Wow, this is really good, Jake."

He smiled. "Glad to hear it. I've never fixed breakfast for anyone but Gabe and myself."

"Really? I figured you'd be sharing this treat with all your lady friends." I teased.

He groaned. "Uh, no. Not going to happen. No sleeping over and for sure no breakfast."

That struck me as odd. Jake didn't have women sleep over? Ever? So I was the first woman that'd slept there? And the first one to enjoy his cooking? Warmth spread over me at his words.

"That's unusual." I commented.

"How so?"

"I don't know. Just seems strange that you wouldn't let your girlfriends stay the night, that's all."

His jaw tightened. "First of all, I don't have a girlfriend, and second, this is my personal space. You have to be pretty damn special to be able to stay."

Holy shit. He was dead serious. "I'm sorry; I didn't mean to upset you Jake."

"I'm not upset, those are just the rules." He stood to clear the dishes after we were done.

I tried to help him clean things up but he refused to let me so I went to the living room to relax on his sofa. I picked up a guy's automotive magazine and flipped through the pages, quickly getting bored with it. As I sat there, I ran my tongue over my teeth and it hit me that I hadn't brushed them since the day before. "Jake, do you have a toothbrush I could use? My mouth feels gross."

"You can just use mine, it's in the holder by the sink."

I left the living room and went back to the bathroom. I stood there brushing my teeth with Jake's toothbrush which in itself was an intimate action When I felt freshened up I went back to the living room to find him. I rounded the corner and stopped.

"Well holy shit. Jake, you didn't mention you had company." Gabe was sitting on the couch giving me a knowing look.

"Hi Gabe." I mumbled and took a seat in a chair across from him. Jake came in from the kitchen.

"I'll be sure and send out an announcement next time." Jake sarcastically said. "Gabe came by to deliver the auction item I won."

"Oh really? What did you win?"

"The luxury box at Yankee Stadium." Jake smiled.

I was disappointed that I hadn't won it, but was glad that Jake did. It was probably more of a man's item anyway.

"How was everything after we left last night, Gabe? The fire department didn't have to be called in, did it?"

"Nope, I handled everything just fine. I did manage to take a sexy as fuck blonde back to my hotel room, though." Gabe looked proud of himself.

"Oh goodie." I rolled my eyes and could hear Jake chuckling.

"Well if you two love birds will excuse me, I need to get back to the hotel, I'm sure Missy, or whatever her name is, is ready for round seven." Gabe got up and left, leaving Jake and me alone again.

"Sure am glad I won this." Jake tapped the envelope with his auction prize in his hand.

"Yeah, suck it." I stuck out my tongue in jealousy.

"What? Oh, did you want this?" Jake teased.

"You obviously saw my name on the bid sheet, Jake."

He came over and grabbed my hands, pulling me from my chair. "Well, maybe I didn't want you to have it. Maybe I wanted to win it so I could take you on a date." He smiled and laid a soft peck on my cheek.

"Really?"

"I figured you'd never been to a game before and I wanted to take you."

Excitement filled me. "Eeeeek!" I screamed and hugged him.

I pulled back and looked at his handsome face. "Jake, why did you donate so much money?"

"I think after you told me what'd happened to you, and then Gabe told me about the charity, I wanted to help. I didn't always have the money to help, but now I do and wanted to."

"Thank you. That money will help so many people and make a difference in their lives."

"I know it will. Now, get your ass downstairs, get dressed and whatever other girly things you do, and meet me back here in an hour. I'm taking you out for the day and I won't take no for an answer."

"Yes sir." I gave him a mock salute, and as I walked away, Jake playfully swatted my butt.

∞ *Twenty* ∞

ONCE I MET JAKE BACK in his apartment we left the building and started walking. Heat moved through me as he reached down and twined his fingers with mine, making us look like one of the couples I'd previously been envious of. Things just felt *right*.

"Where are we going?" I knew Jake liked giving surprises, but I wasn't a surprise kind of girl. I wanted a plan; that way there was less chance for disappointment in the end. I'd pretty much lived my life that way. But I knew that no matter what, there was always some form of displeasure in the end anyway. But with Jake beside me, I wasn't sure I could be unhappy.

"I'm not telling you; you'll just have to see." He teased.

We continued to walk hand in hand until we were at the entrance of a building in our neighborhood. The outside was rather unassuming until I looked up to see a banner hung over the entrance of the building. I paused when I read it: *Ground Zero Museum Workshop, Artifacts from the Recovery.*

Somberness floated over me as I looked up at Jake. His expression was much like mine. "I know it isn't really a tourist thing to do, but this is a huge part of the city. I wanted you to see it."

"Okay." I tried to keep the sadness from my voice.

We walked into the museum, Jake paid the admission and I took a deep breath trying to prepare myself for what I would see inside. My own problems seemed like child's play compared to the things I was seeing. The entire place was quiet and subdued. Patrons solemnly walked around, taking in the rather grim objects on display.

Jake didn't say a word when he led me over to a distorted chunk of metal. I read the signage beside it and gasped when I saw that the piece was taken from the Towers and had once been part of a beautiful standing structure. It was dotted with black burn marks and ash, and I couldn't believe how mangled and twisted it was. For something that stood so strong and sturdy at one time to be warped and shaped into something so unrecognizable was just unfathomable. It took my breath away to be so close to a piece of history that destroyed so much and left so many in a forever period of mourning.

Jake took my hand silently and then led me to a room that held framed photos and artifacts from that fateful day. A shadow box held a single dated flip calendar, which was recovered from one of the many debris sites. It was permanently set on the date 9/11, immortalizing the day plainly and simplly. Charred cell phones, desk phones and even a newspaper with torched edges were among the many pieces pulled from the rubble. Broken glass, a clock that was stopped at the exact time that the first tower was hit were hung thoughtfully on the wall. So many memorials to the first responders of the city were set up. Some of them contained helmets, badges, and turnout gear of firefighters who had lost their lives on what was supposed to be just another day at the office. We scanned the plethora of photos that would be a permanent reminder of the day that would change our country forever. I was glad that Jake had taken me there, but wondered why he had. What was his reasoning for needing me to see something like that?

As we strolled through the museum in silence he finally spoke. "The day after this happened, Tyler enlisted in the Marines. He was pissed that someone could do this to so many innocent people. Mom was so upset with him for going, but he had it set in his mind that it was something he needed to do. I was so mad at him in the beginning; I'd felt like he was signing his own death certificate. But when I sat back and thought about it, I understood."

I then understood the reason for our visit. Jake was close to his brother, and I could tell that having Tyler overseas was hard for Jake. "I'm sorry, Jake."

He looked down at me. "No need to be sorry, I'm proud of my little brother. I've come here several times over the years to remind myself why he's over there. And I know it's worth it. It's just difficult sometimes to think that he's over there and I can't help protect him." I saw a tear slip from Jake's eye; he swiped it away quickly, thinking I hadn't seen it.

"But he has other *brothers* to help keep him safe. And he'll come home and the two of you can sit and tell stories about everything that's happened in the past few years."

"I look forward to that day." Jake smiled. "Are you hungry?"

"Yes." I tried to smile and be strong for him. It was hard though. The family bond between Jake and Tyler was astonishing even though I'd never seen it firsthand. It was a beautiful and inspiring thing to behold. He had something so special with his brother, something that thousands of miles couldn't break no matter how hard they tried.

We left the museum and the beaming sunlight of the day hit my face as I stepped outside. I raised my chin to soak it all in, letting the rays warm my cheeks.

"You look beautiful with the sun hitting you like that." Jake pulled our clasped hands to his lips for a lingering kiss. Once again I felt on fire with the way he touched me. I couldn't stop myself from kissing him back. I stood on my toes and pressed my mouth to his. It wasn't a deep passionate union, but perfect all the same. Jake unlocked our hands and placed his hands on each side of my head, putting his forehead to mine. "The things you do to me, Emily." He stated breathlessly.

The next thing I knew, we were in a cab, and Jake had instructed the driver to take us to Central Park. I flashed back to the times we'd visited there in college and the images brought a smile to my face.

"What're you over there smiling about?" Jake asked.

"I was just thinking about our trips to the park when we were in college."

"We did have a lot of fun back then. I figured we needed to go throw some coins in the fountain for good luck."

I couldn't wait to do it again after all those years of wishing he was still in my life. I didn't know if it was his plan to take me down memory lane and make me remember the great times, but I was thankful for it.

The cab moved along and when we got to the entrance to the park Jake paid the driver and gave me his hand to help me out. We walked again hand in hand on the winding path, watching runners, parents with children and couples just like us out for a Sunday stroll through the lush green naturalness. I'd always felt like the city melted away when I was in the park, it was an entirely different world there. Kids played on the grassy knolls and flew kites in the slight breeze while their parents sat close by on a blanket, holding hands or burying their noses in a book.

The air was warm which made me glad I had decided to throw on a sundress and wedged sandals before we left for the day. The breeze occasionally fluttered the hem, tickling the skin of my legs lightly. Jake looked so carefree in his loose khaki cargo shorts, cerulean blue polo shirt and light brown dock shoes. The blue of his shirt caused his eyes to turn a shade of blue that didn't even look real. They sparkled in the sunlight looking like azure gems.

We reached the Bethesda Terrace and walked underneath the intricately carved archways, which led to the fountain. I'd always loved the way the terrace was made. It reminded me of something I'd read about in a Jane Austen novel during my teenage years. The stone pathways, the pillars that looked as if they were brought over from a castle somewhere in Europe and the fountain itself were stunning.

Jake led us over to the edge of the fountain and we stood there admiring the creation and all of its massive glory. The two-tiered structure sat above a pool of glistening water where several people were gathered just like we were. The regal angel who sat with wings spread was like a guardian to the park and terrace, showing everyone how her pristine glory really was supreme. Cherubs took up the space on the second tier, looking playful and almost hiding underneath the water that poured from just above.

"Are you ready?" Jake dug around in his pocket, jingling loose change. He pulled out a penny for me and one for himself. When he handed one to me I clutched it in my palm and closed my eyes like I'd done many times before in the same spot. When I opened my eyes I grabbed the coin in my other hand and gave it a good toss toward the middle of the fountain. I watched as it disappeared below the water, taking my hopeful wish with it. Jake did the same and then looked at me.

"What did you wish for?" He asked.

"If I tell you, it won't come true. You know the rules." I giggled.

He laughed and pulled me close to his chest. "I think you wished for world peace."

"Maybe I did, and maybe I didn't. But you'll never know," I smiled.

The next thing I knew, we were kissing. A full blown, knock your socks off, who cared if anyone was watching us, kind of kiss. I was breathless by the time we were done. Jake pulled back and looked me in the eyes. I again saw something in them that gave me pause. I wasn't sure exactly what it was because I'd never seen it before from him, but *whatever* it was caused goose bumps to spread wildly over my entire body.

"Let's grab some lunch," he suggested.

"I think we should grab something from that cart we passed on the way in."

Jake looked surprised that I'd suggested it. "Wow, you'd actually eat something from a cart?"

"Sure why not?" I shrugged.

"I just didn't picture *you* as a cart food sort of gal."

"Are you calling me a snob, Mr. Bradford?"

"Yup." He joked but I took what he said seriously. Jake could see the hurt on my face. "Emily, it was a joke, I didn't mean it to hurt you," he said seriously.

"It just aggravates me when people assume I'm a spoiled rich girl. That's not me at all, Jake. Sure, I grew up in the lap of luxury, but that's not who I *really* am."

Jake stopped and turned to face me. "First of all, I've never looked at you like that—I was kidding. And I *know* the real you, I happen to like the real you…all of it." I totally picked up on his innuendo. It made me wish we were someplace more private so I could again show him *all* of the real me.

We went back toward the entrance to the park and found the cart I had spoken about. The line of people near it and the wonderful smells wafting through the air told me I'd made the right choice. When it was our turn to order, I stepped up and placed mine. The vendor handed me a huge hot dog on a warm bun with relish, ketchup and mustard. Jake grabbed his and had onions, sweet peppers and some sort of unrecognizable sauce spread all over it. I walked away and shoved the end of my dog in my mouth. Jake hadn't taken a bite of his yet but watched me as I damn near devoured mine. I was famished.

He looked at me with wide eyes as the frank slipped past my lips and onto my tongue. He started coughing like he was choking.

"What?" I said with my mouth full of food.

"Oh, nothing." He grinned and started to eat his food.

It took me a few seconds before I realized what his reaction was about. "Typical man. You all think alike, you know that?"

"Hey, I didn't say anything."

"You didn't have to, Jake." I laughed.

"The only thing I'm guilty of is thinking how sexy you look while eating that thing."

"And it has nothing to do with the fact you think my mouth would look good on other things too?" I raised my eyebrows.

"You said, it not me."

"But you thought it, which is basically the same thing."

"So what if I did think it? Is that such a bad thing?"

"I guess we'll find out eventually now, won't we," I teased.

"Is that a promise, Miss Mills?"

"Maybe." I threw my napkin in the trash and walked away with an inviting sway to my hips.

I was starting to feel bolder around Jake. The way he talked and acted made me feel like a desirable sexy woman. I liked those feelings; they were growing on me.

Soon the day was coming to a close and we ended up back at our apartment building. I punched in the code to let us in the building and we went up the steps, stopping at my door. Jake stood so close I became nervous, not knowing what to do. Should I ask him to come in? Or should I say good night and let him go upstairs to his empty apartment. I hated choices.

"Invite me in."

I couldn't say no; I wanted him to come in. I wanted him to never leave, too, but that wasn't the type of relationship we had. It was supposed to be simple and uncomplicated; I had to keep reminding myself of that fact before I did something really stupid and messed things up between him and me.

I unlocked my door and went inside, Jake followed. I flipped on a lamp to give just a bit of light to the room and turned to see Jake with his back leaning against the door. He looked perfect standing there in my apartment, all masculine and sensitive at the same time. I knew what I wanted to do, so I needed a few minutes alone.

"Um, can you wait in the living room? I just need a few minutes." I asked.

"Sure, take your time." He pushed off the door and brushed past me on his way to my living room. I took the opportunity to hurry to my bedroom and get things in order. I shut the door and went to my walk-in closet. I started searching for the items I needed. I pulled them out and headed to the bathroom attached to my bedroom. I let my sundress pool at my feet, and then removed my strapless bra and underwear. I pulled the clip from my hair, letting my blonde locks fall around my shoulders in soft glistening waves. I'd bought the bra and panty set at La Perla one day after work thinking I needed to treat myself for a change. I gently removed the tags as not to damage the fabric and then slipped on the panties. I drew the bra over my breasts and fastened the clasp behind my back thinking of how sensual it felt when Jake had removed my bra the night before. I wanted that again. Once everything was in its proper place, I glanced in the mirror and smiled. The deep red lace of both items stood out against the pale porcelain of my skin making me look like some sort of sex siren. *Perfect.* I stuck my head out of the bathroom door to make sure Jake hadn't snuck in. When I knew for sure I was still alone, I darted back across the bedroom to the closet once more. I found the perfect pair of sexy heels to complete what I'd hope would turn Jake on. I slipped them on my feet and looked down. The red suede matched my lingerie perfectly. This was it. I would walk out there in hopes to seduce Jake into my bed for the night. There was a chance he might laugh his way out the door but I prayed he wouldn't.

I opened my bedroom door and clicked my heels on the hardwood floor on my way to him. My hands were shaking with each step I took that would take me closer to the man I wanted to do so many naughty things with. When I turned the corner his back was to me as he sat on the sofa. I didn't want him to turn around yet. "Don't turn around please." I spoke in a seductive voice that'd taken over.

He didn't say anything back so I continued to walk around the sofa and stood just on the other side of the coffee table. Jake lifted his head and his eyes glazed over with lust. "Holy shit. Are you trying to give me a heart attack?"

"No, not really." My face dropped. I had a feeling he wasn't pleased with my little show.

"Turn around." He sexily ordered.

My pulse kicked up a thousand notches and I did what he said. When my back was facing him I heard him suck in a breath. I faced the windows and tried to calm my breathing. Just when I thought I might bolt back to the bedroom for comfort, Jake came up behind me and brushed my hair away from my neck. He placed a tender kiss between my shoulder and the base of my neck causing sparks to shoot down in between my legs.

"Do you have any idea how long I've waited for this?"

"No." I whispered.

"A long damn time." He moved his hands around me and placed them on my exposed stomach. "You have the softest skin." He ran his fingers over my flesh making me moan in delight. My head fell back onto his shoulder as his fingers trailed lower. He slipped his fingers inside the lace band of my panties and touched my clit, causing me to jolt in satisfaction. He didn't force anything; he leisurely stroked my wet skin until I was on the edge. My body became rigid in his arms, and he held me close to him so I wouldn't fall. I reached behind me and twined my arms around his neck, tickling the soft hair at his nape. He groaned in pleasure as we stood there in my living room. Jake kept up his delicious dance over my flesh and I felt the waves of pleasure begin to overtake me.

A shout left my throat as my body clenched and pulsed, throwing me into what had been the second epic orgasm Jake had given me. As he took me down from the waves, his kissed the skin of my neck over and over again causing residual shudders to wash over me. When it was completely over, Jake turned me around and grabbed my hand. My heels once again tapped on the floor on the way to my bedroom.

When we got there, Jake picked me up and carried me toward the bed, placing me down lightly. Still fully clothed, he hovered over the top of me, so I began to tug his shirt up his torso. He sat back on his heels and pulled it the rest of the way off, exposing his sculpted chest for my appreciation. His shirt hit the floor and soon he stood up, undoing the button of his shorts. They slid from his trim hips and pooled at his ankles, he kicked them off along with his shoes and stood there in just his tightly fitting boxer briefs. My mouth began to water as I noticed the bulge pressing the front of the black fabric.

Before he bared himself to my gaze though, he came back to me and slid my red panties down my thighs. He then reached underneath of me to unclasp my bra, and it joined the other scrap of lace on the floor. I was gloriously naked, lying on my bed, waiting for him to reveal himself to me. We didn't speak as he hooked his thumbs in the waistband of his briefs and pushed them down his toned thighs. When he stood back up, my eyes went wide and I automatically licked my lips. He was gorgeously erect, his cock jutting out and up, landing near his belly button. The head was swollen and almost purple, with a drop of pearly liquid seeping from the tip. *Oh god.* The silly thought of how he would fit his entire glorious length inside of me passed through my head, but I didn't have time to dwell on it, Jake had climbed back onto the bed and was looming over me.

His eyes connected with mine as he leaned down to kiss me. My hands wandered to his back where I drew lazy patterns with my fingers over his taught skin. He moaned as we kissed each other in a desperate plea for something more. I was ready. I wanted him so damn bad that I would've begged and pleaded to have him. He suddenly broke the kiss and swore. "Dammit."

My eyes became wide. "What?" I was worried that he'd changed his mind.

"I need to run upstairs, unless you have a stash of condoms here?" He looked hopeful.

"I don't, I'm sorry."

"No worries, I'll just be a few minutes." He tried to get up and I stopped him with my hands on his back.

"Wait, I...you don't have to use one if you don't want to, Jake."

"Emily, you don't have to do that."

"No, it's okay, I trust you. And I'm on birth control." When the word *trust* passed my lips I was taken aback. I hadn't been able to tell someone I'd trusted them in so long, but I did trust Jake to know he'd never hurt me like that. Maybe I was stupid for taking that chance, but I couldn't help but want to feel his bare skin on mine.

"Are you sure?" He looked in to my eyes and questioned me.

"Yes."

"I just want you to know I've never had sex without a condom."

"Me either." And I hadn't. Even in the committed relationship I was in with Michael I insisted we use them. I think I somehow always knew things wouldn't work out. I didn't want the chance that an innocent child would be created and brought into a situation like that.

Jake smiled and settled himself back between my spread thighs. I felt the head of his cock brush my drenched skin as he worked to coat himself with my juices. My back arched and I tilted my hips up in invitation. The waiting was killing me. I needed him inside of me. I sucked in a breath as he finally started to push forward into my tight opening. He stretched me as he slowly, inch by inch seated himself into my waiting body. The burn of the invasion caused me to cry out but he didn't stop; he moved until we were completely connected.

I tried to wriggle a bit. I needed him to move.

"If you keep doing that, this will be over in a matter of seconds, Emily." He warned.

I held still and he rewarded me by withdrawing and inching forward again. Soon he was creating a steady pace of delicious lovemaking. Each solid thrust scraped my sensitive flesh eliciting moans from my throat.

Jakes voice came out ragged when he spoke. "You feel amazing. Better than my wildest dreams."

I closed my eyes at his words. He'd dreamt about me like I had him? He'd been my biggest fantasy for so long, and there I was living it.

Time slipped by and I wasn't sure how long we'd been there, receiving so much pleasure from each other. It was like I was lost in a world where space and time didn't matter anymore; the only thing that mattered was that Jake was there, with *me*.

My body began to tighten, the sign that I was getting close to what I knew would be an amazing orgasm. If I ended up surviving it, I would've been surprised. I gripped his shoulders as I began to flutter. "Jake, I'm going to come." I whimpered.

"Me too, come with me." He started moving harder and faster inside me, hitting the spot that made me go liquid around him.

I felt him harden even more and then he yelled out. "Ah fuck!" I knew he was there.

My body began to clamp down on his and I screamed out until I was hoarse. My orgasm was never ending as his pushed himself forward, filling me up with each thrust.

Our breathing was labored and our bodies sweat covered as we came back down from bliss.

Jake raised his head to look at me. "I don't think anything could *ever* compare to that." He whispered and then kissed me. Our tongues said things that words couldn't in that moment.

When he pulled his mouth from mine he spoke again. "I don't wanna move." He whined.

"Then don't, stay right here all night."

"Okay." He laid his head on my shoulder and rested.

We stayed like that for a while until Jake pulled out of me and picked me up off the bed. "Shower time." He said as he carried me to the bathroom.

He was right, I didn't think anything could've compared to what we'd just shared. But I was afraid that I was already getting in too deep. What was supposed to be simple for me had just turned into something much more.

∞ *Twenty-One* ∞

THE SUNLIGHT FILTERED THROUGH my bedroom window and I felt a warm body snuggled tightly next to me. *Jake*. During the night he woke me several other times to worship my body. I could feel every minute of our night's activities in my sore muscles and I smiled to myself in celebration. I rolled over to find him wide-awake looking at me with those sexy blue eyes. He looked incredibly hot with his hair mussed from sleep, his five o'clock shadow outlining his chiseled jaw and his bare chest showcasing his ripped abs. I couldn't think of a better sight to wake up to. It was the best wakeup call I'd ever had.

"Good morning." He said softly while brushing a kiss across my lips.

"Good morning to you." I blushed. This was still Jake and I was a little embarrassed that he was in bed with me. Even though I wouldn't have changed anything about last night for all the riches in the world.

"Sleep well?" he asked.

"Yeah, actually I haven't slept that well since I moved here."

"Must have been your sleeping companion." he winked.

I let out a laugh. "Must've been. How long have you been awake?"

"Not long, your snoring woke me up. And then there was the drool on your pillow, which was a little disturbing."

"I don't snore!"

He rolled on top of me and started tickling me. "Yes. You. Do!"

"Prove it." I challenged.

"Okay, next time I'll record you with my phone. I might even post it to YouTube."

"You wouldn't?"

"You're right, I wouldn't do something so mean. But I would do this…" He reached down again and started vigorously tickling me right under my arms. He had me laughing so hard I felt like I was going to pee myself.

"You'd better stop that! I need to pee!" I kept cackling.

"Okay, okay. I don't want to clean that mess up." He rolled back over and smacked my ass. "Go."

"I'm going to hop in the shower, it's six-thirty." I pointed to the alarm clock.

"Yeah, back to the daily grind, huh?"

"Afraid so." I frowned.

I really didn't want to go to work, staying in bed with Jake for the entire day sounded like a much better option. But calling in on my second week of work just wouldn't do.

"Want coffee?" He asked.

"Yes, please. Caffeine is my drug of choice."

"I'll make some while you get ready, we can share a cab if you want, since I'm the boss, I'll just go in later." he suggested.

"Sure, that sounds great."

Moving across the room I felt every sore muscle protest. I ached in places that I didn't even know existed, but it made me smile to know how the soreness came about. I shut myself into the bathroom and gazed into the mirror.

"Holy shit," I breathed.

My hair was a knotted mess, sticking out in every direction possible and my face still had the red impression of my hand where I had slept on it. Dark circles loomed under my eyes like I hadn't gotten enough sleep the night before, and I realized it was true. I was busy doing other things rather than sleeping. *Just great.*

Jake had woken up to Medusa lying next to him. I imagined he probably wasn't making coffee; he was most likely running for the hills at the sight of me looking like a hot fucking mess. Stepping into the shower, I tried to clear my head of the picture I presented to him. Surely he didn't turn to stone after I left the room…*right*?

I told Jake that I'd slept well; I *did* when he wasn't making love to me, but an all-night sex marathon was something new to me. I couldn't seem to get enough of him no matter how sore my body was. Jake was quickly becoming an addiction I didn't know that I could break.

Each time he would wake me up, it was something different. His hand between my legs, his lips on my breasts and even him entering me, bringing me awake instantly. After last night I had no doubts about being in love with Jake. I knew it was something I would have to push away, though; I wasn't ready for something like that. And Jake didn't deserve someone so broken.

It took me about thirty minutes to clean up, fix my hair and makeup, and then dress for the day. The place was silent, but I smelled the welcome brew of coffee. Okay so he started the coffee and then escaped. *Well played.*

I walked into the kitchen and luckily Jake was standing there looking oh so enticing in nothing but his shorts from the day before and a smile. He turned around when he heard the click of my heels on the wood flooring.

"Hey...wow, you look amazing!" he said.

"Thanks, quite a change from waking up next to the queen of the undead earlier, huh?"

He let out a belly laugh. "You did look a bit scary, I'll admit."

I punched his shoulder playfully. "Thanks, asshole!"

He leaned in and kissed my temple. "You are beautiful, whether you look like a zombie or dressed to the nines, Sweetheart."

How could something so silly make me feel all warm and toasty inside? Jake always knew the right things to say and each time it made my ego soar. I gave him the once over, eyeing him from head to toe.

"You going to wear *that* to work?" I asked.

"What?" He looked down at his wrinkled shorts, and ran his hands down his muscular chest.

"You look...wrinkled and half naked."

"I thought about it." He gave a boyish grin.

"Better think again, wise guy, they throw people in jail for stuff like that now."

"You're right. But you know we could just play hooky and stay in bed all day. I wouldn't need clothes for that..." He suggested while wagging his eyebrows playfully.

"Jake, I would love to, but I really have to get to work. Sorry." I gave a sad face.

"Then I'll just have to take a rain check." He promised.

Jake went upstairs to quickly shower and change then he was back at my door waiting. He looked positively divine in his charcoal grey suit, black dress shirt and solid grey tie. He grabbed my travel mug of coffee and we headed out the door together. It felt so domestic and natural. It was like we'd been waking up, drinking coffee and chatting like that every morning of our lives. For the first time since college I felt content. The thought hit me that I shouldn't be that happy. The other shoe would drop and something shitty would happen to screw everything up. It always did.

While we stood on the curb waiting for a taxi to come by I caught myself staring at him.

"If you keep looking at me like that I'm going to have no choice but to hold you hostage in my apartment today." He joked.

"Is that a promise?"

"Don't test me…"

We hailed a cab and climbed in. As we took off down the street, Jake grabbed my hand in his. "I had a great time last night."

"So did I, Jake."

"Do you have plans for tonight?" He asked.

"Jake, I'm not sure this thing between us is such a great idea… maybe we should slow down a bit." I needed to slow things down between us before the happy train derailed and killed every person on board.

"Why would you even say that? Am I the only one who felt amazing last night?"

"No, but Jake, I have so many complications in my life right now. It's just not fair to drag you into it."

"What if I *want* to be dragged into it—isn't that my prerogative?"

"No it's not, Jake. You don't understand…"

"Then enlighten me Emily, make me understand why we shouldn't keep seeing each other? God, Emily, I haven't been able to see you for years and I'm *not* walking away now."

"I can't explain it right now. This is getting too damn complicated; it's not supposed to be like this!" I yelled out and the driver looked back at the both of us.

"Listen, you were the one who laid down the terms here. And now you want to slow things down? I don't get it."

How was I supposed to just come out and tell Jake that I had feelings beyond the "friends with benefits" agreement I'd suggested? Of course I knew in the beginning that I did, but I wasn't going to come right out and tell him. I was trying to get my life straightened out. If I'd spent every waking moment with him, I wouldn't have been able to tell heads from tails.

"I know I was, Jake. I'm just scared."

"Of what?" He asked.

"That things between us will go down in flames, and I won't have you as a friend anymore. Does that make sense?"

"Emily, I get it, I really do. But you have to understand, I don't give up that easily. I haven't seen you in ages. Do you think one damn night will make a difference?"

"I don't know. I just need some time to sort some things out, please just give me that?"

"Okay, you win. Take whatever time you need. But just know I'll be here when you're ready, I'm not going anywhere."

"Thank you, Jake." I whispered while I placed a tender kiss on his cheek.

The cab pulled up in front of my work building and I hugged Jake and got out. He looked like he had been hurt deeply as the car drove away with him in the back seat. I was so pissed at myself for not taking a chance and seeing where things would lead us. I didn't want to set myself up for failure. If that made me a selfish asshole, then fine. I just needed some time to decide if it was all worth it.

The truth was I was scared to death of what happened between us the night before. There was a chemistry that I couldn't deny. Something inside me that had been dormant cracked wide open and left me exposed and vulnerable.

I wanted Jake in my life more than anything, but first I had a lot of things to let go of and fix before I could make him a part of it. He said he wouldn't go anywhere, and I believed him with all my heart.

I rode the elevator to my floor and headed right to my office when it got there. I shoved my purse in a desk drawer and plopped in my chair.

Molly came in and took her usual spot across from my desk. "Wow, you look like someone poured sugar in your gas tank. What's wrong?"

"Why does life have to be so complicated?" I whined.

"Tell me about it. I have a house full of crumb snatchers and one in my gut that plays hockey with my liver. What seems to be the problem?"

I rubbed my forehead. "I took your advice—the whole *friends with benefits* thing…"

"Holy shit, did you do the nasty with Mr. Bradford?" Molly looked shocked.

"Yeah."

"Can I give you a high five or something? How was it? Never mind, don't tell me, I'll just become jealous and angry."

"I just don't know if things are going to work like that, Molly. Jake means more to me than that."

"You're in love with the guy, aren't you?" Her expression softened.

"I have been since college." I admitted.

"Then tell him."

"I can't. Things are difficult in my life right now. I have the Bar coming up, I just moved here and I have this thing with my parents that I don't wish to discuss."

"First of all, life isn't easy. We get handed a bag of shit on a daily basis. If you find the opportunity to be happy, you've got to jump on it. Things like that don't come by every day. Would you rather take the chance and have it not work out, or let it pass you by and regret that you didn't try?"

"It's a lot to think about." I sighed.

"And I'm glad you're the one who has to think about it and not me." She joked.

She was right, I had a decision to make and it wasn't going to be easy. Did I want to keep doing what Jake and I were doing and eventually tell him my true feelings? Or end things and one day regret that I let him slip through my fingers, not once, but twice. The lot of it was giving me a migraine.

∞ *Twenty-Two* ∞

I SAT AT MY DESK realizing what a total bitch I'd been to Jake by trying to drive him away. He had been nothing but kind and caring to me, and I blew him off like a speck of lint falling from my shoulder. Everything that had happened in the week since I'd been in New York was nothing shy of a disaster. Jake was my only solace in all of it. It was like he was my salvation in a life that was meaningless.

I hated myself for the way I acted like none of it mattered. We shared such a beautiful night together and I ended it by telling him I needed to think about things. The truth was, it mattered more to me than anything. I wanted it to last forever.

I hadn't planned on him waltzing back into my life. To see him again and be involved intimately was mind blowing. I didn't see him as just a friend anymore; last night changed all that. He was someone I wanted in my life permanently. But how was I supposed to make that leap of faith and trust him completely? It was so much to think about. It wasn't like I didn't know him. Heck, I'd known him so well in the years we spent at college together. It was like we'd already had a relationship back then.

He still managed to scare me with his smoldering looks and his beautiful words. It was like he saw right through all my pain. I'd never been this worked up over a man, Even when the *incident* with Michael happened, it was easy to turn tail and run the other way. With Jake it was different; I felt *pain* when I hurt him. And I didn't want to do that to him. He didn't deserve to have someone shut him out; he deserved to be treated with everything I felt for him and more.

I wanted to confide and open up to him. He knew about my past with Michael, but he didn't know about my parents. He'd seen the reaction

I'd had when my dad showed up at the fundraiser, but I'd never told him *why* I had reacted like that. He'd probably just thought I'd been happy to see my dad, but in all reality, I was just *surprised* to see him. I was sad that he had to fly back to California so soon too. I would've liked to spend more time with him, but I knew his plate was full with work. It crossed my mind to tell Jake what was going on in my family life, but I wasn't so sure he needed to know the details just yet. From the outside looking in I'm sure he thought things were picture perfect, but so many deep-seated issues lay just below the surface.

Before I expected to move forward in my life, I had to let go of the things that were sinking me. It was time to patch up the hole in my boat and paddle to safety. First, I needed to forgive those who I'd felt had wronged me. The first was Michael. I dreaded even going within three feet of the man, but in order to gain some piece of myself back, I had to take the leap.

I sat at my desk and opened my email program. Michael's email address was saved so I clicked it to fill in the blank line at the top of the page. My fingers hovered over the keys for what seemed like an eternity before they began to type black letters on the white page.

Dear Michael,

I hope this letter finds you well. I've been doing so much thinking, and I needed to get some things off my chest. First of all, I don't hate you. I wish I could, but I just don't have the time or energy to do so. It would take too much of the happiness that I do have to spend the time constructing hate toward you. I feel like the things that have happened in the past have led me to the place I am now, and I suppose it was all a lesson in my life. I wish I didn't have the reminder every day of what happened, but my scars remind me that the past will always be there. I can only move forward and forgive those who have wronged me. That being said, I wanted you to know, that I do forgive you. Will I forget? No. I don't want to; I want what happened to make me a stronger person and to live my life for myself and not others. I truly hope that happiness finds you. As a human being, you deserve that as much as the next person. I'm considering this my forgiveness for your past transgressions toward me, and I hope you feel the same.

E.M.

I sat back and read over the letter before hitting "send." I knew once I hit the button, a small part of the anger I'd been hanging onto would dissipate. It would never be completely gone, but as I'd written, I didn't want it to. I knew that the things I'd experienced in my life were for a reason. I hoped that reason was me coming back to New York and taking charge of the life I wanted for myself.

My finger hovered over the computer keys; I closed my eyes, took a deep breath, opened them, and hit send. The confirmation popped up that the letter had in fact been sent, so I let out a sigh of relief.

My relationship with Michael was the biggest hang up I'd had in trusting anyone. My mother was the reason I felt like I wasn't worthy of love. Was I willing to take the step toward forgiving her? Not entirely. She needed to sweat things out like I had for years.

I left my office and went in search for Molly; she was sitting at her desk knitting what looked like tiny baby slippers. She must be on her break. "Hey."

"Oh, sorry." Molly looked up and put her project down. "I swear, Pinterest is so addicting. I found the instructions for these knitted baby sandals on there last night…" She held them up. "And as you can see, they look more like mittens. I wish I had been born with a crafty bone in my body." She let out a sigh and shoved the project in a desk drawer. "But enough about me, what can I do for you?"

"I was wondering if I could take the rest of the day off? I have some…personal business I need to see to."

"Does this have to do with Mister sex on a stick?" Molly waggled her eyebrows.

"Maybe, but could we keep that between you and me?" I cringed as I was asking Molly to basically lie for me.

"I might be persuaded, if…there was to be a box of doughnuts and a jar of pickles on my desk sometime this week." She smiled.

"Ah, bribery, I like your style. Consider it done," I agreed.

"In that case, I'm *so* sorry you have a stomach virus, Emily, why don't you go on home and get some rest." Molly spoke loudly and exaggerated the fib.

"Thanks." I smiled and trotted down the hall to grab my purse.

I grabbed the elevator to the lobby of the building and as I walked through, I noticed Grant pass by. He didn't notice me though. He looked more than pissed so I decided to high tail it out of there. No way was I going down that road again. I ducked into a cab just outside the building and gave the address for Jake's office. The entire ride there I rehearsed in my head what I might say when I got there, but I couldn't think of a good script. I decided I'd wing it; it was better to speak from the heart. If Jake couldn't accept the things that came with my whole package, then maybe he wasn't the man I once thought him to be.

I paced outside of his office building when the cab dropped me off. I looked down to make sure I hadn't worn a hole in the concrete below me with how much walking back and forth I was doing.

"Emily? You're Emily, right?" I turned to see Jake's secretary watching me as she walked up to the building.

"Yeah." My cheeks turned red from embarrassment.

"Mr. Bradford isn't here, he's in court today. Is there something I can help you with? Or you can leave a message?"

I knew I should've called, but stupid me wanted to surprise Jake. "Um, yeah, I'll leave a message." I followed her into the building.

Once inside she slid a pen and sheet of paper over her desk toward me. I held the sturdy pen in my hand and thought for a moment what I wanted to say. I couldn't think of anything; I went completely blank. I slid the items back across the desk.

"You know what, I think I'll just wait until I see him later." I smiled and started to walk away.

"Can I say something?" She stopped me.

"Sure." I turned back around to face her.

"I may be out of line here, so feel free to tell me to shut my trap. But since you've been around, I've never seen Mr. Bradford so happy. The guy practically sounds like a Disney character, all whistling and humming all the time. Please don't hurt him."

She had balls; I'd give her that. I admired that about her.

"That man has worked his ass off the past few years to prove something and whatever it was, it had to have been something big."

I said the most natural thing that came to the tip of my tongue. "I don't hurt the people I care about." I threw my hair over my shoulder and left.

∞ *Twenty-Three* ∞

SINCE JAKE WASN'T AT HIS OFFICE, I headed back to work for the day. I was certain Molly hadn't told Marvin I was gone, he'd been in a meeting all morning. I stopped by a bakery and a deli on my way to pick up the essential bribery material for Molly too. A dozen doughnuts and a big jar of kosher dill pickles. That woman sure had a weird pregnancy craving.

When I returned to the office I headed straight for Molly's desk, she was bent over in her chair. "Molly, are you okay?"

She popped up and had her desk phone stuck to her ear, with her hand cupping the bottom like she was trying to keep her voice low. "What are you doing here?" She hung up the phone and whispered.

"Jake wasn't at his office, what's going on? What's with the MacGyver stuff?" I motioned to the fact that she was still hunched over in her chair.

"Marvin was asking for you. I was leaving you a voicemail." She was still whispering.

"Oh, okay." I shrugged my shoulders.

"Miss Mills, I need to see you in my office, *now*." I heard Marvin sternly say behind me. I turned around and my heart dropped into the pit of my stomach. Of all worst-case scenarios, this was the one I could have done without.

Grant was walking out of Marvin's office with a smirk on his face. *The rat bastard.* I would've had to be completely ignorant to not know why he was here. I should have known that I hadn't seen the last of him after the fundraiser.

I watched him calmly walk down the hall and step into the elevator. Molly was now upright in her chair with a depressing look written all over her face. I knew when I stepped into Marvin's office, my life would once again be turned upside down. I wasn't sure if I had shitty luck, or if I was just an idiot who couldn't get my life figured out.

I followed him into his office and shut the door. Marvin sat behind his desk, rubbing the beads of sweat from his forehead with a dingy handkerchief. I took a steady breath of air and waited.

"Emily, I'm pretty sure you're not stupid, you know why Grant was here, right?" Marvin looked almost sad.

"I think so." I answered him.

"Is it true?" He pinned me with a stare.

"Is what true, sir?" I wanted to hear it from his mouth before I admitted to anything. Innocent until proven guilty and all that shit.

"You beat the shit out of Grant Saturday night?" I could see his lips turn up at the corners in a slight smile.

"Maybe…" I kept my face completely serious.

"Well, he alleges that you did. He said he will not file suit or press charges, *if* you turn in your resignation. I on the other hand think that he deserved everything he got…if in fact you did what he's accusing you of doing."

"I won't apologize for what I did; Grant *did* deserve everything he got. And if I had it to do over again, I would've done much worse."

"So I'm assuming you're not turning in a resignation?"

"No sir, I will not."

"Fine. This could bring down some bad press on the firm; I need some time to think things through. I'm putting you on leave until I figure out what to do about this situation. I hope you understand." He managed to sound sympathetic.

"Yes sir." I did understand. I understood that my job was now in jeopardy because of my trying to stand up for myself. What I *didn't* understand was why Grant didn't reveal that he and I practically had sex in a vacant office right down the hall, just the week before. He could've made things so much worse for me, but he didn't. It left me scratching my head.

When I left the office, I felt defeated once again, even though it was of my own doing. I was woman enough to accept the responsibility for what I'd done, and so my punishment began. I would go home to wallow in self-pity about the entire ordeal and try to get at least a bit of studying done.

When I got back home, I walked around my apartment like a zombie. I wasn't sure what path to take. Each time I took one, I ended up with *more* emotional baggage. The thought crossed my mind that maybe I should just move back to L.A. I wouldn't have to become a lawyer. What would that prove anyway? Who would give a damn besides me? No one, that's who. I had friends there—not the closest of friends—but they were there for me at least. But I questioned myself about that too. I was questioning *everything*.

The more I walked around the more pissed I became at myself. I wasn't upset at anyone but the person that stared back at me in the mirror every day. I'd made the decisions that put me on the path I was on. Maybe it was time to stop blaming everyone else for my disasters and point the finger at the person who did the most damage...*myself*. At that thought I became enraged. How could I have let myself slip back into the turmoil that I was always running from? It was like I was this child who didn't know how to face an issue head on. I ran.

I wanted so bad to hit something in that moment. I needed to vent my anger so as I passed by the kitchen, I grabbed the first thing I saw. It was a crystal vase that I'd bought a few years back. In that moment, that vase represented the things I hated about myself. The greediness, the emptiness and the fact that I couldn't manage to be transparent with anyone. I was always hiding something. I tested the weight of the object in my hand and without really thinking, I lifted my arm and tossed it across the room as hard as I could manage. Just as I did, a knock came at my front door. I stood silent for a bit hoping that whoever it was would just go away.

"Emily? Are you okay?" It was Jake.

I didn't answer; I just stood there frozen in place.

"I know you're in there, I was upstairs when you came home. Open the door." Jake continued to bang on the door.

I was beside myself by that time. Tears sprung from my eyes, blurring my vision and making me feel as if I might hyperventilate. I grabbed the counter for support when my legs felt like they might buckle, causing me to tumble over. Jake stopped knocking and then I heard the familiar sound of keys jingling. Of course, he had a master key to the apartments. *Damn it.* I watched in slow motion as the doorknob turned and swung open, Jake stood there with a look of frustration painted on his face.

"Jesus, Emily, I heard something shatter and thought you were hurt when you didn't open the damn door." Jake looked at me and as soon as he saw my face, he rushed over to me. "You *are* hurt. What happened?" He started to look me over.

"I'm fine." I pushed him away.

Jake looked over at the pieces of crystal shattered all over the floor. He ran a hand through his hair and looked back at me. "Want to talk about it?"

"Not really." I started walking toward my bedroom. I didn't want to talk to anyone; I wanted to get shit-faced and pass out for a week or so. I didn't get far though; Jake grabbed my arm and swung me around to face him.

"Well that's too damn bad, because you're going to talk about it. I don't give a flying fuck if I have to tie you to a chair and make you talk, Emily." He looked pissed.

"Do you really want to know?"

"I wouldn't still be here if I didn't." He let go of my arm.

I stepped around him and went to my living room. When I got there I plopped down on the sofa and hung my pounding head. "I was suspended from work today." I couldn't look him in the eyes.

"Why?"

"Because I fucked up, Jake, because I *always* manage to fuck things up." I shouted.

"That's a little vague, Emily." Jake sounded irritated.

"Grant showed up today. He told Marvin about me knocking him around the night of the fundraiser."

"So Carlton is punishing you for defending yourself? That sounds like a load of shit, Emily. Why didn't you tell him to piss off? He can't suspend you for that."

"Maybe not, but he *can* suspend me for practically having sex with a client in the office, Jake."

"Wait. What the hell are you talking about now? I'm confused."

I jumped up from my seat and stood by the window. "I made a stupid mistake. I tried to break things off with Grant and I failed miserably. It just *happened*."

The room became silent, but then Jake's voice came out with a deadly serious quality. "Please tell me you weren't with him while we…"

"No! I would never do that!"

He slumped into a chair and looked relieved. "Thank fuck."

I couldn't believe he would even assume I would do something like that. What kind of person did Jake think I was? I wasn't a two-bit floozy who got her jollies by screwing several men at the same time; I was loyal to a fault. The thing with Grant had been a mistake I wasn't proud of. It was in a weak moment that I gave into something I had no business doing.

"I'm so tired of feeling like a failure all the time, Jake. I just get my head above water and someone dunks me under again. Maybe it's time to realize I don't belong here, I've had nothing but disasters thrown at me ever since I stepped off that plane."

"So, I'm a disaster?" Jake looked hurt.

"Jake, you're the one thing that's been amazing here; I didn't mean it to sound like that."

"Look, you can either pack your shit, run back across the country with your tail between your legs, or you can fight for what you want. I told you that back in college Emily. If you look at everything with negativity, you're going to have negative results." Jake was now standing so close behind me I could feel the heat radiating off his body.

He was right though; I wasn't seeing the bigger picture in any of it. I was letting the negativity tear me down instead of using it to build myself back up again. How did he know me so well? It was like he crawled inside my brain, swam around for a bit and came out knowing things about me that I wasn't even sure of.

"So, what's it going to be?" Jake prompted.

"You're right. I can't keep running when things get terrible."

Jake wound his arms around my midsection and hugged me from behind as a show of comfort. I'd never felt safer than when he held me close like that. "Good, now I have plans for us tonight." He smiled a boyish grin.

"Should I be worried?"

Jake reached inside his jacket pocket and pulled out something small and rectangular. "I thought tonight might be a perfect night to use these…"

I quickly snatched whatever it was out of his hand. When I saw what they were I screamed. "Really?"

"A Yankees game should take your mind off of things for a few hours. But there is one condition. I invited Gabe and my secretary Eliza to tag along." Jake sounded a bit uncertain of my reaction.

"Sounds like fun." I would've rather spent the time alone with Jake, but I admired Eliza for her directness, and Gabe...well Gabe was just part of the package. I wasn't overjoyed at spending an evening with him, but he did save my ass at the fundraiser. I could at least be civil, unless he decided to act like a total jackass.

"Well then, I'll let you get changed. Game time is in T minus two hours." Damn. Jake looked delicious smiling like he'd just won a golden ticket to Wonka Land. His cheerfulness was infectious and I found myself laughing and smiling back. There was just something about him that made me look on the brighter side of things. I'd decided to stop feeling sorry for myself and live a little.

After Jake left I hurried to my closet to find something suitable to wear. I'd never been to a baseball game, so I wasn't sure what was appropriate. I dug around a bit and finally decided on a navy blue sundress with a pair of sandals. I threw my hair into a quick ponytail, brushed on some powder and headed to the kitchen. I was grabbing a bottle of water when a knock came at the door.

"Come in, it's open." I yelled.

Jake strode in wearing a team jersey, ball cap and a pair of jeans.

"You should really think about locking your door." He scolded.

"I knew it was you. Besides no one can get in the building without the code, Jake. Quit being so paranoid."

Jake snuck up behind me and wrapped his arms around my stomach. "Maybe we should just stay in tonight." He started kissing my neck lightly, sending shivers through my entire body.

I playfully pushed him away. "No, I've been dying to go to a game and I'm going. With or without you."

"Damn. Well I guess we'd better get going." He stuck out his bottom lip like a child.

"Big baby." I laughed. Jake retaliated by sticking out his tongue. "Wait, can I get a picture of that? I'm sure it would make a nice ad for your firm on the side of a bus or maybe a park bench."

"Sure, if I can get one of you naked. But I'll be sure to keep that one for myself." He winked.

I liked the playful side of Jake. "I'll think about it."

I passed in front of him on the way to the door, and as I did, I felt him plop something on my head. I reached up and felt a ball cap. "What's this for?" I turned to face him.

"That's my lucky hat, and you look cute in it." Jake leaned forward and kissed the tip of my nose.

Each moment I spent with him made me feel like I was getting in over my head. I knew how I felt about Jake; I couldn't deny it anymore. But I still didn't feel it was the right time to act on what I felt. We'd agreed that the friends with benefits thing was the way to go. Jake had his career, I was trying to build mine and there was still my issues looming underneath the surface. Either way, I told myself that just spending time with Jake was enough. But I had to keep asking myself, how long would it *be* enough?

∞ *Twenty-Four* ∞

I HAD TO ADMIT I was excited about going to my first ballgame and since it would be with Jake, I was even more pumped. I wanted the genuine experience of being in the ballpark, drinking a cold beer and cheering on a team. I could remember peeking around the corner of my dad's den as a kid while he watched ballgames on ESPN. I would watch in awe as the pitcher hurled that tiny white ball towards the man with a bat, wondering how the hell they even did that. I wouldn't get much time to watch though, as my mother would somehow find me every single time and scold me for looking at something which had no bearing on my life whatsoever. She would say that proper ladies shouldn't watch things like that; it would only taint our brain and make us less ladylike. I would have loved to sit and watch a game with my dad, just him and me staring at the TV screen, having some time together. But I never did.

I smiled to myself as the cab took us to the stadium. So much had changed; I wasn't the same person my mom thought I should've been. In a way I was better. I wasn't perfect by any means, but still, I was starting to understand that life was just passing me by. I was determined to not let that happen. Things weren't exactly lined up perfectly but I was starting to have faith that someday they just might be.

I reached up and straightened the ball cap on my head, making sure the bill was centered. Jake slapped my hand away and pulled it to the side.

"Hey, why'd you do that?" I gave him a dirty look.

"Because you have to have everything so damn perfect all the time. Jeez, Emily."

"No, I don't." I defended.

"Uh, yes, you do. Perfect hair, perfect face, everything has to be in its place all the time. Why can't you just let things be the way they are?"

"I like my life to have order, what's so wrong with that?"

"I didn't say anything was wrong with it, I'm just saying that you would have more time for fun if you would lighten up a little."

I let out a puff of air and looked out the window on my side of the car. "Fine. I'll stop being so fussy."

"Good."

I wasn't sure why Jake was picking on me. I wasn't a perfectionist. Sure, I liked things to be in a certain order, but my life was far from being the way it should've been. If I'd gone with my life plan, I would've been married already, practicing law and probably had children by now. But here I was riding in a cab with the man I'd fantasized about for years, going to a ballgame and wondering if I still had a job.

"I'm glad you think my life is so perfect, Jake. If you knew the truth, you would be shocked." He still didn't know about my family. I wanted to tell him, but wasn't sure when was the right time.

"Then enlighten me."

"Maybe someday." I left it at that.

We stayed silent for the rest of the ride and I was fairly certain Jake was upset about something. I knew he was trying to get me to open up to him, but damn it— I just wasn't ready. Maybe I wanted him to believe my life back home was just peachy. Maybe I thought that if I told him how fucked up it really was, he wouldn't think I was such a novelty. Everyone wanted a piece of someone who lived the glamorous life, someone who rubbed elbows with the elite of society and film stars. If he really knew that I despised my life, hated being thrust in front of the flash bulbs and had a terrible relationship with my mother, well he might not think of me as the perfect Emily anymore. I hated that thought. I just wished I could be more like him. He was so focused, but yet had this fun and carefree side. I on the other hand had a stick up my ass that seemed like it would never come out.

"We're here." Jake said.

I looked up and sure enough we were in front of Yankee Stadium. It was bigger than I pictured, almost resembling an ancient coliseum of sorts. Jake got out, paid the driver and extended his hand to help me out. I took in the sights of fans strolling around wearing their team gear and yelling chants for good luck. I couldn't help but smile. It was all so exciting.

"There's Gabe and Eliza." Jake pointed down the sidewalk.

Gabe spotted us and started walking in our direction. Eliza followed, but had a look on her face that said she wasn't happy about being there. I was pretty sure Gabe had something to do with that; he was usually the cause of *someone's* ire.

"Hey, Emily." Gabe greeted.

I said hi and went around him to talk to Eliza. "Is everything okay?" I asked.

"It would be if *he* wasn't here." She pointed to Gabe's back with a snarl.

"I'm sorry. Maybe we girls can hang out." I tried to smooth things over.

"As long as he stays away from me, I'll be fine. If not, I'd keep all sharp objects away from me or he might find his balls cut off and used for batting practice."

I was correct in my assumption; Gabe had already done something to piss Eliza off. I wanted to be nosy and find out exactly what that something was, but I didn't want the drama. I just wanted to have a good time and be with Jake for the evening. I hoped that Eliza and Gabe wouldn't ruin things.

The four of us went to find a ticket taker and Jake let him scan our tickets. We were then led to a section of the park that housed the luxury suites. With each step we took I felt myself become giddy with excitement. Something about being there made me feel *normal* for once. I was doing something that regular people got to do, and it was in a way thrilling. We all walked down the blue-carpeted hallway seeing pictures of players past hanging on the walls. There were several other groups of individuals heading to different suites also, but most of them were in business attire. Our group looked a little out of place, and judging by the looks we received, the other people thought the same.

When we finally reached the doors to the box, the attendant opened them and let us in. I was amazed at the space provided. There was a bar area with granite countertops, leather furnishings, a private bathroom and sliding glass doors that led to more seats outside to watch the game. Flat screen televisions were hung throughout the room for a closer look at the goings on below, pictures and posters boasting the team accomplishments were scattered throughout the room and menus were placed around with special food selections for the group. I felt like we were living in the lap of luxury while being in there.

As the guys talked about all things baseball, I snuck to the sliding glass doors and pushed one open. The fragrant air of the park hit me in the face as I stepped out onto the patio and closer to the railing. I grasped the metal and looked down. Fans were crowding into their seats, vendors were selling food and drinks, and I could hear kids laughing and having a blast. The field itself was amazing. The way the green stripes were mowed into the grass so precisely, the stark white of the bases and the NY logo painted into the field made me feel even more elated to be there.

"Hiding out here?" I turned to see Eliza.

"No, I've never been to a game before. Just taking in everything." I smiled.

"I've only been to a Braves game back home. But that was years ago when my dad was still alive." I could see sadness on her face when she talked.

"Oh, I'm sorry."

"It's okay. I've learned a lot after losing my dad—never take things for granted because you never know when you'll lose them."

Eliza's statement hit home for me. She was right. I'd lost so much, and I didn't stop to think about how I *was* taking things for granted. I was taking Jake for granted, just like I did in college. I always expected him to be there, and after we graduated, he wasn't. Did I expect him to stick around now too?

"Can I ask you something?" Eliza asked. I nodded.

"Do you love Jake?"

I was taken aback by her question. I felt like the floor had been jerked out from under me. How was I supposed to answer her? Be truthful? Or keep my mouth shut? Surely she wouldn't say anything to Jake if I told her the truth. "I have since college. But please don't say anything," I admitted.

"Yeah, I could tell. And don't worry, my lips are sealed." She shrugged.

"Why did you ask then?"

"I wanted to hear you say it. Do you want to hear a secret?"

"Uh, okay." I was leery but curious.

"Don't tell Jake I told you this, but one day I went into his office for some paperwork while he was in court and he'd been doing an online search of you. It was about three years ago, but he Googled your name." I was floored at her revelation. Why would Jake do a search on me? That was just crazy. Surely he wasn't trying to contact me...right?

"Look, I really don't know what's going on between the two of you, but I can tell you this, that man in there doesn't just think of you as a friend." Eliza stated. "And I know I'm being nosy, but I see the two of you together and it looks like the real deal. I'm actually quite jealous."

"Why would you be jealous?"

"Truthfully, when I first started working for him I was crushing on him big time. Here I was fresh from Georgia, moving to the Big Apple, and Jake took a chance and gave me a job. He was so nice and yes, I'll admit, sexy as hell. I guess when you came into the office that day with paperwork I saw how he looked at you. Kinda' made me envy you a little."

"Jake and I are just friends, Eliza. Well, friends with benefits, nothing more. Jake has never looked at me in any other capacity. Besides, I have too much shit in my life to even worry about having an actual relationship with someone."

"Yeah, but isn't that what a relationship is? Sharing everything with that special someone? Letting them help you through it with love and support?"

"I can't do that to Jake. He deserves someone who can emotionally be there for him. That person isn't me. Jake is an amazing man, Eliza; I just don't see how it would really work."

"But you said you loved him...isn't love all about overcoming obstacles together?"

"I guess so."

"Then it sounds like you need to think hard about what you really want, and not what you think is best for Jake. He's a grown man, let him decide what he wants."

Eliza was right again. "Are you always this direct with people?" I had to ask.

"Mostly." She smiled.

"Then I think you and I are going to become great friends."

I was surprised when she leaned over, wrapped her arms around me and hugged me. I'd never had a friend besides Jake do that. It felt nice to have someone to chat with. Someone who *did* tell it like it was. Eliza had no qualms with that. She opened her mouth and the truth poured out. I liked her even more after our conversation.

"What are the two most beautiful women in the world up to out here?" Jake popped out of the doors.

"Boss, you don't have to compliment me, I work for you, remember? As long as I get a check each week, I'm not going anywhere." Eliza joked. "I'm going to find a drink." She headed back inside and shut the doors, leaving Jake and me alone.

"Was she out here telling all sorts of lies about me?"

"Nope, nothing but the truth. I really like her." I complimented.

"She's a good kid."

"Kid?"

"She's only like 25 or 26, I think. Pretty young for moving here by herself. Her mom still lives in Atlanta and Eliza actually sends her part of her paycheck to help out. Don't tell her this, but when I found out she did that, I raised her pay. I figured it would help out a little more."

"Wow, Jake that's really sweet."

"Eliza deserves it, she puts up with my shit."

I couldn't help but hug Jake at that moment. I was seeing so many different facets to the man who stood before me. He was ruthless in the courtroom but practically a saint in his everyday life. He liked to joke and be a big kid, but he was also an amazing lover and friend.

I turned toward the railing again and let out a sigh.

"What's wrong?" Jake stood closer to me.

I took a deep breath and prepared myself for what I would tell him. "I know you think I had a perfect life, Jake, but you don't know how wrong you are." He didn't say anything. "I'm sure it looked like I had everything—money, material possessions, social status—but there was so much going on behind the scenes that people never saw."

"Look, Emily, I have never judged you or thought anything about your personal life."

"Sure you have, everyone does. They see a spoiled rich brat who parades around in front of the cameras and has the world handed to her on a silver platter."

"Don't put words in my mouth. Have you ever heard me say that?"

"No."

"Then don't presume to know what I've thought." Jake turned away.

"Then why were you my friend in college, Jake? You knew who I was back then; you knew where I came from and who my parents were. Why?"

"First of all, if you think I was around you to gain some sort of fame or be in the spotlight, you're dead wrong, Emily. I genuinely liked you, I still do. So you need to stop thinking someone is always after you for what they can get. Maybe there are some people that really give a damn about you." Jake stomped back inside.

I slumped into one of the seats behind me and hung my head. Why did I go off on him like that? Why was I pushing him away when just moments before I admitted to an almost stranger that I was in love with him? And why the hell did I always sabotage the happy times in my life? We were having a good time, and then I had to open my big trap and upset Jake. I needed to apologize to him. I couldn't keep doing things like that and expect him to just forget it.

I got up to go back inside. When I slid the door open I was shocked to hear yelling. Jake was on one side of the room holding Eliza back, and Gabe was on the other with a busted lip. My eyes went wide, wondering what the hell had happened in the short amount of time I was outside.

"Keep him the fuck away from me!" Eliza screamed.

Gabe wiped his bloody lip. "You're fucking crazy!" he yelled back.

I wasn't sure what to do, so I went to the bar to find some ice and a towel. I quickly made an ice pack and took it to Gabe. He snatched it from my hand and pressed it to his face.

"Are you okay?" I pulled the towel away from his lip and looked at the cut.

"No, I'm not okay. She's nuts," he spat out.

"I'm nuts? You're the one who just asked me to have a quickie with you in the bathroom, you asshole." Eliza bit out.

"The both of you need to calm down now," Jake chimed in.

"Fuck this, I'm outta here." Gabe hurried toward the door.

"Me too." Eliza followed suit.

The room was silent while Jake and I stood there staring at each other.

"I hope one day he gets his shit straight." Jake ran a hand through his hair looking frustrated.

"Did she seriously punch him?"

"Sure did. Eliza doesn't take shit off anyone. She tells it like it is and doesn't take any prisoners."

"Wow." I couldn't think of anything else to say.

"Someday something epic is going to happen in his life, and hopefully then he'll see he can't treat people like they're disposable." Jake walked to the bar and pulled out a beer.

"Jake, I'm sorry for earlier. I shouldn't have said the things I did. I get so paranoid that people only want to be around me because of who I am. I wanted to move here for a clean start and get away from all that."

He looked up. "What was it like? Living in the spotlight? I never really asked you."

"At first it was fine; I actually liked the attention. But then it just became too much. My parents didn't care about anything except the movie business. I was pushed to the side."

"Is that why you have trust issues?"

I was floored that he pegged me so clearly. "I learned to depend on myself. My parents didn't show me the kind of love parents should. When the thing happened with my ex, they weren't there for me. My mother sided with Michael and left me to feel like I deserved what I'd gotten." I could see the fury building on Jake's face. "My dad let her dictate everything; he never stood up for himself."

"Is that why you were so emotional when he showed up at the fundraiser?"

"Yeah. I'd gotten an email from my dad saying that he and my mom separated. He said he was tired of letting her tell him the way he should feel about things. I guess he wanted a relationship with me, and she didn't think he should since I had moved away. He chose me."

"I'm sorry to hear they separated, Emily."

"I'm not. My dad's a wonderful man and I think now he and I can have a father/daughter relationship. I've been wanting that forever." I felt a tear slip from each eye.

Jake came to me and pulled me tight to his chest. "I hate to see you cry. God, if I could fix everything for you and take away your pain, I would in a heartbeat, Emily."

"I know you would." I looked up through tear-soaked lashes.

"I know this probably isn't the right time to ask you this and feel free to say no, but I want you to come home with me to visit my parents. I always go visit in the summer for a week and they'd love to have you."

"Jake, that's your family time; I'm not going to intrude on that."

"You wouldn't be. I've already talked to my mom about it. She wants you there."

"Really?"

"Yes, really. I used to talk about you all the time when I was in college. Hell, she practically knows you as well as I do."

"Are you sure, Jake? I would love to go, but please don't take me because you feel sorry for me."

"Emily, I'm not asking you because of what you just told me about your parents. I've been meaning to ask you for a few days now. When you told me about what happened at work, I figured you needed some time away. If you don't want to go, its fine."

"No, I *do* want to go. I just want to make sure you're fine with it, Jake."

"I wouldn't have asked if I wasn't fine with it," he assured me.

"Then I would love to."

Jake wiped away the last of the tears streaming down my face, then leaned in and brushed his lips against mine. Again I felt the familiar sizzle between our bodies. It wasn't something I could explain, it just…*was*. Each time Jake touched me it felt like he was reaching inside my soul. He could read me and know exactly what to do or say to make things better.

What started out as an innocent, sweet kiss though quickly morphed into something passionate and lust-filled. I wasn't sure which way was up when his hands slid over the fabric of my gauzy dress, or how I could even breathe when our tongues twined hotly with each other's. It was as if something took over my body and turned me into a desperate wanting female. I wasn't sure if I'd ever get enough of him.

As we kissed, nipped and drank of each other, I felt my body being lifted off the floor and my legs went around Jake's waist. I was jolted slightly when I felt him plop down on the sofa in the room. The leather squeaked beneath the weight of our bodies settling on the large piece of furniture. I lifted myself up to better straddle Jake's lap as he grabbed my waist and pulled me tighter to him. The kiss went on and on, and I found myself rubbing against his obvious hardness concealed behind his zipper.

He pulled his mouth from mine and breathlessly spoke. "If you keep doing that we're going to have a problem."

I gave him a sexy grin and pushed myself back and stood. I lowered myself to my knees on the plush carpet below and ran my hand over his growing erection.

"Oh, fuck." Jake threw his head back and moaned.

I reached up and undid the button to his jeans, followed by his zipper. I watched his face as he tried to reign in his composure while I slowly tortured him. I grabbed the waist of his jeans and underwear, giving them a tug. He lifted up so I could pull them further down and as I did his beautiful cock sprang free, causing me to lick my lips in anticipation. I couldn't wait to taste him on my tongue, to feel the silken skin glide along my taste buds. But I wanted him absolutely crazy before I did any of that. I gingerly slid my palms up his taut thighs and with one hand, grabbed his cock and began to slowly stroke him from root to tip. With each movement I could hear the breath rush from his chest and small gasps escape his mouth. His eyes were closed tightly as I continued to run my hand over him.

"Jake, open your eyes." I whispered.

He slowly opened them and when he did, I leaned forward to run the tip of my tongue across the bead of moisture seeping from the engorged head. His masculine flavor exploded on my tongue and had me craving more. I kept sampling just the tip for a few licks, but soon needed all of him in my mouth. I opened wide and slid my lips down the hard shaft until I could take no more. I hollowed out my cheeks and sucked as I pulled back, feeling more of his essence release into my mouth.

"Damn, that feels amazing." I heard him moan.

His encouragement made me want to please him more so I quickened my pace and soon felt him go harder in my warm mouth. I knew I had him on the razor's edge but he lightly grabbed the sides of my head and pulled me from his cock. It popped from my mouth and I felt disappointed.

"As much as I want to come in your mouth, I really need to be inside of you."

Jake then motioned me to stand as he stroked himself. "Lift your dress." I did as he said, baring my pink panties. "Are you wet?" He asked.

"Yes." I whispered.

"Come here." He held his cock up in an invitation.

I was so ready to have him again. I put my knees on either side of his thighs and held my panties to the side. Before I could settle down on him though, Jake reached forward and trailed a finger through my folds. I was already so sensitive; I knew it wouldn't take long to make me go off.

"Fuck, you *are* wet." He pulled his hand back and I was surprised when he brought his finger to his mouth and sucked my juices from it. It was one of the sexiest things I'd ever seen, and it had me dripping even more.

I couldn't wait; I needed him inside me so I grabbed his cock and positioned it at my slick entrance. I wasn't willing to go slow; I needed something hard and fast and was hoping that Jake did as well. Once I had him where I wanted him, I slammed myself down on him and almost screamed when he filled me completely. The feeling of being so full was outstanding. I just stayed still for a bit, soaking up the fact that we were connected in such an intimate way.

When I finally felt like I wanted to move, I placed my hands on Jake's shoulders and rocked back and forth, massaging his cock against my hypersensitive flesh. My clit was rewarded with friction against him also, and each sensation had me wanting to fly over the edge. I rocked back and forth, madly wanting to drive him and me crazy and it was working. I was out of my mind, and Jake held so tightly to my hips that I was sure there would be bruises the next day. I didn't care; I just kept on riding him and feeling him inside of me.

"That's it, Baby, fuck me." Jake encouraged.

His dirty words were like music to my ears and I couldn't help but continue to vigorously fuck him. Sweat was starting to bead on my forehead as I rode him closer and closer to the edge. I could feel my body so in tune with his and wanted him to follow me over the cliff we were standing on. I whimpered as the first flutters cascaded through me.

"I'm going to come, Jake."

"Do it, come on me." He gripped my hips tighter and forced me back and forth against himself.

I let myself go, throwing my head back and screaming his name. His warmth flooded me as he poured himself inside of me with a hoarse cry of his own. My own orgasm lasted for what seemed like an eternity. When I felt that I had nothing more to give, I collapsed against his chest where I could hear the pounding of his rapid heartbeat against my eardrum. I stayed there for a few moments as I tried to get my emotions

under control. It was on the tip of my tongue to blurt out that I loved
him. I wanted to so badly, but it wasn't the right time. So I kept my mouth
closed and reveled in the glow of what'd just happened between us.

"You're amazing." Jake kissed the top of my head and lifted my
chin so I could look into his glowing eyes. "Just when I think I know
you, you seem to peel back another layer and show me more, Emily."
He smiled and it melted my heart even more.

I knew there would never be another man for me. Jake was it. He
wasn't there to save me, he was there to be a part of my life and I hoped
that someday he might care for me as much as I did him.

∞ *Twenty-Five* ∞

I'D BEEN AWAY FROM WORK for a few weeks and as distraught as I was over the situation with my new job, the thought of getting away with Jake was a welcome distraction. It was exciting to know I'd be able to see where he came from and meet his parents. Though the thought of the latter made me slightly nervous. They had to be great people though, because in my opinion Jake had turned out to be a wonderful man. Someone like him could only have come from a wonderful upbringing.

But was I going to be intruding on his family time? He did say he only visited them for a week in the summer ...I was having second thoughts. I didn't want to feel like the fifth wheel on a car. Hell, I'd felt like that enough growing up, I wanted to avoid feeling like that now too.

I paced my apartment chewing what nails I had left, thinking that I should just back out. Jake sat comfortably on the sofa watching me worry a hole in the floor.

"Jake I'm really not sure I should go..."

"Look I hate to be a demanding son of a bitch, but you're going and that's final. Now go pack your stuff, our flight leaves in a few hours."

"Yeah but this is your time with family, I'm going to be in the way. You should just go and enjoy them."

He jumped up from his seat and stood in front of me. "I'm not opposed to kidnapping you, Emily. Stop being so stubborn, stop worrying and go pack."

I continued to make excuses for why I couldn't go. "But what if Marvin wants me back soon? I can't be in Texas if he calls."

"I don't care if the president calls and needs you to wipe his ass Emily, you either go pack your stuff, or I'll go pack it for you. I don't think you'll like my way of doing it though." He gave a sinister grin.

"Fine, I'll go." I sighed heavily.

Walking to the coffee table I pulled out my laptop and started to boot it up. "What are you doing?" Jake closed the screen and looked at me strangely.

"I need to buy a ticket for the flight."

"I've already taken care of it, just get yourself ready. I'm headed upstairs to finish packing a few things."

He kissed my forehead and headed out the door. Something inside my chest pulled at the sight of him leaving. I knew he would be back, but the image of him exiting almost caused me to burst into tears. The thought crossed my mind again that maybe I should tell Jake how I truly felt about him. But what if he didn't reciprocate those feelings? I know we shared something special, but did he feel the same things that were churning through me? What if he tossed my declaration back in my face just like everyone else had in my life? I wanted a guarantee that my fragile heart wouldn't be crushed into tiny shards, so it was best that I keep my lips sealed. I would enjoy the time away with him...as friends, with benefits.

I pulled my luggage from the closet, and opened it on the bed. I packed enough clothing and other items to last me for the week and then zipped the bag up tight.

I heard a knock at the door just as I lugged the bag from the bed. "Coming." I shouted from the bedroom. When I opened the door Jake was waiting with a huge smile on his gorgeous face. Would I ever tire of seeing him?

"Ready?"

"Yeah, just let me grab my purse."

"Let's go, then." he grabbed my suitcase while I found my purse and wheeled it out the door.

I knew it was crazy but every time I entered an airport terminal I felt like I was running from something. This time things felt different. I was happy, happier than I'd been most of my life, and I had Jake to thank for that.

Somehow he knew how to drag me kicking and screaming outside of my self-induced shell. I still wasn't ready to completely let everything go, but I was on the right path to doing so and it felt liberating. I just wished I had the courage to say what was lying just below the surface.

I felt like a damn coward for holding back. But I needed to in order to protect myself. Jake was slowly chipping at the walls I'd built and with each piece; he managed to find a side of me I wasn't even aware of. Some I liked and some scared the hell out of me. I knew they were all a part of me no matter what, but figuring out how they all fit together to make me whole was a task I wasn't sure I was up for.

After we checked our luggage Jake took my hand and led us through the terminal to our gate. We waited for them to announce boarding while sipping on our cups of coffee we'd managed to snag at a Starbucks inside the airport.

"You look like you're going to puke." Jake ran his thumb over the back of my hand.

"I feel like it too." My stomach had been unruly for the past few days; I chalked it up to nerves.

"Can I get you something?" Jake offered.

"No, I'll be fine. I'm just nervous."

"There's no need to be, my parents will love having you around. Mom's excited; our house was only ever filled with men. Having another female around will be a nice break from all the testosterone." He laughed.

I smiled but it still didn't help the queasiness that rested in my stomach. I took a deep breath and mentally calmed myself down.

As we boarded the plane we were ushered to the first class cabin where we took our seats and waited for the plane to taxi onto the runway.

"Thank you, Jake." I leaned over and whispered.

"For what?"

"For letting me come along, I know this is your family time, and I promise I won't get in the way." I smiled.

"You're *never* in the way, Emily," he reassured me. "It's nice to have my best friend back; I missed you when you moved back to California."

"I missed you too."

I leaned over, placed a quick kiss on his cheek and laid my head on his shoulder.

"You'll probably feel better if you take a nap."

"Good idea." I yawned, not realizing how drained I felt.

Soon I felt myself drifting off comfortably while feeling Jake next to me.

When our plane landed at Dallas/ Ft. Worth International Airport, my nervousness began to make an appearance. I had to fight to push the sick feeling down. I wasn't usually this high strung when it came to meeting new people, but this wasn't the same. It was Jake's *family* he was going to introduce me to, and I wanted to make a good first impression for some odd reason. The entire situation just felt *important*.

After finding our bags at luggage claim we headed to the rental car counter to pick up the vehicle Jake had reserved for our trip. Once we were settled in, he began to drive south from Dallas. The ride was pretty silent at first, and all I could seem to do was ring my hands together nervously in my lap.

"Okay, your hands are doing some sort of crazy dance over there in your lap. What's on your mind?" Jake broke the silence.

"Would you believe me if I said I was *still* nervous?"

"Yes I would, because I feel the exact same way." He tried to sooth me with a short laugh.

"That's should be comforting on some level but it's not."

"Yeah, well, I've never exactly brought anyone home to meet the parents. But everything will be fine, just trust me, please."

"Jake, if it's that big of a deal I can stay in a hotel or something; I don't want to be a burden on anyone..."

"Are you kidding? If my mom found out I made you stay in a hotel she'd have my balls in a vice. It'll be fine...I promise." He raised my hand from my lap and laid a tender kiss on the back of it.

This was obviously a huge thing for Jake; I was the first woman he'd brought home. I did feel honored that he would invite me, but I still felt strange about it. I hoped that I wouldn't seem like an outsider. I'd never been on a ranch before; I worried that I would seem like an idiot trying to fit in for the week.

I tried to strike up more conversation as we drove. "When's the last time you visited your family?"

"Last summer. It's hard to take time off to travel, but I make sure I block off a week every year. I've tried to get my parents to fly to New York but they're stuck in their ways. They have a lot going on with the ranch, too." I could tell in his voice that he missed his home there.

"Are you planning on moving back here someday? I know that was your original plan..."

"I think I will eventually. With things the way they are right now, though, I'm not sure when that will be."

I knew how it was to have a plan and not know how or when things would work out. I was in that position with my entire life. I did hope that Jake got to move back home though, as great a lawyer as he was in New York; I knew he would be amazing wherever he ended up.

"When does your brother get to come home?"

"I'm not really sure, he's re-enlisted twice now. I think he'll probably do it again when the time comes." There was a note of sadness in his voice.

"That must be tough for your mom, having one son halfway across the country and one halfway around the world."

"Yeah, she handles it pretty well, though; she's always been the cornerstone of the family. I know she writes to Tyler quite frequently, I think it gives her some reassurance that he's all right. I've tried to teach her how to use Skype, but she still thinks that computers house the devil inside them."

"Were you and Tyler close when you were kids?"

"As close as two brothers can be without killing each other. Tyler wasn't the most sociable guy; he pretty well kept to himself until he met his wife."

"That must be hard for her with him being gone all of the time…"

"I suppose it would be if she were still alive, but she was killed in a car accident. The sad part about it all was that she was expecting their first child."

"Oh my God, that's terrible!"

"Poor guy was overseas when he got the news; I'm really not sure what kind of man to expect when he gets home though."

"Sounds like he might need his family to rally around him."

"I suppose so."

As Jake drove us about thirty miles outside of the city he turned onto a dirt-coated road marked with a rustic wooden archway that boasted his family name hanging from a carved wooden plaque. There were fences connected to the weathered wood, and they stretched as far as the eye could see into the horizon. Rich farmland with tall grass and trees waving in the slight breeze dotted the surface of everything. I should have felt strange being in such a remote place, but instead I felt at ease, almost like a sense of serenity passed over me. It was all so different from where I grew up. I was accustomed to tall buildings and miles upon miles of concrete freeways. This was relaxing and perfect.

He drove down a dusty road about three quarters of a mile when we came upon a picturesque two-story log cabin, complete with a wraparound porch and antique style rocking chairs.

"Jake, this is beautiful!" I exclaimed.

"Home sweet home." He smiled.

His face produced so much joy; I could tell he loved this place with every fiber of his being. Even though it was my first time there, I loved it too. It was serene and welcoming.

I could see numerous barns and outbuildings scattered about the property, and horses were busying themselves trotting and neighing proudly in the vast pastures. This was a place I could stay forever, so placid and unspoiled, unlike the concrete jungle I felt enslaved to.

Jake unfolded his frame from the car and lifted our bags from the trunk. I slowly climbed out too and breathed in a whiff of the sweet country air surrounding me like a welcoming relative. It was so refreshing—no smog or smoke to clog my nose and no honking of horns to interrupt my thoughts. It felt as if my senses were heightened to an all-new level. As I stood there and marveled at the charming sights around me, I heard a female voice call out behind us.

"Jake!" I turned to see a gorgeous woman in her fifties barreling down the steps of the wraparound porch, with a gleeful smile lighting up her entire face.

"Hey, Mom." Jake yelled.

"Oh, Jake, it is so good to see you again! It's been too long, Honey." She threw her arms around Jake.

"Yes it has, Mom. You look great." He kissed her on the cheek.

During their pleasantries I felt like a fourth wheel on a tricycle, but didn't want to interrupt their reunion. It all made me envious though, *My* mom would've never given me a welcome like that, and in fact I would've been lucky if she were even around when I arrived home.

"Mom, this is Emily." Jake stood by my side and wrapped his arm around my waist in a protective measure.

His mom turned to me. "Well look at you! Such a stunning little thing." She turned to Jake. "Isn't she?"

"I couldn't agree more."

I beamed at their compliments and felt my cheeks flame. So this was what it was like to have a loving family? My parents loved me but not in the way the Bradfords shared their love. This was true affection, not the plastic recycled affection I was used to.

"Well I'm sure you two are exhausted from your flight, why don't the both of you head upstairs and get settled in. Jake I made up your old room, you can just throw your bags in there and dinner should be ready around six."

"Thanks, Mom. I think I'll show Emily around a bit before dinner, if that's okay with you." He looked at me.

"Sounds like fun." I smiled.

Upon entering the house I could smell something sweet permeating the air around us making my stomach growl.

"Whoa, calm down there." Jake joked.

"Something smells amazing."

"More than likely one of my mom's desserts, she's actually won ribbons at the county fair with some of her recipes." He sounded so proud.

"Well if the smell is anything to go by, she's already won first place with my stomach."

We walked through the house some more, and I tried to take in everything around me. The walls were covered with family photos and the furniture, even though it wasn't brand new, looked so cozy and inviting. Everything had a rustic appearance making it all fit in with the log cabin it was housed in. I fell more in love with each step I took.

Jake led us up a beautiful handcrafted staircase and down a long hall. At the end was a large room that felt so comfy and inviting when I stepped through the door. There was a mahogany four-poster bed as the centerpiece, and at the end was an antique trunk that looked as if it held treasures from another time and place. The bed was covered with what looked like a handmade quilt with matching pillow shams and I couldn't help but run my hand across it to find if it was just as soft as it looked.

"My grandma made that," Jake said.

"It's gorgeous, Jake."

Jake watched me check out the rest of the room and the adjoining bathroom. It was just as welcoming. The walls were done in a dark wooden panelling, and the floor was tiled with light brown stone. The pedestal sink was perched beneath an antique iron trimmed mirror, and the bathtub and shower were set back in the wall.

"Ready for a tour?" Jake called from the bedroom.

"Yeah, I just need to freshen up a bit; I always feel like a mess after I fly."

Jake crossed the room and sauntered toward me. He looked like a lion going after its prey, and my belly began to flutter. When he reached me, I tilted my head up to look at him and he gave no warning. He crashed his mouth over mine, taking me on a dizzying tango of our lips. He tangled his hand in my hair and cupped the back of my head while the other was grasping my hip so tight I could feel his fingers dig into my flesh through my jeans. His kiss was desperate and scorching, pulling me into him further and further. I wanted nothing more than for him to throw me on the bed and take me to the edge of absolute bliss, but he quickly pulled back and pressed his forehead to mine, trying to catch his breath.

"You're really hard to resist, Emily." He breathed.

"Then don't resist me, Jake." I joked.

"I would love nothing more than to christen my bed, but my mom is downstairs. I'd hate to get caught." He tapped a soft kiss to the tip of my nose.

"I can be quiet."

"Liar." He tugged me toward the door and into the hallway. "Come on, I'll show you around."

We trotted down the steps and Jake led me outside. We walked toward a huge red barn and entered a small door that was latched closed with a piece of worn lumber. As I stepped through I was delighted to find several horses waiting in their respectable stalls.

"Have you ever ridden?" Jake opened a stall and pulled on the horse's halter.

"Yes, but probably not in the way you're used to." he waited for me to continue. "I was taught to ride in shows; it's more formal than riding for fun."

"So you never rode for fun?" Both of his eyebrows lifted in curiosity.

I laughed. "Not really. I had a horse in the family stables, but I wasn't allowed to ride her for pure enjoyment."

"Wow, that's sad." He looked at me with a frown. "How about we ride for pure fun today? It'll be easier than showing you everything on foot."

"That sounds amazing." I beamed.

Jake soon chose a horse for me and she was a beauty. Her coat shone like the summer sun, and she displayed a heart shape on her forehead that made me smile. Jake saddled her up, and helped me climb on.

"This is Berkley; she's a good ole' girl." He patted her flank.

"She's perfect." I smiled.

"Go ahead and take her out, and I'll be out there in a few."

"Okay."

I grabbed the reins and led Berkley out of the stable door and into the gated area ahead of me. I rode her around in circles for a bit, trying to get a feel for her while I waited for Jake. When I turned her around to face the barn, Jake rode out on his horse.

"You have *got* to be kidding me..." My mouth fell open.

"What?" He asked innocently.

What indeed. The man was riding on a solid white horse and all that was missing was a sword and some shining armor. Even though there was so much irony in his actions, I couldn't help but feel giddy seeing him up there. He truly looked like some mythical savior coming to rescue me from a fire-breathing dragon. .

"Oh...nothing. I'm ready."

I could see a sly grin turn up the corners of his mouth. "Giddy up, Cowgirl."

As he rode off ahead of me, I shook my head and followed close behind. What were the odds?

∞ *Twenty-Six* ∞

RIDING OUT IN THE OPEN with the wind whipping through my hair made me feel like a completely different person. I was surrounded by nothing but nature as my horse trotted down a worn path on Jake's family land. I was practically giving myself whiplash with the way my head moved back and forth trying to soak in every part of the stunning scenery around me. It was nothing shy of spectacular.

"You look happy over there." Jake pulled the reins of his horse and came up beside me.

"I am. This is all so beautiful; thank you for making me come with you."

"See, I told you it would be nice to get away. Sometimes you have to trust that others may know what's best for you Emily."

"That's not such an easy thing to do though."

"Letting go and taking a leap of faith isn't easy, but sometimes the risk is worth the rewards in the end."

Jake always gave me tidbits of advice to think about, he wasn't pushy with things he told me, it was like he dropped hints knowing I would absorb his words and take them into consideration. And I did. I thought about things he told me probably more than he thought I did. But Jake was about the only person I took advice from. He was a smart man, and not just book smart either. He knew how to handle things, sometimes with a little force, and sometimes he knew when to back off and be gentle with everything. I admired him more than he knew.

"Would you ever live in a place like this?" He looked over to me and asked.

"I think so, it's so different from what I'm used to, but there's something about it that whispers *home*."

"It has a way of getting under your skin quickly. I like New York, but this will always be my home."

Jake knew where he wanted to be in his life and I wished I had direction like him. I was like a lone leaf hanging from a tree branch, wondering if today would be the day I'd fall from my spot and drift somewhere else. To wake up and have so much security and an actual home would've been a dream come true.

We continued to ride through the property and soon came to a picturesque creek; Jake stopped his horse and grabbed the reins, tying them to a low hanging tree branch. When he was done, he came over to me, helping me slide down from my saddle and tethering my horse as well. I followed him to the edge of the water and we stood there in silence for a few minutes.

"I've been offered the district attorney position in Dallas." He kicked some dirt and rocks with his boots.

"Wow, Jake, that's fantastic. Congratulations." The news was good news, but inside I felt like I'd been kicked again.

"I'm not sure if I'm going to take it yet though."

"Why wouldn't you? It's a great opportunity, Jake."

"If I accept it I'd have to be moved back here in the next six months."

I didn't know what to say. I was happy for Jake, I really was, but maybe I was being selfish. I didn't want him to leave. But what reason did he have to stay? It wasn't like I was anything special to him; our relationship wasn't even a *real* one. We hung out, had sex, and that was it. It hit me that maybe it was time to once again let go of Jake. He had an opportunity to do something amazing with his life; I couldn't be the one to hold him back from that.

"I think you should do it." I blurted out.

"Yeah?"

"Yes, I mean, I like having you in New York, but I don't think you should pass this up. It's what you've worked for, Jake. This will give you the chance to be with your family and have your dream job."

"Yeah, I guess it would. I don't know, I'm still thinking it over. They've given me two weeks to make my decision."

Two weeks. Just knowing he only had that amount of time to make a decision was heartbreaking. What was I supposed to say to that? I'd told him my thoughts, but truthfully I wanted to scream it from the rooftops that I needed him to stay, for me. As selfish as it sounded, I'd waited so long to have a chance with Jake, now I only had a short period of time to either say how I really felt or walk away once more. If I walked away, I wasn't sure I would be able to survive. I'd learned so much about myself with Jake.

"Could we head back now? I'm not feeling the best." Nausea hit me all of a sudden.

"Sure. Is there anything I can get you?"

"No, I think I need to lie down for a bit. I should feel better later."

What I needed to do was cry, but I wouldn't do that anymore. I had to figure out what was truly important and decide whether to act on it or not.

We rode back to the house in silence. After Jake put the horses back in their stalls, I headed back upstairs. Jake didn't follow me, and it was a good thing too.

When the bedroom door was closed behind me, I broke down. Tears sprang from my eyes like an emotional flood and I shook uncontrollably. Why couldn't I just tell him that I wanted him in my life, I would've been willing to move, hell, I'd have moved across the world to be with him. Jake didn't know that though, he only knew that I'd made a stupid deal with him and there we were. That was it.

As I stood there bawling my eyes out, I felt sick to my stomach again. I tried to swallow the ill feeling down, but before I could talk myself out of it, I ran to the bathroom and threw up. I hugged the toilet, letting the contents of my stomach empty out until there was nothing left. What was wrong with me? I never got sick. I stood up and turned on the water to rinse my mouth out. As I was dabbing a towel on my lips a strange thought hit me. I threw the towel down and ran to find my purse. I grabbed my phone and scrolled through my calendar app. Each week that I counted back made my stomach flip more. It couldn't be, could it? I counted again just to double check. I was late. *A freaking week late.*

"Emily, are you okay in there?" Jake called from the other side of the bedroom door.

"Uh, yeah." My voice came out raspy.

What was I going to do? I began to internally panic. I had to know for sure.

I went to open the door to let Jake in.

"Hey I was just...you don't look so good. Are you sure you're fine?" He brushed my hair away from my face.

"I think I have a stomach bug. Is there a pharmacy anywhere close?"

"Yeah, about ten miles south, grab your purse and I'll take you."

I put my hand on Jake's chest. "No, I can find it. You stay here with your mom; I'm sure she'll have dinner ready soon anyway."

"What if you get lost? You've never been here before."

"I have GPS on my phone, I'll find my way." I assured him.

"Okay, well if you have any problems just call me." He pulled the rental car keys from his pocket and held them out.

"Thank you." I grabbed the keys and my purse and practically ran down the steps. I made it to the car, started it up and drove back down the road from which we came. When I got to the end I searched in my phone for a pharmacy and set my GPS to the address it provided. Luckily the timer said it was only a fifteen-minute drive.

The entire drive I tried to calm myself down. Maybe there was a chance I was wrong, maybe I really was sick. But what if I wasn't *just* sick? What if my life was about to change in a way I wasn't prepared for?

∞ *Twenty-Seven* ∞

I MADE QUICK WORK of finding what I needed and driving back to Jake's parents' home. I hid my purchase deep inside my purse, hoping that when I got back I could just sneak upstairs and do what I needed to, undetected. I didn't need a big scene; I just wanted to find out if my life would be...*different* from that point on.

I pulled the car back next to the house, got out and shut the door.

"You didn't get lost." Jake was waiting on the steps.

"Nope, I didn't." I tried to walk past him and he grabbed my arm, startling me. When my body jumped, my purse went flying off my arm. It was like watching something happen in slow motion, the contents of my bag were scattered about on the dirt and grass below, while my stomach dropped to my feet. I closed my eyes hoping that maybe I was lucky and the *one* thing I wanted to keep hidden would've just stayed safe in the bottom of the bag.

"Shit, I'm sorry." Jake bent over to pick up the contents of my purse. I couldn't watch. I knew if it weren't for bad luck, I'd have no luck at all. I could hear my heartbeat roar in my ears as the extreme nervousness hit me. "What the hell?" Jake was behind me, but I knew without a doubt what he was talking about.

I slowly turned around and when I faced him, he was of course holding the purple box tightly in his hand. I wanted to start running and never stop. This wasn't the way I wanted to approach the situation, I wanted something more inconspicuous. "Jake." I breathed.

"Upstairs, right now." He grabbed my elbow and led me inside the house. I didn't know if it was anger rolling off of him or what, but I was scared.

We made it to the bedroom and Jake sat down on the end of the bed. I stood there watching him flip the sealed box between his shaking hands while he looked intently at it.

"Why didn't you tell me?" He looked up and pinned me with a serious stare.

"Because I didn't know anything Jake, I still don't."

"Are you late?"

"Yes, but only a week. It could just be stress, though."

"I guess we'll find out soon, huh?" He stood and handed me the box. "If you think you're doing this alone, you're wrong, Emily."

I nodded and walked a few steps into the bathroom. I closed the door and locked it, leaving Jake on the other side. I stood there, opened the box and read the instructions since I'd never taken a test like that before. Three minutes, that's all it would take to find out if our lives would change forever. Did I want this? Was I ready for something that epic to happen? I didn't have the answer; I was still in shock that this was even happening. I pulled the stick from the plastic wrapper and sat down on the toilet. I did as the directions indicated and replaced the cap on the test. I laid it on the side of the bathtub so it would have a flat surface to do its job. I then opened the door and walked past Jake who was leaning against the doorframe. Normally three minutes would have flown by. It would have been just a blip on the radar of my normal day, but not then. Three minutes in that instant felt like hours were ticking by, like sitting there watching flowers sprout from the ground. I don't think I'd ever been so nervous in my life, or scared out of my wits. I couldn't talk, I could barely breathe.

I sat there on the bed wondering what was running through Jake's mind as he checked his watch every five seconds. He was in deep concentration, but almost looked pissed off. Maybe he had a right to be.

"It's been three minutes." He looked up at me.

I couldn't move. My body became paralyzed with fear of the unknown.

"You check it." I put my head down.

I could hear Jake move into the bathroom and then he came to sit near me on the bed. He held the white stick tightly in his hand not saying a word at first.

"Whatever happens, Emily, I want you to know that I'm here, okay?"

I nodded again right before he opened his hand to reveal the results. I took a deep breath, closed my eyes and opened them again. When I looked down at his hand I wasn't sure what sort of reaction to have.

"It's negative." I breathed.

Jake said nothing. He got up from the bed, threw the test into a nearby trashcan and left the room. He had to have been relieved, right? Something like that could've ruined his plans and tied him to something that would've changed the course of his life. He didn't need that. Truthfully, if he hadn't found the test in the first place, I don't know that I would've told him right off. It may have made me the world's biggest asshole to keep something so important from him, but Jake had so much ahead of him. I knew he would've given up everything to make things right, he was a standup guy like that. But I could've taken care of myself. I wouldn't have wanted to do things alone, but if it meant that Jake could have his dreams, I would've done it.

I had to talk to him. We needed to say something, anything about what'd happened. I went downstairs to find him. When I passed by the kitchen his mom was stirring something on the stove.

"Excuse me, have you seen Jake?" I asked.

She turned around and smiled. "I think he said something about needing some fresh air."

"Oh, okay, thank you."

I went to the front door and looked out, hoping to see Jake pacing somewhere. When I didn't, I walked outside and started searching for him. The gravel of the driveway crunched under my feet while I walked further hoping to find him. I was starting to panic when there was no sign of him anywhere.

"I'm up here." I heard Jake's voice call.

I looked around and still couldn't see him.

"In the barn." He called again.

I finally looked up and could see Jake's silhouette in the loft door of the barn that housed the horses. I followed the path inside and found a ladder that lead to the same place he was. Cobwebs clung to my fingers as I scaled each wrung of the wooden ladder trying to reach the top. When I did, I stood up and brushed myself off.

"Tyler and I used to come up here and hide from my parents when we did something bad." He chuckled.

"And why are you hiding here now? Did you do something bad?" I walked over and sat beside him on a square hay bail.

"Not really. I just came up here to think."

"Jake, I'm sorry."

"Don't apologize. I'm the one that should be sorry, Emily. I should have stayed and talked to you about what happened."

"You were relieved, I get it. You needed some time to unwind."

"Relieved? No, more like disappointed." He grabbed my hand in his.

"I don't understand. Why would you be disappointed, Jake?"

"I know it's not the ideal circumstance, but someday it would be nice to have a baby."

"Sure it would, Jake. When you find someone amazing who you want to spend the rest of your life with, then you do the whole marriage and kids thing."

"And what if I've found that person already?"

I jumped from my seat and turned my back. "Don't say things like that, Jake. We are nothing more than friends with benefits," I scolded.

"That's bullshit and you know it, Emily. Don't sit here and tell me you don't have any sort of feelings for me. If you even try, I'm calling you a bald-faced liar."

"Even if I did, it wouldn't matter. You have an amazing life ahead of you. You need to go live it, Jake."

"So you're not denying it?"

"I don't know what I feel. I've been forced my entire life to feel the way others expect me to. I haven't had a chance to figure out what I want."

"That's an excuse. You know exactly how you feel, but your problem is, you're too damn scared to let yourself have any sort of happiness. You think that if you get comfortable, someone will always come by and rip it away. How can you live like that? How can you face yourself every morning knowing that you've let so many things pass you by because you'd rather stick your head in the sand than face them."

"Shut up, Jake!" I yelled.

"No, Emily. You need to hear the truth. Yes, you got the short end of the stick with your previous relationship, and damn it, I'm sorry, but I'm not him. I will not sit here and let you blame me, *or* yourself for anything that happened to you. If you can't get beyond the shit that happened in the past, then you need to leave. I refuse to live in the past, Emily, *my* future doesn't lie there."

"You're giving me an ultimatum," I stated.

"I'm giving you a choice."

"That's not fair, Jake."

"I think it's plenty fair. You've done nothing but blame others for everything that's happened to you. When is it time to put the past behind you, Emily?"

"You have no idea what I've been through." I bit out.

"I know that you're a spoiled brat who thinks life should be fucking perfect. When will you understand that it's not? When will you finally realize that you deserve to be happy?"

"I can't do this anymore." I walked over to the ladder and started my decent. I held my tears in until I reached the bottom. I could hear Jake muttering something as I left the barn, but refused to go back. I needed to leave; I couldn't stay there and let him treat me like that. I thought he knew me, I thought he understood the things that made me tick, but I was dead wrong. He was just like everyone else, a judgmental asshole.

I tried to calmly go back in the house but was stopped by Jake's mom on the front porch. She had a look of sadness in her eyes.

"Emily, could we talk?" She asked quietly.

I didn't want to, I wanted to go upstairs, pack my things and find the first flight back to New York. This wasn't how the week was supposed to go; it was supposed to be a nice relaxing time away from my troubles and worries. Instead, it turned into something from which I wanted to run...again.

"I don't think that's a good idea." I wiped the tears from under my eyes.

"Maybe not, but I think you need to talk instead of running away."

I nodded and followed her into the house and into the kitchen. She set a glass of iced tea in front of me, and I took a cooling sip.

"Jake deserves better." I lifted my head and looked toward her.

"Is that your assumption, or his decision? Is it fair to him for you to decide what he needs?"

"I guess not. But he has an opportunity to move back here and have the career he's wanted, I can't get in the way of that."

"I really don't think that's the issue here, Emily. This is what I see. I see a woman who's possibly been hurt in the past, who's so afraid to trust people that she's missing out on something that *could* be the best thing that's ever happened to her. Now, I think you need to think about what you want, stop worrying about what's best for others and decide if you're willing to take the risk to be happy. If you aren't, that's up to you. But Jake has waited so long to find happiness. I've never seen my son smile like he does when he's with you. And you're the first woman he's ever brought home." She reached across the table and grabbed my hand.

"How am I supposed to let go of everything from my past and move forward?"

"It will take time—things don't fix themselves overnight. But sometimes having someone who cares about you near can make a world of difference."

I gave her a watery smile and stood from my chair. I did have a lot to think about but sitting there wasn't the place to do that. There was one thing that had to be done, and it was the thing that would help me move past everything.

I headed upstairs to pack my bags. If I was going to open my heart and be happy, I had to take the steps toward doing it.

∞ *Twenty-Eight* ∞

I COULDN'T EXPECT TO SIT BACK and wait for everything to just fall in line and fix itself. If I wanted something to go right, I had to make it right. So that was my plan. I had to face the one person who I was allowing to hurt me…my mother. Even though I'd walked away, I was letting her stick with me. I carried so much hate and hurt around every day. I was using her as an excuse and I didn't want that anymore. I wanted to face her, talk to her and ultimately forgive her for what she done. Sure, to some it wasn't that big of a deal. But to me, I felt like the love she'd held from me made me doubt that I deserved love at all. I wasn't jaded enough to think talking to her would fix everything, but I knew that I could say what I needed to and move on.

As I sat in the airport in Dallas, I waited for my flight number to be called. I wasn't sure what I'd say when I got there just yet, but something told me to speak from the heart, something I had a hard time doing so far in my life. I'd let so many great things pass me by and I wasn't doing it again. I hoped that after I sealed up the loose baggage I carried, maybe things would be semi-normal.

The nearly three-hour flight took no time at all, and soon I was grabbing my things in baggage claim at LAX. I wheeled my bags through the airport and quickly found a ride outside. I gave them the address of my parents' house, hoping my mom would still be there. If I knew my dad, he wouldn't have kicked her out, he would've continued to make her comfortable in the home they had shared for so many years. As bad as things had gotten, my dad would've still had compassion for her; after all, they were married for so long and still had *me* connecting them.

I checked my phone as the car took me to my former home, but no one had called or texted me. I was saddened to see that Jake had just given up, but he had every right to since I had walked away. I couldn't tell him what I was doing, either. He would've wanted to tag along and try to make things better for me. In all reality, I was the only one who could fix things. I couldn't drag him into it. This was the *one* time in my life that I had to woman-up and face things head on.

When the car drove up to the massive iron gates that guarded my parents' estate, I was overcome with anxiety, but I pushed it down. It was time to stand up and face my demons even if they were tearing me apart. I refused to let them do it anymore.

I reached out of the window and punched in the 9-digit code for the gate and watched the decorative bars slowly swing open. The car inched forward as they did, revealing the driveway that led to the house. I looked out the back window as we passed through, the gates closing quickly behind. I sat forward once again and took a deep breath as the house came into view. Once upon a time I'd loved coming through that gate, I thought I was so privileged to have such wealth and opulence in my life, but now it just reminded me of the things that were so wrong with my life. The house represented a time passed that I wasn't a part of anymore, a time where I let things slide by me while I was blind to everything. Jake was right, I did deserve love. I deserved to be able to hold my head up and have happiness. I know I messed things up with him, but I thought that maybe someday we could be friends again. The chance at something more with Jake had passed, and yes, that saddened me. But it was of my own doing. I was paying the consequences for things I said and *hadn't* said. I didn't want to live with regret, but it was just part of the cycle I'd been putting my life through.

The car stopped in front of the house and I reached over and pushed the door open. When I stood from the car, I looked up and was stunned to see my mother standing on the steps in front of the double doors that led into the house. Her facial expression gave nothing away as to what she was thinking, but I could tell she was without makeup, and her clothing told me she was in one of her depressed moods. A loose T-shirt hung from her shoulders and a pair of black yoga pants streamed down her trim legs. Her blonde hair was piled on top her head haphazardly and her feet were bare of any footwear. This was not the same mother I'd been used to seeing every day. This woman didn't even look like she belonged in this home.

I paid the driver and soon he was heading back down the driveway. My feet were planted in their spots as I stood there staring at what looked like a shell of my mom.

"You might as well come in, Emily." She crossed her arms and turned her back, going into the house.

I guess that was my invitation. I pulled my bags behind me and followed her inside. As soon as I shut the door behind me, a smell hit my nose and made me gag.

"Mom, what *is* that smell?" I looked around at the disarray around me. Clothing was strewn throughout the house, dust was caked on every visible surface, and it smelled like something died in here.

"Your father fired the maid and I've had to fend for myself." I trailed her into the sitting room and watched her lazily plop down on a chaise lounge. "I think he's punishing me. He knows I can't do this shit by myself." She grabbed up a martini glass and took a big swig of its contents.

"When's the last time you've eaten anything?" I asked."

She held up the glass. "Does alcohol count?"

I pushed myself forward and stood in front of her, jerking the glass from her hands and sloshing the drink all over the floor. "No, Mom, it doesn't." I was so angry I threw the stemmed glass across the room, shattering it on the fireplace mantle.

"Well then, it's been a while." She tried to laugh but I could tell she was almost too weak to.

"You don't get to give up, Mom, not anymore."

"And I've given up in the past?"

"Hell, yes, you have. You've given up on everything. Dad, yourself and me. When will you realize that some people *need* you?"

"No one *needs* me, Emily, I'm just a fixture that's been here for so many years, but now everyone's shown me that I will never be needed."

"Stop feeling sorry for yourself, Mom. You did this. Not me, not even Dad. You stood by and pushed everyone around hoping we would just keep sticking by you. But we didn't, did we? We figured out that there was a life beyond you, Mom."

"Well what was I supposed to do?" She bit out.

"You were supposed to give a damn! When we needed you, you were supposed to be there, Mom."

"I was there!"

"No, you weren't, you were anywhere *but* where we needed you to be." I sat across from her, really noticing the lines and wrinkles that plagued her face.

"I've tried so hard to be the best wife and mother, but no matter what I did, I failed."

"Mom, the fact of the matter is this. We can't be perfect, we are going to make mistakes along the way but you can't just give up."

"She's right." I whirled around to see my father standing in the doorway. He stepped forward. "I'd thought that things could be perfect, but quickly realized they couldn't. I've spent my life in the office trying to build a career and make sure the two of you had enough money and things to make your lives comfortable. But I wasn't giving either of you what you really needed. I've missed so many milestones and events in your life, Emily; I should have been there. Your mother doesn't deserve all the blame here either. She thought her job was to look good on my arm all these years, and I let her believe that."

"But you could've been a parent to me, Mom. Why weren't you?" I had to ask.

My mom and dad looked at each other like they were hiding something. "I was afraid to," she whispered.

My dad sat beside me and started to talk again. "Emily, I met your mother when I was twenty-six, she was only nineteen at the time. She was this beautiful young woman whom I fell for instantly. I knew right off I wanted to marry her, but she refused. She said she couldn't drag me into her mess. I had no idea what she was even talking about at the time. When I figured it out, I made the decision to be with her anyway."

"I don't understand." I looked between them again and confusion rolled over me.

"Your mother was pregnant when we met...with you. I told my parents that you were mine, and we were married a few months before your birth."

"Wait, are you telling me..." I was almost speechless at their bombshell.

"I'm your father in every way that counts, Emily. Even though I haven't been the best father, I am yours. We didn't think it was ever a big deal. Your mother and I were thrilled to have you."

"But why were you afraid to be a parent to me, Mom?"

"I'd always felt like I messed up, like your father took pity on me for what I was going though. Every time I looked at you, I hated myself. You were my reminder every day of how I had screwed up my life. At first I tried, but the more time I spent with you, the more I hated you. But it wasn't your fault; you were an innocent child who didn't know anything about the situation."

"Do you hate me *now*?" A tear slipped down each cheek when I asked the question.

"No. I hate myself for what I've done to you. I hate that I wasn't there for you when you needed me the most, Emily." She said with conviction.

"Why weren't you there for me when everything happened with Michael?" I needed answers.

"The truth is, I *wanted* to see you hurt. I felt like you'd hurt me by messing up my life, and it was my way of thinking you deserved payback."

I buried my face in my hands and cried. It was all so much to lay on me at one time. To know my parents kept a huge secret from me all those years, and to finally know why my mom treated me like I was nothing to her. In her eyes, I was a mistake.

"I don't expect you to forgive me, Emily. I wouldn't forgive me. All I'm asking is that you understand *now* why I was the way I was."

What was I supposed to say? I was feeling so many emotions that I couldn't make sense of any of them. I wanted to scream, to hit something, but what would that prove?

"Do you realize what you've done, Mom? You've damaged me to the point that I can't have a normal relationship with anyone. I don't trust people; I think that they'll always hurt me." I jumped from my seat and stood by one of the floor-to-ceiling windows looking out to the garden outside. "I can't even let the man I love, love me."

"I'm so sorry." I heard my mom start to cry.

I realized that I couldn't hate my mom anymore and I couldn't hate myself either. It was time to let go of the past and start to claim my future. I was still shocked from the news my parents had revealed, and it would take some time to sort through the feelings I was experiencing, but I was relieved on some level because I understood why things had happened.

∞ *Twenty-Nine* ∞

I'D SPENT A WEEK with my parents in Los Angeles, and for once it was nice to sit around and just talk things out among the three of us. I'd learned that my biological father was killed in a car accident right before my mom found out she was pregnant with me. He was an actor trying to find a job in Hollywood when my mom met him. They had dated for around eight months, and from what my mom said, he was her first love. She did love my father now, but I understood about never forgetting the person your heart belonged to first.

I admired my dad for marrying my mom even though she was pregnant with me, he didn't have to do that, but he loved her. And I could tell even though they had issues now, they still cared deeply for each other. On the second to the last day I was there, my mom took me to the place where my biological father was buried.

It was a cemetery in the Hollywood Hills and I was touched when she told me that my dad paid for his burial plot and headstone. She said that he offered to do it because he refused to have his daughter's real dad be buried somewhere unassuming. Mom told me that she would visit the grave a few times a year and place a bouquet of fresh white roses there because when they'd met, he could only afford one white rose to give to her.

I also learned that my middle name was the name of my real father's mother, Irene. I was honored that she gave me something of his to carry with me. My father told me that he was all for letting her give me the name as long as he was able to give me my first name. He was so supportive of everything during the time my mom carried me. He went to every doctor's appointment, would go out in the middle of the night to find the things she craved, and he was the first to hold me when I was born.

My dad never once made me feel like I was a burden while he talked about things that happened with my mom and him. He talked as if I *was* his child no matter what, and really, I was. I didn't doubt that he loved us both enough that he would risk everything to give us a life. And he proved it too. His parents doubted that I was his, they threatened to take away his stake in the family business, but my dad held strong and claimed that I was without a doubt his. For someone to love two people so much meant the world to me. I just hoped that it meant something to my mom.

I didn't hate her for the things she revealed. I was angry that it was all coming to light now, but I was grateful that I had an understanding and could grasp things better. I sat down with my mom and got so many things off my chest that were eating at me and she was more understanding then she'd ever been. She apologized for the things she'd put me through. She knew it was wrong to treat me as if I was her *problem* instead of her child, but I think in the end she knew how much it had affected me.

Over the week I talked about my goals of taking the bar again. I told them about the things that had happened in New York, and I shared the fact that I was in love with Jake and how badly I had hurt him. I still cried every night for what I did, walking away like he meant nothing to me. But I knew that eventually I'd be able to heal and at least tell him how I felt. Even if he turned his back, I could maybe sleep at night knowing I'd done what I could to make things right. It would still break my heart if he didn't want anything to do with me, but I couldn't blame him for making that decision.

By the time I boarded the plane back to New York, I'd felt immensely better about the relationship with my family. My dad decided to move back into the house with my mom, he hired the housekeeper back and the place didn't smell like something had died there anymore. I knew it would take some time for things to be completely healed, but they were well on their way. I promised them that I would visit often and they also said they would come to New York to see me. I was free—I'd finally learned the truth, I'd forgiven the past and I was looking forward to actually having a future. What that future entailed, I wasn't sure. But I was no longer afraid of it. I knew it wouldn't ever be perfect, but whatever it was, I would grab it with open arms and be happy that I was given the chance to live it.

∞ *Thirty* ∞

WHEN I GOT BACK TO NEW YORK, I settled into my apartment and waited to hear if I still had a job or not. I told myself that either way I would pick myself up and move on from whatever happened. I could only learn from the things I'd done and not keep punishing myself for them.

The weeks went by and the air outside became even hotter as the middle of July approached. The city's air was full of change but I looked at it as a good thing. The wind was becoming damp with humidity and everywhere you went, you could see people donning clothing that kept them cool under the sweltering sun. I found myself taking walks around my neighborhood in the evenings just to feel the last glimmers of summer sunlight on my face before the sun went down.

Toward the middle of July I was sitting in my living room checking my emails when my phone rang. I reached over to answer it. "Hello?"

"Emily, this is Marvin Carlton." I suddenly became nervous.

"Yes sir, how've you been?"

"Just fine, thank you. Listen, I know it's been a few months, and I'm really sorry I haven't gotten back with you, but I was wondering if you would be interested in coming back to work?" he offered.

I couldn't keep the excitement out of my voice. "Absolutely, sir, that would be wonderful." I smiled.

"Great, I hope tomorrow isn't too soon?"

"Tomorrow is perfect. Thank you so much."

Relief hit me as soon as I ended the call. It wasn't like my job defined me, but knowing I could be closer to my dream filled me with elation. I was set to take the bar exam at the end of the month and being able to study with the other grads and work a bit would be a relief. I'd been hitting the books and trying to take practice exams online since I'd been back from California, but I still wasn't feeling as confident as I should've been. And to add to everything, I couldn't help but be sad when I saw a moving company pick up Jake's things and drive away with them just three weeks before. I wanted to knock on his door and tell him that I needed him but he'd made his choice. He apparently had taken the D.A. job in Texas, and on one hand I was happy for him, but on the other, I was stricken with grief. I no longer heard his footsteps upstairs, could no longer pretend that he was just a few steps away and had lost my chance to say the things I should've said. He was just...*gone*.

I reassured myself that I was doing the right thing though. I was on track to be what I set out to be, and I knew that doing so would be the first step in being happy. I talked to my parents frequently on the phone or corresponded with them via email, and each time I did I felt like small pieces to my life's puzzle were falling into place. Someday I would sit back and look at everything that had happened and be thankful for it all but for now I would continue to chip away at the chunks of myself that I could and be better tomorrow then I was the day before.

The next day I got up with a sense of self-worth and went to work like I'd never been gone. I took the elevator to my floor and stopped at the door to what was, I hoped, still my office. Taking a deep breath I pushed it open.

"Welcome back!" Molly was waiting on the other side and practically attacked me with a welcoming hug. Her very pregnant belly smashed into me as she pulled me close.

"Thanks, Molly. How've you been?" I grabbed her by the shoulders and looked her over.

"Same shit, different day. I'm about ready to give myself a C-Section if this kid doesn't make an appearance soon." She looked worn out.

"How much longer is it supposed to be?"

"Only a week, but damn, I feel like I've carried this little one for three years."

I reached down and patted her tummy. "All in due time." I laughed.

"I'm going to tell you the same shit when you're carrying a damn watermelon around under your shirt."

"Oh, did you ever find out what you're having?"

"Nah, we figured it would be a good surprise. That and the little booger keeps mooning us every time we've tried to find out." She put her head down and stuck her tongue out at her protruding stomach.

"I'm going to take a guess and say it's a boy."

"Who knows, there could be sixteen of them things in there with the way I look. But anyway, how have things been with you, Emily? I've been so worried."

"Actually, the time off really put things in perspective for me. I was able to spend time with my parents and learned a lot of things that made sense."

"Well that's good, I suppose. What about Mr. Hottie? Spend any time with him?"

I went around my desk and sat in the chair. "Yeah, a little, but that chapter of my life is over. Things didn't work out." I distracted myself by booting up my computer.

"So that's it? Just the old, *things didn't work out* spiel?"

"Yup, but it's okay."

"Huh, I would've thought the two of you were planning a wedding and babies with the way you felt about him. Guess I'm off my game. Must be this pregnancy — it's messing me up."

"It really is okay, Molly. I have so much on my plate right now anyway. The bar is in a couple of weeks and hopefully I'll be celebrating afterwards."

"Okay, if you say so. I'd better get back to work; Marvin is in meetings all day so if you need anything just grab me. Oh, and there is a box of files in his office, he wanted me to have you put them away in the file room."

"Okay, I'll come grab them in a few, just let me down this cup of coffee and get my computer all squared away."

Molly left my office and I spun my chair around to look outside. I warmed my hands with the paper cup of coffee as I sat there trying to think of anything other than Jake. I knew Molly would ask about him and me; she was nosy like that, but I thought I had given a good answer. Yeah, it was kind of lame, but it was all I could think of. What was I supposed to say? "Oh yeah, well, you see I ran away from Jake because I'm a complete idiot who doesn't know a good thing when she has it." Somehow I didn't think Molly would've liked that explanation. She would've probably smacked me and then pushed me to the ground while kicking me with her swollen feet. No, I was not ready to take the abuse that Molly would dish out because I was a dumb ass.

I sipped my coffee until it was finished and threw the cup into the trash. I stood from my chair and headed out of my office toward Marvin's to grab the box of files. When I was a few feet away from Molly's desk I stopped abruptly. She was standing by her desk with a look of confusion on her face.

"Everything okay, Molly?" I asked as I walked closer.

"Uh, not really. My water just broke." She looked up at me with wide eyes.

"What?"

"Water broke. Baby is coming." She spat out just as she doubled over in what looked like excruciating pain.

"Oh my God! What should I do?"

"Get me to the hospital!" She yelled.

I grabbed her purse from her chair and led her down the hall toward the elevator. The moans and groans coming from her mouth told me she was in terrible pain. I pulled out my phone. "What's your husband's number, Molly?"

"He's not in town...*fuck,* this hurts!" She screamed. "He's working. In. Phoenix." She clung to the railing inside the elevator for dear life.

I tried to keep calm but every fiber of my being was screaming just as much as she was.

"Okay, no big deal." The doors slid open and I rushed her through the lobby and outside. The heavens must've been shining down on us because a cab was waiting right by the curb. I flagged it down and ushered Molly toward it. I opened the door and practically pushed her in.

"Whoa, Lady, is she...?" The driver turned around and looked plum freaked out.

"Yes, now please get us to the hospital." I ordered.

He put the car in gear and sped through traffic. At times I was scared for my life and others I was scared that I'd never regain feeling in my hand. Molly gripped it so tight that the tips of my fingers were turning white.

"Just breathe, Molly." I tried to calm her down.

"Don't tell me to breathe, damn you!" She looked like something from a horror movie.

"I'm sorry! I don't know what to say!" I yelled back.

I watched as she struggled to keep what composure she had, but she was in so much pain that I was hurting for her. Relief hit me when the cab buzzed through the entrance of the hospital. The taxi came to a screeching halt in front of the emergency room doors and the cabbie was nice enough to get out and open the door to help Molly from the car. I removed myself on the other side of the car and ran to help her too. Soon there were nurses at our sides with a wheelchair, and I stayed close by Molly's side. Her eyes kept rolling back in her head each time a contraction took over her, and she would grab her stomach and scream.

When the nurses finally got her to the maternity ward of the hospital she was taken into a private room and lifted onto the bed. I hung back by the door as I watched them place a fetal monitor on her stomach and check her vital signs.

"Get your ass in here!" I heard Molly yell.

I knew she was talking to me, but I felt awkward being there. I wasn't family, I was just a co-worker.

"Molly, I don't think I can be in here." I slowly walked to the side of her bed.

"The hell you *can't*. I don't have anyone else here, so you're it, Emily." Her eyes crossed as another pain hit her.

I looked to one of the nurses and she nodded her approval for me to stay. I was so nervous; I'd never seen a child being born. "Okay, I'm here." I grabbed Molly's hand and reassured her.

I stood there with her while the staff made work of removing her underwear and throwing her legs into the fold-out stirrups from the bed. A cart was brought in with all sorts of instruments placed on it, and soon an important looking man made his way into the room. He sat at the end of the bed and looked between Molly's legs and back at us.

"It's great to see new age couples having children together, congrats to the both of you." He commented.

Molly and I looked at each other. "Oh no, we aren't...her husband is out of town, I'm just filling in." I blushed.

"A little less talking and a lot *more* getting this thing out of me, Doc!" Molly screamed at him.

"All right then." He looked down again. "Looks like you're fully dilated, are you ready to push?"

"Does a bear shit in the woods? Of course I am!" I couldn't help but laugh at Molly's demeanor. This was certainly a *different* experience.

I watched in awe as Molly grunted and pushed, trying to give birth to her baby. I held tightly to her hand with each effort she made, while trying not to be overcome with emotion. It wasn't long before the doctor spoke again. "One more push," he encouraged.

Molly pulled her head from the pillow beneath her and gave one more heavy push. The room was silent except for the screaming coming from the tiny human being that the doctor held in his hands.

"We have a girl." He exclaimed.

"Oh Molly, she's beautiful!" I started to cry from sheer joy.

The doctor cut the umbilical cord and wiped the baby off, then wrapped her in a tiny pink blanket. One of the nurses stepped in and placed a small knitted hat on top of her bald head and held the tiny being up so Molly could see her. I saw tears streak Molly's cheeks as the baby was placed in her arms and she gave the little one a kiss on her pink cheek.

"She's perfect." Molly cried.

She was right. I'd never seen something so perfect in my life. Her tiny fingers stretched out like she was trying to grasp something, her eyes were wide as if she was taking in everything new around her and her small wails were like a sweet song among the chaos of the room. Molly held her close like she was the most precious thing in the world.

"Do you want to hold her?" Molly looked over at me and asked.

"If it's okay with you." I wasn't quite sure; I'd never even held such a small baby. I didn't want to break her.

I stepped forward and placed one hand under the tiny girls' neck and the other snugly under her back. When she was in my hands, I pulled her close to my chest so she could feel my warmth. The newborn cooed as I lightly bounced her in my arms and whispered to her. "Welcome to the world, Little One, you're going to have an interesting life with a mommy like that." I smiled at Molly. "But don't let her fool ya'. She has a scary bark, but she's like a marshmallow on the inside."

"Hey, don't tell her that. She needs to know that I'm a badass."

"I'm sure she'll figure it out. So what's her name?" I looked over at Molly.

"Kaylynn Marie. My mom's name was Kay, and Carl's mom was Lynn. And my middle name is Marie."

"I love it. *Kaylynn Marie*." I tried out the new name just because. "Well, I think I'll let you two get better acquainted." I handed her back to Molly and leaned over to give the new mom a hug.

I turned to walk toward the door. "Emily." Molly got my attention and so I turned back toward her. "Thank you for being here for me. You've been an amazing friend." She smiled.

"It was my pleasure." I waved goodbye and left the room.

In a way I was envious of Molly. She had a brand new life to take care of and a husband who would more than likely be thrilled with his new daughter. I wasn't even near that point in my life yet. I told myself that someday I would be.

∞ *Thirty-One* ∞

NERVOUS DIDN'T EVEN BEGIN to describe how I felt while sitting in the testing area at the end of July. I was getting ready to decide my own fate right there on the screen of my laptop. This was it, I would find out if I had studied hard enough, wished long enough and had what it took to become a lawyer. I said a silent prayer in my head as the clock began to tick down the minutes allowed. I had only seven hours on the first day to complete part of the test and two more days ahead of me. I was ready. I thought back to everything I'd learned, recently and from college, as I answered the multiple choice questions and typed out the essays required. I second-guessed myself several times as I scrolled through the pages on the screen in front of me but ended up going with my gut instinct. The red hands of the large clock seemed to fill the room with a loud ticking sound as I nervously tapped my nails on the mouse pad of my computer.

"The time is up, ladies and gentleman," the proctor at the front of the room proclaimed.

I closed my laptop and breathed a sigh of relief. The first part was over. Before I'd come in I told myself that even if I didn't pass this time, I would try again. I wouldn't give up, and it didn't matter how long it took me. I would be back in that spot again if need be. I owed it to myself to not give up on something I wanted so badly.

After it was over, I went outside where the sweltering summer air did nothing to cool my already warm skin.

After traveling back from the testing site I spent the rest of the day in my apartment, just relaxing and trying to calm myself down. It was hard wanting something so bad but not knowing if I would have it or not. I called my parents later that evening to let them know I had taken the test, and both of them wished me well.

Around seven p.m. the buzzer for the downstairs door went off. I pressed the button to see who it was. "Hello?"

"Hi Emily, it's Eliza, can I come up?"

I wondered what she was there for; we hadn't spoken since the incident at the ballgame. "Sure, come on up." I buzzed her in and waited with my apartment door open.

When she reached the door, she threw her arms around me and pulled me in for a huge hug.

"It's so good to see you," she proclaimed and slipped past me into the apartment.

"You too, how are things?"

Eliza tossed her purse onto the counter and turned to face me. "Oh, ya' know, busy busy. I hadn't heard from you and wanted to make sure you're still alive."

"Yeah, I'm here." I laughed. "Can I get you something to drink? I have wine," I offered.

"Wine sounds great." Eliza made her way into the living room while I found my opened bottle of wine and a couple of glasses. I poured equal amounts in each one and hurried to the living room where she was. I handed her one and she took a huge gulp.

"What have you been up to?" she asked.

"Just working, oh, and I took the bar exam today. I'm crossing my fingers." I held up my crossed fingers to drive my point home.

"Have you heard from Jake?" She didn't waste any time getting to *her* point.

"No, I haven't."

"He's okay, I mean, I've seen him better, but all in all I think he's alright."

"Oh, so you've talked to him since he moved to Texas?"

"Texas? What makes you think he moved there?"

"He was offered the district attorney position in Dallas, I just thought since he didn't live upstairs anymore that he'd moved there." I was confused.

"He turned that down. He didn't leave New York, he just moved closer to the office. He has a real sweet penthouse a few blocks from work."

"Why would he have turned that job down? That was a great offer. I would've thought he'd have taken it."

"Nope." Eliza drained the last of her wine and plunked the glass down on the coffee table. "He said there were some things he needed to take care of here. I didn't really question it or anything. When that man gets something in his head there's no reasoning with him. But you know that."

"Yeah, I guess I do." I was shocked that Jake was still in the city. I thought for sure that when I saw his things being moved out that he was gone. I didn't know what to say.

"I can give you his new address if you want it," Eliza offered.

"No, it's okay, but thank you." I turned her down.

"I swear the both of you are made for each other. I've never seen two more hard-headed people in all my life."

"Eliza, things didn't work between us. They never will."

"Why? Because you think he shouldn't love you?" She hit the nail on the head causing me to go silent. "Bingo! Listen, Jake is nuts for you. The man turned down his dream job because of it, and that has to tell you *something*."

"Did you come over here just to put this thought in my head?"

She jumped from the couch. "Pretty much! And now that my job is done, I will leave you alone to think, or act…whichever one you'd like to do." She laughed and grabbed her purse. "See ya' around, Emily." And with that, the feisty red head was gone.

She came in like a damn tornado, upending my sense of calm, whirling out the door with the quickness. I couldn't decide yet if I loved her or loathed her. But her information did bring more thoughts of Jake to my head, which was something she completely intended on doing. What was I supposed to do? I had this information, and in a way I was mad at Jake for not accepting his dream job. He could've moved closer to his family and had a prestigious career, but instead he chose to stay in New York. What the hell was wrong with him?

Part of me wanted to call Eliza and get Jake's address, but the other part wanted to leave well enough alone. If he'd wanted to contact me, he obviously knew where I lived. He didn't even say goodbye when he moved. But in all fairness, I never said goodbye when I'd left him in Texas either.

I grabbed up my glass of wine and threw back the rest of the dark purple liquid. I slumped back onto the sofa and threw my arm over my face. What the hell was I going to do?

∞ *Thirty-Two* ∞

THE NEXT WEEK went by at a snail's pace while I mulled over what I should do about Jake. I traveled back to the testing site for the other two days of the exam and was filled with utter relief and exhaustion once it was all said and done. The days I wasn't doing the testing I worked to keep myself occupied and paced the floors of my apartment during the evenings because I wasn't sure what else to do. The rest of the next week had flown by and soon it was Saturday. I needed so badly to get out of the walls that seemed to be closing in on me. I got myself up and dressed, grabbed a travel mug of coffee and headed downstairs... I needed some open space and nature to calm my overworked brain.

I hopped in a cab a few minutes later and asked to be taken to Central Park. The air outside was still sticky and the sun shone brightly with the unmistakable signs that summer was in full swing. I looked out the windows on the ride to the park, watching people move about among the crowds trying to get to their Saturday destinations just as I was. I wondered if any of them were as confused as I was. Did they have a huge decision lying on their shoulders too? Or were they just living in the moment, going about their lives and taking what they were given day by day? I still hadn't gotten to that point yet. I worried all the time about stuff I couldn't control, but I also knew that's what made me human. Even though I couldn't control it, that didn't mean it wasn't okay to ponder it.

The cab pulled up to the entrance to Central Park, I handed the driver some cash and got out. I could smell the fragrance of hot dogs cooking and immediately thought of Jake again. The sounds of him laughing as I shoved the hot dog in my mouth, the way he made fun of me for even *wanting* to eat something from a cart—it all made me smile. I walked by the cart and took a whiff of the offerings, telling myself that I would grab something on my way back through. I continued forward along the path noticing less people about than when Jake and I had been there earlier in the summertime. A few families were scattered about, but mainly it was die-hard runners or pet owners taking their dogs out for a walk. I couldn't blame the ones who weren't out, though; the sun was downright blazing like an inferno hanging in the sky above us.

But I kept on going, needing to find that one special place in the park that always meant so much to me. As I kept walking I'd come up behind a couple that had to have been in their eighties. They held hands and walked so close like they were new lovers out for a stroll for the day. I smiled as I thought of Jake and me walking hand in hand in the park too. The way my small hand fit into his larger one, the way my body seemed to lean into his and match his stride even though his was so much faster. God, it was perfect for the time it lasted.

When I came upon my special place I stood back, taking everything in. The trees around me were boasting the brightest shades of green, the blades of grass reached toward the sky, begging for a drop of rain to quench its thirsty roots and the visible areas of dirt looked cracked, waiting for some relief just as everything else was. I knew that in a few months, none of it would look the same. The leaves would be tumbling toward the ground, and the crowds would thin while people stayed inside cozied up with their families. It was strange how everything would change, but underneath it would always stay the same. It would emerge essentially brand new and full of more life and vigor than it had in the previous seasons.

I trudged forward across the brick pathway, digging in the pocket of my jacket for the change I'd placed there earlier. When I found what I was looking for, I stepped to the edge of the fountain that held so many memories for me. I couldn't be sad about this place because it was something that represented happy times, times that I could look back and smile about and know that no matter what I *was* happy.

I held the weathered coin in my cupped hands and brought it to my lips. I closed my eyes, as I'd done so many times before and secretly made my wish. I opened them up and tossed the silver into the water with a resounding plunk. I sighed as I watched it fall to the bottom to join so many other wishes. When I knew it was among the rest, I turned around to walk away.

"What did you wish for?" My head jerked up at the sound of the most familiar voice.

"Jake."

"I'll tell you my wish, if you tell me yours."

"Then they won't come true."

"Maybe that's the trick, though." He stepped closer. "Maybe all this time we've thought that by keeping them secret, they'd come true. Maybe it's the other way around."

"So if I tell you what mine was, it should come true?"

"There's a chance, I suppose."

"Okay then, I wished that you'd forgive me." I whispered, feeling embarrassed.

"Huh, that's a pretty good one. But I've already forgiven you, Emily."

"You have?" I looked into his sparkling blue eyes.

"Yes I have. I understood why you left—you needed time. And I needed to give it to you."

"But I've been terrible to you Jake, why would you even give me that?"

"Because I refuse to give up, I've waited forever for you to come back into my life and what's waiting a little longer," he shrugged.

"Thank you for understanding, that means so much." I smiled.

"Wait, how did you even know I would be here?"

"I might have followed you." He moved his feet nervously against the brick below us.

"So you're stalking me?" I gave him a horrified expression.

"Hey, I was just trying to track you down to talk to you."

"I guess that isn't such a bad thing, then," I smiled. Just then my phone beeped with an email notification. I pulled it from my purse and opened my Yahoo account. I felt my nerves come to the forefront as I saw the New York Bar Association as the sender of the email. "Is everything okay?" Jake stepped close enough that I could smell his man soap and cologne mixture.

"Yeah, it's just my test results." I sighed.

"Aren't you going to look at them?" His eyebrow rose.

"I'll do it later." I started to shove my phone back into my purse.

Jake plucked it from my hands before I could, though. "I'll do it." He slid the lock button to the open position on the screen.

"Okay, fine! I'll open it." I grabbed it back and took a deep breath. I hit the email app again and closed my eyes for a second. Whatever was in that email, I told myself I would be fine with it. It didn't matter; there were more important things in life than passing a test. I clicked the email and started to read. Each word bled into the next as I scrolled further down, but the one word that stood out in all of it was…"Passed." I breathed.

"You passed?" Jake grabbed my phone from my shaking hands. "I knew you could do it." He threw his arms around me and hugged me close to him. "Congrats, Emily." He kissed the top of my head.

"Thank you." I was speechless.

"This is amazing, I'm so happy for you." He pulled back and looked me in the eyes.

"Jake, why did you turn down the job in Dallas? That was your dream." I had to know.

"My dream is a lot bigger than a job, Emily."

"Oh."

"Aren't you going to ask me what I wished for?"

"Uh, okay, what did you wish for?" I played along.

"I wished that you'd say yes."

"Yes to what?" I was yet again confused.

"When I did this…" He knelt down on one knee and pulled out a black velvet box from his pocket. He popped the top open to reveal a shimmering diamond set atop a thick platinum band. "Will you marry me, Emily?"

My entire body shook with so many emotions, I was terrified, excited, but most of all, I was happy.

"Yes." I said loud enough for everyone around us to hear.

A huge smile spread across Jake's face as he stood back up and slid the stunning ring onto my finger. The next thing I knew, I was being pulled in for the most passionate kiss I'd ever felt from him. Our lips pressed together in a sign that we were going to be stronger than ever. That our friendship would be one that would last for the rest of our lives. But most of all, it showed that through everything, there was always a second chance…*our* second chance.

∞The End∞

Acknowledgments

There are a group of people I need to give a shout out to. First and foremost I would like to give a huge high five to my amazeballs team at Booktrope. Jennifer Gilbert and Samantha Williams, my dynamic duo of book/project managers. They have listened to me laugh, cry and complain more than anyone on this planet in the past few months. Next is my phenomenal editor Allie Bishop. Allie helped take a jumbled pile of words and morph it into an awesome story that we can be proud of. To Greg Simanson, my cover designer, who I am convinced is also a mind reader. Cindy Slator, who revealed the fact that I am indeed a comma whore, in her proofreading efforts.

I would also like to thank those who have been on this crazy ride from the first words I ever put on a page. My fabulous sister-in law Candie, who is my biggest fan. My best friend Nicole who has to listen to my crazy ideas while pretending to understand what the hell I'm talking about. My sister LaRae, who told me that I need to put down Pride and Prejudice and read erotic romance novels. And last but certainly not least is my Hubby Paul. Thanks for putting up with me babbling about fictitious characters and letting me keep you up at night with my constant clicking of the computer keys. You are the bacon to my BLT.

*Read further for a sneak peek of "Left to Chance,
Book Two in the "Chances Are" Series*

Preview of Left to Chance
"Chances Are Series"
Book Two

*Content subject to
change in editing*

~Chapter One~

THE DAY SEEMED TO BE so incredibly flawless; the clear warm weather in Texas was downright pristine for a picture perfect June wedding for Emily and Jake. I couldn't help but admire the atmosphere and the way things had played out during the day. I always loved weddings and what they represented, the love, the devotion, and the passion between the Bride and Groom on their special day.

I was honored that Emily asked me to be her maid of honor; we hadn't really known each other *that* long, but had formed an instant bond either way.

"You must be Eliza?" Jake's mom sat down at the table with me.

"Yes ma'am that's me. How're you doing today?"

"Oh I suppose I'm alright. A little sad but I think I'll survive."

"I'm hoping that it's a happy kind of sad?" I watched Jake's mom dab her eyes with a tissue.

"Of course it is. One of these days you'll understand when you have children of your own." She gave a pat to my hand. "Well I'd better go dance with my son before they head out for the night. You take care young lady." I watched as she rose from the table and headed over to the beaming couple.

I understood what she was saying, but I didn't want her to know that there'd be no chance of me having children in the future. Not because I didn't *want* any...I just couldn't physically have them. Unfortunately an accident when I was a kid took that privilege away from me. I tried not to think about it too much though, it only made me envious of the one thing I knew I could never have.

I suppose that's why I hadn't even tried to date as much as I probably should've. I didn't want to explain every personal little detail to a stranger. But these were the days where you'd ask for someone's credit report before even going on a first date. If guys knew I wasn't capable of having children, they would run in the other direction. Sure there was probably someone out there that wouldn't care, but I refused to take that chance. Humiliation didn't seem like a fun and inspiring past time.

I think that's why I found the day so endearing. For two people to pledge themselves to each other for the rest of their lives was the greatest gift anyone could ever hope to receive. It was almost like watching some sort of real life fairy tale unfold in front of teary and joy filled eyes.

I would've been some sort of monster if I didn't get emotionally caught up in all of it. It was just a natural reaction.

But maybe *I* was the one with rose-colored glasses comfortably perched on my nose. Did I *really* not see the ultimate picture after the big fluffy event? It wasn't all matching bathrobes and long walks on the beach was it? Maybe I'd become cynical about the institution of marriage; after all, one couldn't truly be happy with *one* person for the entirety of their natural born lives! That had the mark of insanity written all over it, complete with coordinating strait jackets.

I could probably blame my opinion of relationships on the fact that I was *always* unlucky in the romance department. I had my fair share of boyfriends, but no one fit into what I thought was *"the one"* category. Maybe I was being stubborn. It could've been possible that I was setting the bar too high. Quite possibly I needed to lower my standards. But why should I? Didn't I deserve to have someone cherish me? So *what* if it all ended in disaster and heartache, at least I could mark it off on my "to do list".

The lot of it took a toll on my self-confidence, and left me wondering if I had some sort of genetic defect that attracted assholes. My case in point, the king of assholes that I had the unfortunate pleasure of being escorted down the aisle by. Gabe Ellingsworth.

The guy was such a douche bag; he lived his pathetic life not giving a shit about anyone else but himself. He was the spoiled rich boy, with the proverbial silver spoon in his mouth and expected everyone to bow down to his greatness. The man held his nose up so far, that if it'd come a torrential downpour in the next five minutes, I was sure I'd be watching him gasp for air. The worst of all of it was the wildly know fact that he used women like they were just another play toy in his life of discards.

The man never hung onto a woman longer than it took to screw her brains out and send her packing. As long as I'd known him, that was his pattern. Gabe left a rip tide of panties in his wake no matter where he went, if my suspicions were correct, he would find a panty dropper here too, just like he did at every event.

It always pissed me off when I'd met people who did nothing but "take" in their lives. They never decided it was right to start giving back and they hurt so many people in the process. Gabe was the poster child for that, he took everything from everyone and just kept walking. I tolerated him only because he was Jakes best friend, but the man had burned me and I would rather pour gas on him if he were on fire, than find water to douse him with. One word summed him up…asshole.

He wasn't the ideal person in my mind to escort me as a bridesmaid, but this was Jake and Emily's day, so I sucked it up and went with it. It wasn't my day so the decisions weren't in my hands. But now that the wedding part was over, I sat at my table nursing a glass of chilled champagne. The reception was in full swing and I couldn't take my eyes off the happy couple on the dance floor. They were so complete together, like two halves of a whole. I felt myself becoming envious of them. Jake was a great man, I'd worked for him in his law firm for five years and I could only describe the job as wonderful. He was always kind and caring, and when my cat died last year, he actually adopted a new one for me. He gave her to me as a Christmas bonus, and I'd never been happier.

Emily and I had become the best of friends. She loved Jake with such intensity that couldn't be rivaled anywhere. The way she spoke about him, and the way she looked at him, was something to behold. Today was no different, the image of them together made me burn inside. I wanted that, I wanted to feel my skin on fire with love and passion, but the prospects were slim pickings.

"May I have this dance?" I heard a familiar voice behind me.

I turned to find Gabe standing there. "Go fuck yourself Gabe."

"Okay I deserve that, but seriously Eliza are you going to hold this shit over my head forever?"

"Probably so Gabe, that's the way I roll." I spat out flatly.

"Well that sucks." He said almost under his breath.

"You have no respect for anyone's feelings Gabe, so go find someone else to bother."

"Are we really going *there* today?"

"Why not Gabe?"

"Well I would rather not have your emotional tirades thrown at me during my best friend's wedding."

"Emotional tirades huh? Well then, I have nothing more to say to you, so like I said before Gabe…Go fuck yourself!"

"Fine, whatever." He said while walking away.

Gabe just didn't see it, He wanted to place blame on everyone else but himself. He could have learned some manners, I mean, who stands in a luxury box at a Yankees game and asks someone for a "quickie" in the bathroom? Hadn't he ever heard of romancing a woman? There were other ways to get in someone's pants besides acting like a tool. I wanted to think that he'd maybe changed over the past few months but then I realized…men like Gabe *don't* change.

"Hey Eliza, what are you doing all by yourself over here?" Emily sat down.

"Just trying to stay out of the way."

"Is everything alright? You look pissed."

"I'm fine Emily, I'm trying not to scratch Gabe's eyes out."

Emily let out a laugh. "You wouldn't be the first woman who wanted to do that."

"He's just such a prick, why does he think he can use everyone as his personal doormat and then throw them away like they don't even matter?"

"I think that's what he's used to, he doesn't know any better."

"He needs to grow up!" I said a little too loudly.

"I agree whole heartedly with you on that, but that's not for us to make him do, you know?"

"Yeah I get it; I just wish someone would knock him in the head and fix him."

"Someone will someday. Something huge will happen in his life that will make him see the error of his ways. When that happens, Gabe will have no choice but to grow up. It will happen, it always does." Emily winked.

"Yeah, I suppose you're right. But enough about captain douche bag, I have a question for you."

"Okay shoot?" Emily raised one perfect brown in curiosity.

"It's your wedding day, and you aren't drinking, you didn't even have champagne when Jake made his toast."

"Um, yeah about that." Emily rubbed her belly.

"Oh. My. God! Are you pregnant?"

She smiled and her cheeks turned a slight tinge of pink. "Yes!"

I threw my arms around her. "Holy shit! Congratulations, does Jake know?"

"I just told him after we came back down the aisle."

"Is he okay with it?"

"Of course he is, he's over the moon at the idea. I mean we wanted to start a family eventually, and yeah it's really soon, but I love him and he loves me, so we're excited." Emily beamed.

"Oh Emily, I'm so happy for you." I felt tears sting my eyes.

"No crying! This is a happy day, so I order you to get off your ass and go dance...or drink."

She was right this was a happy day; I needed to get past the fact that Gabe was a douche canoe, and have some fun. "You're right! Here I go!" I steadied my resolve and headed for the bar area. I wasn't going to let the small stuff get in the way of me having a great time. When I got to the bar I ordered a Jack and Coke...my drink of choice.

"Pretty strong drink for a little thing like you." I heard Gabe say.

"What's it to you?"

He held up his hands in a defensive gesture. "Whoa, look Eliza I'm sorry, can we please just call a truce for today?"

"Fine, you're right Gabe, this isn't right to be fighting like a bag of cats at our best friends' wedding." He was right; I couldn't be showing my ass all day. It wasn't fair to Jake and Emily.

"Bag of cats?" He chuckled.

"Okay so the making fun of me begins?" I knew he couldn't be nice for too long.

"No, it was funny that's all." Gabe shot me his signature charming grin that made panties melt off of his victims.

"Sorry, we say goofy stuff like that where I'm from."

"And where is that?" He stared at me with curiosity.

"Atlanta." I tried to state it with as much pride as I could muster. I loved my home state of Georgia, and I missed it every day.

"Huh, I didn't know you were from the dirty south…"

"More jokes Gabe?"

"Okay, okay, I'm sorry. Can we start over?"

"Sure." I eyed Gabe skeptically.

"Would you like to dance Eliza?" He said gentlemanly.

Against my better judgment I agreed. "Alright, why not." I threw back the rest of my drink and slammed the small tumbler on the bar. The remaining ice cubes swirled around the insides of the glass sounding like wind chimes rustling in a slight breeze.

Gabe took my hand in his, and I felt something like a static shock move through my body. Every nerve ending came to life, and I quickly pulled my hand back.

"What's wrong?" Gabe raised his eyebrows.

"Uh, nothing." I shrugged.

I put my hand back in his and the same thing happened again. What the hell was going on? I'd experienced some major weirdness lately but this phenomenon took the cake. I mentally shook it off as some sort of environmental oddity.

Once we were on the dance floor, Gabe pulled me tightly to his chest. A collision of senses started to overtake me and my brain felt like it might explode with things I hadn't felt before. I wanted to haul ass away from the unknown but I always kept my word and right now I promised Gabe that I'd dance with him. I lifted my head to breath in his scent, one that smelled of expensive cologne, and woodsy male. It was intoxicating and made me shiver from the roots of my hair to the tips of my bright crimson pedicure.

"Are you sniffing me?" He interrupted.

I turned beet red. "I'm sorry…It's just your cologne, it smells good."

"Thanks, you smell good too." He smiled and took in a shuddering breath of his own making me tremble that much more.

I couldn't help but blush again; his eyes were taking inventory of every inch of me. As we stepped in sync around the dance floor my gaze was enraptured in his like a fly caught in a spider web waiting to be devoured. In those moments I looked at him for the first time, I mean *really* looked at him. His eyes were the color of a Caribbean ocean, so blue and deep, like he had sapphires for irises. His hair was a shaggy style that hung haphazardly around his strong jawline. He was easy on the eyes, no wonder he had zero issues getting women to swoon after him. I could tell he had secrets, as did I, but in that moment I wasn't seeing "Gabe the player" I was actually looking into the soul of "Gabe the man." And what a man he was.

I brought myself out of my mental observations and tried to focus on the bad things about his though. I didn't want to know the real him, if there even was a real Gabe. The man had too much history of shit I didn't need to be a part of. If I were a smart person I would slap on my running sneakers and high tail it the heck away from him. I couldn't let myself get caught up with Gabe. Even if there may have been a time that I really liked him. Gabe would throw me to the curb after he slept with me. I would just become another notch on his over- priced bedpost. God I had to get away.

"Something wrong?" Gabe asked.

"No I'm fine, I just need a break." I pulled away.

"We just started dancing Eliza." He pulled me closer to him, his heat enveloping every part of me, making me feel like I'd been sun burned to the depths of my soul. It was blatantly obvious that he was turned on too. Funny, because so was I. What a reaction to have for someone I loathed with everything that I was.

"Gabe, this isn't a good idea." I felt so uncomfortable. I wanted to crawl right out of my skin and find a safe hiding place. Gabe was dangerous, not only to my body, but my heart.

He brushed a loose hair from my face causing me to shiver all over. "I know. Just dance with me please?"

I couldn't help but give in. Gabe had woven some sort of voodoo on me and it was impossible to resist his charm. "Okay." I whispered as I looked up into his pained eyes.

Maybe there was more to this man then what was on the outside. Maybe I was only seeing the man Gabe wanted everyone to see. Surly he was more complex than just a guy who screwed for fun and partied until the wee morning hours on weekdays. I was having the most difficult internal battle raging inside of me.

Once the last few notes of the song ended I regretfully pulled away. "I think I'm going to get another drink, do you want anything?" I asked.

"No thanks."

I left him on the dance floor and went back to the bar. His scent clung to me beseeching my body to run back to the man that would only crush me if I dared to play his little game. And that's all it was to Gabe. A Game that he designed. One that only proclaimed a single winner in the end- Gabe.

I ordered up another Jack and Coke, and started sipping it. The bartender looked across the bar at me and could tell there was something wrong. I'd always been the person who wore my feelings all over my face. When I was younger my mom could tell when something was either wrong, or I was not being truthful about something. It wasn't something I could control.

"You okay Miss?" The bartender asked.

"Just fine, well besides the fact I'm not nearly drunk enough." I let out a heavy sigh and pushed a few falling tendrils of hair behind my ear.

He pulled out an unopened bottle of tequila. "Well then, let's see what we can do about that shall we?"

I smiled an evil grin. "Bring it on."

He lined up several shot glasses, and poured the liquid in them one by one, some so full that the tequila sloshed out on the bar. "Here's the game, after you take a shot, you have to say something about yourself that no one knows." He joked.

"Sounds fun." Not really. It sounded like a hangover from hell and a bad taste in my mouth. But why not. I'd been buttoned up Eliza for too long and it was time to let my hair down and have a bit of fun for once.

He sat a bowl of lime wedges on the bar top, along with a saltshaker. He pushed a shot toward me and chuckled. "Bottoms up."

I threw back the shot, and it burned like hell fire all the way down. My throat felt as if it might catch on fire if I breathed wrong. Okay so I wasn't nearly soused enough to do tequila shots, but this little game seemed intriguing.

I spit my first secret. "I have a major crush on Brad Pitt!" I yelled while thumping the shot glass back on the bar.

Everyone at the bar started laughing hysterically. I took another shot. "I have a Backstreet Boys poster on my bedroom wall!" They continued to laugh hysterically at my antics. I couldn't help but cackle along with everyone. This truly was humiliating, but fun either way.

By the ninth shot, I was feeling no pain whatsoever. My inhibitions were completely gone, and I was pretty sure I couldn't feel my face or if I even still had a face for that matter. I grabbed the tenth shot and held it up to my lips. My reaction time was delayed and it was like seeing everything happening in slow motion.

I felt a warm hand on my shoulder, and turned to see who it was. Gabe was standing there with a look of concern on his face. I tossed the shot down my throat, which tasted like pure water at that point. The small crowd I'd drawn was waiting anxiously for my next secret. I swallowed the liquid and shouted out my final secret before my brain could override my mouth.

"I'm a virgin!"

More Great Reads
From Booktrope

Sex and Death in the American Novel by **Sarah Martinez** (Erotic Fiction) When free-spirited erotica writer Vivianna meets award-winning author Jasper Caldwell, she wants to hate him for his role in her brother's suicide. But despite their literary and sexual differences, she finds herself wanting him. Using quotes and references to classic erotic and literary icons, *Sex and Death in the American Novel* is on one level an unconventional romance and on another a discussion of the merits of erotic literature.

Pulled Beneath by **Marni Mann** (Contemporary Romance) When Drew unexpectedly loses her parents, she inherits a home in Bar Harbor, Maine along with a family she knew nothing about. Will their secrets destroy her or will she be able to embrace their dark past and accept love?

Blogger Girl by **Meredith Schorr** (Contemporary Romance) Kimberly Long has two passions: her successful chick lit blog and Nicholas, her handsome colleague down the hall. But when her high school nemesis pops onto the chick lit scene with a hot new book and eyes for Nicholas, Kim has to make some quick revisions to her own life story.

Unsettled Spirits by **Sophie Weeks** (Contemporary Romance) As Sarah grapples with questions of faith, love, and identity, she must learn to embrace not just the spirits of the present, but the haunting pain of the past. Can she accept her past in order to let love in?

Work in Progress by **Christina Esdon** (Romance) Psychologist Reese Morgan refuses to let go of a childhood trauma. When she meets a handsome contractor, Josh Montgomery, she wonders if the walls around her heart can be knocked down to let love in.

Discover more books and learn about our new approach to publishing at www.booktrope.com

CPSIA information can be obtained
at www.ICGtesting.com
Printed in the USA
FFOW03n1700170914
7422FF